Reluctantly EVER AFTER

THE oops baby CLUB

HEATHER ASHLEY

Copyright © 2025 by Heather Ashley

All rights reserved.

No part of this book may be reproduced in any form or by any electronic or mechanical means, including information storage and retrieval systems, without written permission from the author, except for the use of brief quotations in a book review.

ISBN # 9798288381768

heatherashleywrites.com

For everyone who thinks they can hate fuck their enemy out of their system...

Good luck with that.

PLAYLIST

"Fire For You" by Cannons
"Wicked Games" by The Weeknd
"Like a Boy" by Ciara
"bad idea right?" by Olivia Rodrigo
"Talk" by Hozier
"Touch" by Cigarettes After Sex
"Let's Hurt Tonight" by One Republic
"The Night We Met" by Lord Huron
"Liability" by Lorde
"ceilings" by Lizzie McAlpine
"You Were Meant For Me" by Jewel
"The Archer" by Taylor Swift
"Eyes Closed" by Halsey
"Blue Jeans" by Lana Del Ray
"Shameless" by Camila Cabello
"War of Hearts" by Ruelle

1
Wren

I WAKE up to what feels like a herd of elephants stampeding through my skull and the unmistakable taste of bad decisions coating my tongue. The luxury suite's blackout curtains are sort of doing their job, but enough merciless Las Vegas sunshine still manages to break through to burn my brain.

For fuck's sake, how much did I drink last night?

I groan as consciousness crawls back to me sense by sense. And then I become aware of three things simultaneously: I'm completely naked, I'm not alone, and there's something on my left hand that wasn't there yesterday. My heart and stomach both roll as my fingers brush across something smooth and metal.

Is it...?

No.

No.

Yup, it's a ring. On *that* finger.

Coincidence? I sure as hell hope so.

I squeeze my eyes shut, hoping this is just a nightmare, but the warm body blanketing my back is all too real. Whoever he

1

is, he's radiating heat like a bonfire and it's doing nothing to help the gross hangover sweat coating my skin.

I'm sticky and miserable, and this is the very last thing I need.

But my bed buddy doesn't know or care. No, he's too busy breathing deep and even against the back of my neck, peaceful as can be while I'm freaking the fuck out.

And I'm not even going to acknowledge the morning wood poking my ass.

Nope.

There's not enough coffee in the world for this.

His arm is slung over my waist, heavy and—I freeze as I notice the ink. There are colorful tattoos running down his forearm and spilling onto his fingers, designs that I've seen before. Designs that I would recognize anywhere.

No. No, no, *no*.

My stomach gives another threatening churn as I slowly turn over, already knowing what I'll find, but praying to every god I don't believe in that I'm wrong.

Yeah, I'm not wrong.

Kasen James is sleeping beside me, and I've gotta say, I'm jealous. He has no idea of the cataclysmic fuck up that's just patiently here, waiting for him to open his eyes.

Waiting to ruin everything.

Meanwhile, I'm painfully awake, staring it right in its offensively handsome face.

What the hell have I done?

Welp, since this day's already ruined and I've been up less than five minutes, I allow myself a second to do something I never do: I check out my enemy.

His dark hair's a mess, but his body... well, it's the opposite of a mess. He's got defined muscles but not overly so and most of his skin is covered in colorful ink that stands out against the bright white hotel sheets that are tangled around his hips.

Low around his hips, so low that I can almost see—

Nope.

This is *Kasen*. Owner of Timber Brewing. The biggest pain in my ass and also the man who's been trying to undermine my distribution company since day one.

Also known as the most infuriating human being on the planet.

And apparently, my new husband. Maybe.

I'm still holding out hope the ring's for something else.

Literally *anything* else.

Maybe he's messing with me, and this is all some elaborate joke.

He *does* love to piss me off.

It doesn't explain the nakedness or the way our bodies are plastered together, but my brain can't brain right now, so I'm ignoring the Occam's razor of it all.

I'll invent all the complex explanations I want, thanks.

The room spins as I carefully lift his heavy arm from my waist and place it on the mattress. He stirs a little and I hold my breath, but he doesn't wake up. Once I'm free, I sit up too fast in my desperation to get away and the sheet falls.

And I'm naked.

I mean, I already knew I was, but now it's confirmed and without Kasen's body heat, now it's a cold sweat I've got going on.

I yank the sheet up, clutching it to my chest. My head gives a violent throb or seven, but the pain is nothing compared to the panic starting to rise in my throat.

Or it could be vomit. Honestly? I think it's both.

Either way, for a second, I forget that I'm trying not to wake Kasen up for my walk of shame when I spot an official-looking document with a receipt from the Little White Wedding Chapel sitting on the nightstand.

It's a little crumpled, but clear as day are three signatures scrawled at the bottom—one of them mine, the other Kasen's—and a third signed by someone named "Elvis Aaron Presleigh" with a smiley face drawn in the 'g'.

Well, I think it's safe to say panic's about to win the vomit-panic duel happening in my throat.

As my pulse skyrockets, the throbbing in my head only gets worse, and *why am I awake?*

I think a solid plan would be to fall back asleep and hope that when I wake up for real this time, this whole thing was just some nightmare my subconscious cooked up thanks to all the tequila I soaked it in last night.

A middle finger from my brain to teach me to *never* venture away from beer again.

Except no. I can't go back to sleep. Not with *him* in my bed. And you know what the worst part of this is? It's when I sneak another look down at Kasen, and a *shiver* goes down my spine at the sight of all that delicious—

Nope.

Nothing about Kasen James is *delicious*. Not a damn thing. Not his broad chest or the stubble on his jaw or the abs with the real-life V that disappears under the blanket. I glare at him. How does he have *abs,* anyway? A drool-worthy six-pack a guy who likes beer as much as he does should *not* have.

Maybe he sold his soul to the devil. It would explain a lot.

You know what? This is fine. All I need is a plan.

I need to get out of this bed, find my clothes, and get out of this room before Kasen wakes up. Once I have a coffee IV and a shower, I can evaluate what needs to come next.

Taking a deep breath, I blow it out and spin, setting my feet on the floor. Okay, so far, so good. But I've never been that lucky, and the second I stand up, those light blue eyes crack open.

Every muscle in my body locks up as our eyes connect, and I wait to see what he's going to say. There's a wrinkle between his eyebrows, like he hasn't quite registered who I am.

And I almost laugh when the light goes on behind them. Almost.

He jerks upright, reaching to pull the comforter up higher. His eyes dart from my face to my bedhead to the sheet wrapped around me and then back again.

"What the *fuck*?" His voice comes out rough and I'm not sure if it's from sleep or the horror of this situation.

"Good morning to you, too." Now that he's awake, I pull the sheet tighter around me.

He lifts his hand to run it down his face, but then he freezes when he sees the matching ring on his finger to the one on mine. *Welp, guess there goes any hope this was a prank on his part.* "Please tell me this is some kind of sick joke."

I lift my hand and wiggle my fingers so he catches the glint of gold on mine. "Apparently not."

I scoop up the papers on the nightstand and hand them over. Kasen snatches them, eyes scanning the documents frantically. "How drunk were we?"

"Drunk enough to think *this* was a good idea," I say, gesturing between us. Th*is* encapsulates so very many things. The nakedness, the wedding. Whatever happened between last night and right now that I have zero memory of.

I spot my black dress hanging from a lampshade and hurry over to grab it, shimmying into it over the sheet and then letting the sheet drop.

Now where the hell are my underwear?

Kasen runs a hand through his messy hair and I ignore the way it makes his biceps flex. "Did we...?" He gestures between us and I laugh.

"I think it's pretty safe to say we did." If the ache between my thighs and the fingerprint shaped bruises I noticed on my hips are anything to go by, but I don't think he needs the details.

Kasen's jaw clenches, and he looks away. "Jesus Christ."

I find my underwear on the floor by the bathroom, so I grab them and go inside for a little privacy. Flicking on the light, I get the full effect of my bad decisions staring me right in the face when I look in the mirror. My makeup's an absolute travesty, my hair's a tangled, wild mess and there's absolutely no way I'm going to be able to cover the Texas-sized hickey on my neck.

I'm pretty much the dictionary definition of *walk of shame.*

Who the hell even *is* the girl in the mirror because no way is she me. I don't do stuff like this. And I *definitely* do not sleep with the enemy.

Again, we're ignoring the whole *married* thing. Coffee IV first, remember?

While I pee and *ohmygod sweet relief,* I take a second to look around the fancy bathroom. It's got one of those giant jacuzzi tubs that could fit the entire list of characters from a reverse harem in it. And at some point last night, it looks like Kasen and I had some fun in there.

There's a half-empty bottle of top shelf tequila tipped over and spilling out onto the floor, which still has cold puddles of water all over the place.

Say what you want, but at least we didn't drink the cheap shit.

I splash cold water on my face, trying to wash away the evidence of what I've done, but all it does is smear around the mess of my makeup and now the front of my hair's dripping and wet.

Oh, and the light catches the ring on my finger and why the hell am I still wearing it?

I go to take it off, but this dress doesn't have pockets and besides, if I take it off, then I have to deal with what to do with it and...

I can't.

I just... can't.

I do not have the brainpower with this hangover to make decisions.

Not small decisions and not *I probably-definitely married my rival in Vegas and then consummated the hell out of the wedding* decisions.

Just fuck *all the decisions.*

When I get my shit together as much as I'm going to, I step back into the room. Kasen's pulled on his jeans, but he's still shirtless. And I'm pretty sure he's going commando, too.

He's upsettingly hot.

Unfortunately hot.

And he's pacing the room, gripping the ends of his messy hair like he's having some sort of meltdown. I might hate the guy, but I can't blame him. I'm freaking out, too.

I'm absolutely *not* drooling over the tattoos that continue up his neck and disappear into his hairline. I've never seen Kasen without his black beanie and some sort of flannel before, and the sight is...

Well, my nipples would tell you that it's distracting.

Maybe a little sexy.

Just, like, the tiniest bit.

"We need to fix this," he says without looking at me. "Now."

"No shit," I say, searching for my purse. *Where the hell is it?* "I've worked too hard to let a drunken mistake with *you* ruin everything."

Kasen's head snaps up as he lets out a chuckle that's not funny at all. "Of course your first thought would be business. Yeah, I can't be chained to you. I need out."

Ouch, but also same.

"Everything's about business." I find my phone and check it—three missed calls from Kieran, my head of operations slash assistant, and a solid dozen texts. Awesome. "Do you have any idea what would happen to my reputation if this got out? The

7

craft beer industry is sexist enough without adding 'slept her way to the top' to the rumor mill."

Kasen's eyes narrow. "You and that fucking company. That's all you care about."

"Like you're any different," I shoot back. "Timber's your whole identity."

"You don't know the first thing about me."

"Right back atcha."

We glare at each other as the air between us starts to crackle. And am I standing closer to him than I was a second ago? How'd that happen?

My gaze drops to his chest against my will, following the lines of ink that disappear into his waistband. And... yep, that's the outline of his dick. His *impressive* dick, aka the reason I'm walking a little funny this morning.

I force my eyes back up to his face and find him watching me with an intensity that makes my breath catch.

"This never happened," Kasen says, breaking whatever the hell *that* was and I blow out a breath. He takes a step back, then another. "We got drunk, we made a mistake, we fix it, and we never speak of it again."

"Agreed." I nod, relieved that for once we're on the same page. I wanted coffee before acknowledging this whole thing, but it looks like Kasen's the type of guy who tackles problems head-on and as much as I want to run away from this, I can't. I wrinkle my nose at the sentence I'm about to say. "We need a divorce."

"Annulment," he says. "It's faster."

I shake my head. "We slept together. You know, consummated the marriage? I'm pretty sure that means we don't qualify."

The word 'consummated' hangs in the air between us, and things are happening *down below* that I'm going to chalk up to aftershocks from last night and leave it at that. Kasen's eyes darken as he watches me, but then he looks away.

"Fine. Divorce then. The sooner, the better."

I find my heels under the room service cart, which still holds the remnants of what appears to be wedding cake. My stomach rolls again and my mouth starts to water and not in the good way. I close my eyes and take a couple of deep breaths.

"I'll contact my lawyer as soon as we get back to Portland," I say, slipping on my shoes and trying to regain some semblance of dignity. *Yeah, right.*

"No lawyers," Kasen snaps. "The fewer people who know about this, the better. We can file the paperwork ourselves."

"And you're suddenly a divorce expert?"

"I just want to handle it myself." He finally finds his shirt—a dark flannel crumpled on the floor—and pulls it on, covering the ink that I can't stop staring at. "The convention ends today. We go home, file the paperwork, and forget this ever happened."

"That might be the first good idea you've ever had, James." He scowls at me, but I ignore him. "I'm going back to my room to shower off last night. I'll see you when we get home."

Well, the time has come. I'm about to do the official walk of shame from my enemy's hotel room.

I'm really nailing this whole *living my best life* thing.

"One more thing," he says as I reach for the door. "No one can know about this. Not your friends, not your employees. No. One."

"I already agreed to that. Trust me, the last thing I want is anyone finding out I was stupid enough to marry you," I say, and damn, even I can admit that was a really bitchy thing to say.

See? This is why serious conversations should only be had after I've been properly caffeinated.

Something flickers in Kasen's eyes—hurt, maybe?—but

then I blink and his usual scowl's still in place, so I think it must've been a hangover-induced hallucination. Stupid me, he doesn't have human emotions. "Feeling's mutual, Pink."

I hesitate with my hand on the doorknob. Why the hell don't I want to go?

"This is dumb," I mutter, more to myself than to him.

"What?"

I straighten my shoulders and despite the smeared makeup and the fact I can literally *still feel him inside of me,* I give him my bitchy professional smile. "Nothing. Let's never do this again."

I don't wait for his response, stepping out into the hallway and closing the door behind me.

Holy crap.

Did that just happen?

I can't believe I married Kasen James.

2
Wren

THE FLIGHT back to Portland is excruciating. My hangover has evolved from "just let me die" to "functional zombie" territory, but the persistent throbbing behind my eyes makes it impossible to get anything done. Instead, I pop a Dramamine and spend the flight with my sunglasses and headphones on doing my best not to interact with anybody.

I stare out the window at the clouds, trying and failing not to think about Kasen.

We managed to avoid each other for the rest of the convention, though I caught glimpses of him. He's tall, and it makes him easy to spot even in a crowded room. He had that stupid beanie back on his head and his signature flannel stretched across his muscles. Every time our eyes met, a shock of something uncomfortable passed through me, and we both looked away.

Good to know he couldn't help looking at me too, though.

I spin the wedding band on my finger. I still don't understand why I haven't taken it off. I *should* take it off. Now. Immediately. This stupid ring represents the biggest mistake of my life. But for some reason, my fingers won't cooperate.

I've tried to come up with a reason why, but I've got nothing. I guess I like how it feels there even if I can't stand the man who put it on my finger.

For fuck's sake. This is ridiculous. I'll deal with it when I'm back in Portland, where I can lock away this gold band and the entire Vegas disaster along with it.

Until then, I'm in the business of doing anything and everything that feels good and comfortable. So the ring stays.

Just until I get home.

"More water, ma'am?" The flight attendant's question startles me.

"Um, yes. Please." My voice is wrecked. I didn't notice it this morning, what with all the life-changing discoveries and brutal hangover, and now I'm wondering if it's because I was up all night screaming.

In the best and also horrifyingly worst way.

When she moves on, I slouch in my seat and try to forget everything that happened over the last forty-eight hours. I must doze off, because the next thing I know, the captain's announcing our descent.

I press my forehead against the cool window. The sky's gray and rainy as we come down through the clouds, and I love it. The good ol' Pacific Northwest gloom. It feels like home.

It feels like what happened in Sin City was just some sort of fever dream and I'm waking up back in reality.

Twenty minutes after landing, I'm standing at baggage claim watching the same three suitcases circle the carousel. Not one of them's mine.

This is what I get for being an over-packer and having to check a bag.

My phone vibrates in my hand just as I'm taking it off airplane mode.

> Kieran: Where are you?

> Kieran: The MacIntyre meeting's in 45.
>
> Kieran: Do I need to file a missing person's report?
>
> Kieran: Don't make me call you

Shit. The MacIntyre meeting. I completely spaced on it. They're a small but growing brewery looking for distribution—exactly the kind of client Cascade needs. Exactly the kind of brewery Kasen would try to convince to bypass distributors altogether and sell direct-to-bar like Timber does.

> Me: I'm in baggage claim hell.
>
> Me: Stall.

I tap my foot against the tile. "This is ridiculous," I mutter, earning a sympathetic smile from the businessman standing next to me.

By the time I reach Cascade headquarters, I've pushed thoughts of Vegas and Kasen as far back in my mind as possible. I've done what I told myself I would, and when the plane touched down on Portland soil, I took the ring off.

It didn't go far, though, and I slipped it on the simple chain necklace that used to be my grandmother's and tucked it into my shirt. I did a speed change into fresh clothes in the airport bathroom. My hair's pulled back into a ponytail, my makeup's as flawless as it can get, having been done in the back of an Uber (complete with covered hickey), and I'm back to feeling more like myself.

I mean, I'm still a wreck, but no one needs to know that.

My baby, the converted warehouse that houses Cascade Craft Distribution, comes into view, and every time I see it, I feel a swell of pride. I built this business from nothing, fought for every contract, every tap handle, every distribution route.

I refuse to let one stupid decision hurt my baby.

Kieran meets me at the door in a tailored navy Tom Ford suit, a coffee in each hand and a smirk on his handsome face.

"It must've been a good weekend because you look like hell," he says, handing me the larger of the two cups.

"I don't want to talk about it," I reply, taking a grateful sip.

"Exactly how you should walk away from a trip to Vegas."

"MacIntyre?"

"Conference room. They were early, which is a good sign."

I nod, already shifting into work mode as the caffeine works its magic into my bloodstream. "Good. What's our offer?"

Kieran falls into step beside me as we cross the warehouse floor. "Thirty percent distribution with first-year incentives if they hit the targets we set. Exclusive rights to their seasonal releases."

"Make it thirty-five," I say. "I want them to feel we're invested in their growth."

Kieran gives me a searching look. "You sure? That's higher than we discussed."

"I'm sure."

What I don't say is that I need this win today—need something to go right after the clusterfuck that was Vegas. I need to prove to myself that I'm still capable and strong and not the fuckup my weekend choices might imply.

Right before we're about to go into the conference room, Kieran stops me with a hand on my arm. He looks down at me with a frown, his hair swept back off his face. "I know you said you don't want to talk about it, but what really happened in Vegas?" he asks quietly. "And don't say 'nothing' because I can tell something's off." He glances up at the room full of people. "You can't go in there being off."

For a split second, I consider telling him everything. Kieran is the closest thing I have to a best friend, the one person who knows all the sacrifices I've made for Cascade. He's been by my side for all of them. But this whole thing is just too humiliating to admit. At least right now when I've got less than thirty seconds before I need to walk into that room projecting nothing but confidence.

"What happens in Vegas stays in Vegas," I say with forced lightness. "Now let's go sign this brewery before someone else does."

Kieran doesn't look convinced, but he lets it drop. "Whatever you say, boss."

I paste on my *I'm about to own the world* smile as I push open the conference room door, extending my hand to the MacIntyre team. "Welcome to Cascade. Let's talk about getting your beer into every bar in Portland, shall we?"

For the next hour, I lose myself in what I do best—growing my empire. I push thoughts of Kasen and wedding rings and big dicks and Vegas hotel suites to the back of my mind. This—business, contracts, distribution routes—this is what I'm good at. This is what matters.

Not blue eyes or tattoos or a warm body keeping me safe while I sleep.

By the time the MacIntyre team leaves, contracts signed and handshakes exchanged, I've almost convinced myself that everything that happened this weekend was some kind of weird fever dream.

But then my phone buzzes with a text from an unknown number.

> Unknown: we need to talk

And just like that, reality comes crashing back and ruins my good mood. I stare at the message while my heart gallops away. I know exactly who it's from, even without a name.

Kasen James.

My husband.

3
Kasen

Four weeks later...

I SWEAR I see fucking pink hair everywhere.

It's been a month since Vegas, and I still can't get the image of Wren Callan sprawled across those hotel sheets out of my head. Every time I close my eyes, there she is with all her curves and attitude and that goddamn hair fanned out against the white pillowcase.

The divorce paperwork sits half done on my desk at home. I've filled out my portion, but I keep finding reasons not to file it. Either I'm too busy or I need to double-check something. Maybe the courthouse closes early on Fridays. They're bullshit excuses, and I know it.

Ask me if I care.

"The wort's about to boil over," Lake's voice drags me back to reality. "You planning to add those hops sometime today, or should we just brew a different beer altogether?"

I blink, suddenly aware of the weight of the measured hops in my hand and the rolling boil of the wort in front of me. The rich, malty aroma fills the brewery and I inhale. This, at least, makes sense.

"Shit. Sorry." I dump the hops into the kettle, watching the green cones disappear into the bubbling liquid.

"That's the third time you've zoned out this morning." Lake leans against the brewing tank, arms crossed over his chest. His blonde hair is messy and his septum ring catches the light as he tilts his head. "What's going on with you?"

"Nothing." The word comes out too fast.

"Bullshit." Lake's eyebrow quirks up. "This about Cascade again?"

My jaw tightens at the mention. "What about them?"

"Oh, I don't know." Lake checks the temperature gauge, making a note on his clipboard. "Maybe the fact that you've been obsessed with beating 'Princess Pink'—" he makes air quotes with his fingers,"—ever since she swiped the airport contract from under us."

"Don't remind me." I grab the long paddle and stir the wort more aggressively than necessary. "She undercut us, knowing we couldn't match her price without taking a loss."

"And that's bad business... how, exactly?" Lake reaches over to adjust the heat. "Careful, you're going to scorch it."

I ease up on the stirring, focusing on the repetitive motion to calm the irritation bubbling up inside me. It's the same feeling I get every time I think about Wren and her vicious business tactics. Or her mouth. Or how she looked in that black dress in Vegas before it ended up hanging from a lampshade in my hotel room.

"It was a dick move," I mutter.

"Says the guy who's been trying to convince every new brewery in Portland to bypass distributors altogether." Lake snorts. "Face it, man. You're just pissed because she's good at what she does."

I shoot him a glare. "Whose side are you on?"

18

"The side of not watching you being a moody bastard over the same woman for the last year." He checks his watch. "Timer's up. Whirlpool hops go in now."

I flip him off, then reach for the next addition, carefully measuring the hops that will give our new seasonal its signature finish. My hands work automatically while my brain keeps circling back to Vegas. To waking up with a wedding ring on my finger and Wren Callan naked in my bed.

The brewery door swings open and the chime pulls me back to reality. Because I got lost in memories of *her*. *Again*.

Lake glances over my shoulder and grins. "Speaking of women who terrify you—hey, Clover!"

I turn to see my sister making her way through the brewery, baby carrier in one hand, diaper bag slung across her body. Her black hair is piled in a messy bun, dark circles under her eyes, but she's smiling. My nephew, Noble, is in the carrier, out cold.

"I'd flip you off, Lake, but there are innocent eyes present," Clover says cheerfully.

"He's asleep," Lake points out.

"Yeah, well, I'm too sleep-deprived to argue." Clover sets the carrier down on a clean section of countertop. "Less than two hours of sleep at a time for the last week has left me barely functional."

I wipe my hands on a towel and cross to her, dropping a kiss on the top of her head. "You look like hell."

"Thanks, big brother. And you look like you slept in those clothes." She pinches my t-shirt and wrinkles her nose. "How's the new seasonal coming?"

"If your brother can stay focused long enough to finish it, we might actually get it into fermenters today," Lake says.

I ignore him, looking into the carrier at my nephew. Noble's tiny features are relaxed in sleep, one small fist curled near his cheek. Something in my chest constricts at the sight.

"The baby's still breathing, right?" I ask, only half-joking. He's so still.

Clover rolls her eyes. "Yes, Kasen. He's fine. Just tired from screaming his head off all morning." She rubs her eyes. "Banks is on a twenty-four-hour shift at the station, and I needed to get out of the house before I lost my mind."

"You want coffee?" I gesture toward the coffee machine behind the bar.

"God, yes. And an hour of adult conversation that doesn't revolve around breast pumps or baby poop."

"I don't know about the second part," Lake calls over his shoulder, "but the coffee's fresh. Made it an hour ago."

I reach for the baby carrier before Clover can pick it up. "I got it," I say, grabbing the diaper bag too. But that's my sister for you. Trying to carry everything herself even when she's dead on her feet.

Clover follows me to the office, settling into the worn leather couch that's seen us through countless late nights and early mornings. I set down my nephew and the carrier before pouring Clover her coffee, strong with just the right amount of cream and a sprinkle of cinnamon, the way she's always taken it.

"So," she says, wrapping her hands around the warm mug. "What's got you so distracted that even Lake's noticed?"

I busy myself with adding cream to my own coffee. "Nothing. Just work stuff. You know how it is this time of year."

"Uh-huh." Clover takes a sip, eyeing me over the rim of her mug. "It wouldn't have anything to do with a certain pink-haired menace, would it?"

I nearly choke on my coffee. "What? No. Why would you—"

"Because Navy saw you two having some kind of intense conversation at that brewery convention in Vegas last month." She smiles her evilest little sister smile at me. "She said she could actually see the sparks flying between you."

Fuck. Actual sparks would have been less dangerous than what really happened.

"Why was Navy there?" I shake my head. "No, you know what? Navy needs to mind her own business," I grumble, taking a seat behind my desk. "And so do you."

"Oh, *please*. Like trying to dodge the question doesn't just prove my point." She leans forward. "What happened in Vegas? And don't say 'nothing' because you've been acting weird ever since you got back."

I'm saved from the interrogation by a small whimper from the baby carrier. Noble's face scrunches, his tiny body stretching as he starts to wake up. Clover sighs.

"And we were just getting to the good part." She reaches for him, but I'm already on my feet.

"I've got him." I carefully lift my nephew from the carrier, supporting his head the way Clover taught me. He feels impossibly small in my hands, fragile but solid at the same time. "Hey, little man."

Noble blinks up at me, his big blue eyes focusing briefly before his face crumples again.

"Shh, it's okay." I tuck him against my chest, one hand cradling the back of his head, the other supporting his body. Holding him like this makes me happy in a way I can't explain. And he smells weirdly good. "I've got you."

To my surprise, Noble quiets, his tiny hand grabbing onto my flannel shirt. I glance up to find Clover watching us.

"What?" I ask, suddenly self-conscious.

"Nothing." She shakes her head, smiling. "Just... you're good with him."

I shrug, careful not to disturb my nephew. "He's easy. Barely even cries with me."

"That's because you radiate this weird calm energy when you hold him." Clover sips her coffee. "It's the only time you don't look like you're about to punch a wall or brood yourself to death."

"I don't brood."

"You're the king of brooding. I'm surprised you don't wear a crown instead of your beanie."

I roll my eyes but can't help the small smile tugging at my lips. Noble makes a soft, contented sound against my chest, and I find myself rocking from side to side, a natural movement I didn't even realize I was doing.

"So," Clover says, clearly not letting me off the hook, "are you going to tell me what's got you all up in your head, or am I going to have to pry it out of Lake?"

"Lake doesn't know," I say, and then I want to kick my own ass. Why the hell would I admit there's anything to know? Fuck.

Clover's eyes light up like it's Christmas morning. "Ah-ha! So there *is* something to know."

I backpedal. "That's not what I meant—"

"Oh please," she cuts me off, leaning forward. "Navy told me you and Wren were about to kill each other or fu—"

"Don't." I focus on Noble, avoiding my sister's penetrating stare drilling into the side of my face. I won't be thinking about Wren naked while holding my nephew and talking to my sister. Not happening. "Cascade's been poaching accounts we were negotiating with, that's it."

It's not exactly a lie. Cascade has been more aggressive than usual lately, swooping in on bars and restaurants we've been courting. A couple of weeks ago, they landed MacIntyre Brewing, and I'd been working on them for months. I was trying to convince them to follow our direct-to-bar model, but Wren must have made them an offer they couldn't refuse.

It's like she's trying to piss me off. Or get my attention.

"Is it?" Clover narrows her eyes. "Because the way Navy

described it, there was definitely something going on between you two."

"Navy needs to get her eyes checked."

The brewery door chimes again, and a minute later, my best friend appears in the office doorway, dressed in his station uniform - navy department t-shirt and utility pants. He must have stepped out during his twenty-four-hour shift, like Clover mentioned. His face lights up when he sees Clover, and something in my chest twists—half envy, half happiness for my sister and best friend.

Banks's grin widens as he crosses the room. "Hey, Freckles," he says, pulling Clover in for a solid kiss before turning to me and Noble. I try not to gag. "How's my boy doing, Uncle Kase?"

"Just keeping him warm for you," I say with a half-smile, handing Noble over to Banks.

"And he's perfect," I add, just as Clover says, "He's a tiny terror."

Banks chuckles, settling Noble against his chest. "That's my boy." He looks between us with a knowing smile. "So, what were you guys talking about? When I walked in, it looked intense."

"Nothing worth repeating."

"Kasen's thing with Wren Callan," Clover says at the same time.

Banks's eyebrows shoot up as he bounces slightly to keep Noble content. "Your arch nemesis? Still holding that grudge over the airport deal?"

"It's not a grudge," I mutter, feeling defensive.

"Come on." Banks shifts Noble to his shoulder, giving me that knowing look he's perfected over fifteen years of friendship. "You've been obsessed with that woman since she first showed up on the scene. Maybe you should just sleep with her and get it over with already."

My whole body goes rigid, and I can feel heat crawling up

my neck. Noble makes a small squawk, like he can sense the sudden tension.

"That's not—we're not—" I can't even form a coherent sentence.

Banks exchanges a look with Clover. "Did I hit a nerve?"

"You don't know what the hell you're talking about," I manage, my voice tight.

Banks's eyebrows shoot up. "I was just giving you shit, dude." He studies my face, his expression shifting from teasing to something else. "Wait a second..."

"Don't." I glare at him, but it's too late.

"Holy shit." Banks's eyes widen. "Something happened, didn't it?"

Clover's head whips around, her gaze pinning me in place. "Kasen Jessie James, you better start talking."

"Nothing happened," I snap, but the lie feels like gravel in my throat.

Well, if by "nothing" you mean waking up married to the woman I've been feuding with for years after fucking her, then sure. *Nothing happened.*

And fuck her for middle naming me.

"You're such a bad liar," Clover says, with a big-ass shit-eating grin on her face. "You totally banged Wren Callan." Then the smile drops and she gags the way only little sisters can when they're confronted with their brother's sex life.

"I didn't sleep with her," I say, which is technically... well, not true either. Although there wasn't much sleeping involved.

"Vegas?" Banks asks, a hint of admiration creeping into his voice.

"Drop it," I warn, my tone leaving no room for argument. "Both of you. Now."

The office goes quiet, except for Noble's soft gurgles. Finally, Clover stands, taking the baby from Banks.

"Fine. Consider it dropped." She studies my face. "But

Kasen... whatever's going on, you know you can talk to us, right?"

I nod stiffly, unable to meet her eyes. How the hell am I supposed to tell my sister that I drunkenly married the woman I've been complaining about for months? That I've filled out divorce papers but can't seem to file them? That I wake up in the middle of the night, reaching for someone who isn't there?

Who I'm not even sure I *want* there?

"We should get going," Banks says, breaking the tension. "Reed's stopping by the house later to check in on Clover and the baby, and I've gotta get back to the station."

"Everything okay?"

"Just a follow-up," Clover assures me. "Noble had a little jaundice after birth, remember? Reed just wants to make sure everything's good."

I nod, relieved. "Tell him I said hey and that he should stop by after for a beer."

"Will do." Banks starts gathering Noble's things. "We still on for the Blazers game next week? Reed's coming too."

"Yeah, I'll be there." I help them pack up, grateful for the distraction, for something normal to focus on.

As they're leaving, Clover hugs me tight. "Love you, big brother," she murmurs. "Even when you're being a stubborn ass."

I squeeze her back. "Love you too, brat."

Banks gives me a look over her shoulder that says this conversation isn't finished, but he doesn't push it. They leave with a final wave and I blow out a breath now that they're gone.

I stand there for a second, reveling in the quiet. Then I hear Lake call from the brewing area, "Ten bucks says you slept with her!"

"Fuck off, Lake!" I shout back, but there's no heat in it.

I return to the brewery floor, where Lake is checking readings on the fermentation tanks, a knowing smirk on his face.

"Not a word," I warn.

He holds up his hands in mock surrender. "Wouldn't dream of it." He pauses. "Though it would explain a lot."

I grab a clipboard, focusing on the numbers, on the safety of data and measurements. On things I can control, unlike the mess I've made of my personal life.

"Don't you have something better to do?"

"Than watch you squirm? Not really." Lake checks his watch. "But I do need to go check on that delivery at the loading dock. The new glasses for the tasting room should be here."

He heads toward the back exit, pausing at the door. "For what it's worth... I get it. She's hot, smart, and drives you crazy."

"We're not discussing this." And I bristle at Lake calling Wren *hot*. When the fuck has he looked at her?

"Whatever you say, boss." He disappears through the door, leaving me alone with the steady hum of the brewing equipment and my unreasonably jealous thoughts.

I force myself to focus, and before I know it, two hours have passed. I'm feeling almost normal again. The wort is cooling, ready to be transferred to the fermenter. I put Lake in the tasting room to help with the afternoon rush because I didn't want to deal with his shit, and I've been hiding out in the brewing area. It's quiet back here and the repetitive work has cleared my head. It's had the added bonus of pushing any and all thoughts of Wren to the background where they belong.

Until I glance out the front window and see a familiar van parked across the street, the Cascade Craft Distribution logo big and bright on its side.

"You've got to be fucking kidding me," I mutter.

I watch as one of Wren's delivery guys unloads kegs at The Hop Yard, a bar that opened just last month. A bar I've been trying to get Timber into since before they even opened their doors. A bar whose owner assured me last week they were still "considering their options."

My jaw clenches as it feels like snakes coil in my stomach. Before I can think better of it, I'm pulling off my brewing gloves and heading for the door.

The spring air is cool against my skin after the warmth of my brewery. I cross the street without bothering to check for traffic, my focus locked on the Cascade van and the guy lifting kegs onto a dolly.

"Hey," I call out, my voice sharper than I mean for it to be.

The delivery guy looks up, confusion crossing his face when he sees me. "Can I help you?"

"When did The Hop Yard sign with Cascade?" I demand.

"Uh..." He glances at his clipboard. "Last week, I think? Today's the first delivery."

Last week. While I was still waiting for Tom Hayes to 'consider his options,' Wren had already locked down the account. The familiar frustration rises, made worse by the knowledge that we've been avoiding each other for weeks. After that text exchange when I first got back to Portland—setting up a coffee meeting I never showed up for—neither of us has reached out again.

Things are too awkward and I don't want to face her as much as I imagine she doesn't want to face me.

She's good at pissing me off from afar, though. Always has been.

Now when I need to confront her about business, I can't even do that without dragging up Vegas and inevitably her questions about when we're going to file the divorce papers I can't bring myself to fill out.

"Everything okay, man?" The delivery guy is eyeing me warily now.

I force myself to take a breath. "Yeah. Fine." I turn and head back to the brewery, hands clenched at my sides.

Seeing her company logo, knowing she's expanding her

reach right in my own backyard, sets something off inside me. It's like she's deliberately trying to get under my skin.

Back in the safety of Timber, I lean against the wall, taking deep breaths. This is why I need to file those divorce papers. I need to move the fuck on. Forget I ever saw what Wren Callan looks like first thing in the morning, soft and rumpled and more beautiful than she has any right to be.

Before I can talk myself out of it, I pull out my phone and scroll to the contact I'd saved and had to stop myself from texting every single fucking day. The one labeled simply "Pink." My thumb hovers for a second before I type:

The Hop Yard? Really?

I hit send before I can talk myself out of it. Almost immediately, three dots appear. She's typing back.

Yes, really. Why? Did you lick them and they're yours?

I can practically hear her voice, sarcastic and bitchy and why the *fuck* is my dick chubbing up? My thumb hovers over the screen for a long moment before I reply. I consider bringing up what else I licked that's now mine but think better of it. Instead, I type:

> We need to talk about Vegas.

Her response comes almost immediately:

> Wren: Four weeks of silence and now you want to talk? No thanks.

I stare at the screen, frustration and something else—relief?—warring inside me. She's shutting me down, which is exactly what I should want. I should just send the paperwork to her office and be done with this shit.

I don't need gray eyes flashing with anger or lips curving into that smirk that drives me crazy.

But if she doesn't want to meet, why am I so disappointed?

I pocket my phone without responding. Let her think I don't care. Let her think anything but the truth—that I can't stop thinking about her.

"Fuck," I mutter.

Lake pokes his head in from the tasting room. "Everything good? You look like you've seen a ghost."

"Not a ghost," I say, pushing off the wall and heading back to the fermenter. "Just shitty choices coming back to haunt me."

4
Wren

I'VE PUKED three times this morning. Three. And I'm blaming it on bad sushi... that I ate last week.

Yeah.

I wipe my mouth with the back of my hand and stare at my reflection in the Cascade office bathroom mirror. Holy hell, I look like death warmed over—pale and clammy, with circles under my eyes so dark they could be mistaken for actual bruises. Even my pink hair looks sad, the rose gold fading to a washed-out shade that perfectly matches how I feel.

"Get your shit together, Wren," I mutter, splashing cold water on my face.

It's been six weeks since Vegas. Six weeks since I woke up naked with Kasen James's ring on my finger. Six weeks since we slept together, and I have zero idea if we used protection. My gut says no just based on the sheer level of stupid involved in that night.

I'm guessing my gut's right, because it's been eight weeks since my last period.

Nope. Absolutely not going there.

It's stress, obviously. I've been dealing with the MacIntyre deal, expanding distribution routes into uncharted territory, and dodging Kasen's increasingly persistent texts about fixing our "situation." Who wouldn't skip a cycle with all that?

I dry my hands and straighten my blazer, doing a quick scan to make sure I didn't miss the toilet this time because it was close. Yep, I'm definitely *not* falling apart at all.

This is *fine* (she says in a voice like Ross from Friends).

Totally fine.

When I push open the bathroom door, Kieran is waiting in the hallway, leaning back against the wall with one ankle crossed over the other. He narrows his eyes, daring me to bullshit him.

"That's the third time today."

"Yep."

He sighs and holds out a cup. "It's peppermint tea. It'll help."

I take it, grateful despite my irritation at being so transparently mothered. "I'm fine. It's just something I ate."

"For the past week?" Kieran falls into step beside me as we head back toward my office. "You've been 'something I ate'-ing for seven straight days, Wren."

"I've also been closing the Henderson deal while juggling three new breweries and keeping the Johnson route from imploding." I take a cautious sip of the tea. It's perfect—not too hot with just the right amount of honey. "I'm allowed to be a little under the weather."

"A little under the weather," Kieran repeats flatly. "You nearly passed out during the inventory meeting yesterday."

"The warehouse was hot."

"It was sixty-two degrees."

I shoot him a glare, but there's no real heat behind it. He knows me too well. "Don't you have actual work to do instead of monitoring my bathroom habits?"

"Apparently that's part of my job now, especially after yesterday." His expression softens slightly. "Seriously. What's going on with you? And as someone who's spent a lot of energy focused on not knocking anyone up, I'm getting a bad feeling. I'm gonna need you to be straight with me."

We reach my office, the glass-walled corner space that overlooks the warehouse floor. Through the windows, I watch our team loading trucks with kegs and cases. A massive distribution map of the Pacific Northwest dominates one wall, colored pins marking our territory—red for exclusive contracts, blue for shared, yellow for pending negotiations.

There are a lot more red pins than there were six months ago.

I sit behind my desk, setting the tea down carefully. "Nothing's going on except the usual end-of-quarter chaos."

Kieran doesn't buy it for a second. He closes the office door and takes the seat across from me, his expression deadly serious.

"Is this about the airport deal? Because I heard through the industry grapevine that Kasen James is still furious. Apparently he's been trying to convince the airport to allow direct sales from local breweries instead of going exclusively through distributors."

My heart does a stupid little stutter at Kasen's name, and I focus on keeping my expression neutral. *Seriously? Get it together, heart.* That sounds exactly like something Kasen would do. He's like me in that way, and we both refuse to accept defeat.

And that flutter in my stomach? Totally just irritation.

Obviously.

"Let him waste his time," I say, reaching for a file folder to give my hands something to do. "That contract is ironclad. And it's not like we haven't earned it. Half the craft beer sampled at PDX already comes through our warehouse."

Kieran studies me for a long moment. "There's something you're not telling me."

My fingers tighten on the folder. "Like what?"

"I don't know. Something happened in Vegas. You came back different."

I force a laugh that sounds wrong even to my own ears. "Different how?"

"Distracted. And now you're sick all the time. You're a mess, boss. And you lose your shit whenever Timber or Kasen James comes up."

I resist the urge to play with the ring still hanging around my neck. "I don't lose my shit."

Kieran scoffs. "I was at that supplier meeting yesterday and overheard the Eastside Ales guys talking about you and Kasen having some kind of confrontation at the convention. Then this morning, that rep from Evergreen Hops with the porn star mustache asked me if you two were 'still at each other's throats.' Deny it all you want, but people aren't stupid."

Meaning *he's* not stupid. Heat floods my face. "People need to mind their own damn business. Nothing happened. Nothing worth talking about, anyway."

"So something did happen."

Fuck fuckity fuck fuck fuck.

"Nothing happened." The lie tastes like bile. Oh, wait. I think that's actual vomit climbing back up my throat.

Kieran doesn't look convinced, but he mercifully drops the subject when my phone buzzes with a text. I glance down at the screen.

Out of the frying pan, into the freaking fire...

> Kasen: Can we talk about Vegas?
>
> Kasen: C'mon, Pink. You know we can't keep ignoring it

I grit my teeth at the nickname but take a deep breath to rein in my irritation so Kieran doesn't notice.

Pink. Only Kasen calls me that, and somehow he manages to make those four letters sound both condescending and *way* too intimate at the same time. I don't even know what to do with it other than get pissed off.

There *might* be the tiniest bit of me that likes the stupid name, but that part of me can fuck right off.

He's been trying to get me to meet for weeks now, sending texts I've been strategically ignoring. Clearly he's not taking the hint.

I switch off the screen without responding. Dealing with Kasen needs to be future me's problem because right now I simply *cannot*.

"So," Kieran says, blessedly moving on, "we still on for Henderson this afternoon? I've got the numbers prepped, and those custom tap handles just came in."

I could kiss him for changing the subject. This is safe territory. I can handle work.

"Yes, we—" I choke a little as a wave of nausea hits me again and I'm not prepared for it. I swallow hard because if I don't, I'm going to throw up. I breathe through my nose, willing it to pass. It does not, but I get my shit together enough to finish my earlier sentence. "We should lead with the seasonal rotation plan. Henderson wants flexibility with their limited releases."

Kieran narrows his eyes. "You look like shit again. You just got all pale and sweaty."

"Wow, thanks."

He grins, but then it drops off his face. "Maybe you should go home. I can handle Henderson."

"I'm fine," I insist, even as my stomach rumbles out a warning and minty acid climbs up the back of my throat. Turns out that peppermint tea was a bad idea. "I just need a minute."

And about twenty-five Tums and maybe some Dramamine.

Or a nap. Yeah, I could really go for a nap.

Though it's looking more and more like I'll get to take it on the floor in front of the toilet.

He opens his mouth to argue, but I've already lost the battle and I jump up, shoving my chair out of the way and making a desperate dash for the bathroom. This time, I do puke on my shoes. Ugh.

When I finally stumble from the stall, my assistant is waiting with a paper towel and an expression that says he's reached his limit on my bullshit for the day.

"Yeah," he says, handing me the towel. "You're going home. Now."

I start to protest, but another wave of dizziness sweeps over me, and I have to grab the sink to stay upright. Kieran grabs my arm, holding me steady while I rinse out my mouth.

"I'm not asking, boss," he says firmly. "Either you take yourself home, or I'll take you. Better yet, take your ass straight to the doctor."

For once, I don't have the energy to fight, but I give it my best shot anyway. "The Henderson meeting—"

"I already told you I'd handle it."

I nod, hating how weak I feel. This isn't me. I don't get sick. I don't take days off. I don't let anything interfere with the business I've built from nothing.

"Fine," I give in because really I don't have any other choice. "But I'll be back tomorrow."

"We'll see," Kieran says, already pulling out his phone to order the car.

I want to argue but I can't, so I guess that's tomorrow's problem. Hopefully by then this food poisoning or whatever will finally be out of my system.

The ride home is a blur. I curl up in the back seat of the rideshare, trying to ignore the bubbling, gurgling mess of my stomach and the thoughts racing through my head. It's just a stomach bug. Or food poisoning. Or stress. Maybe a disgusting trifecta of all three.

It has to be.

But as the car pulls up to my apartment building, a different explanation—one I've been refusing to acknowledge in any way—pushes its way to the forefront of my mind.

I haven't had my period since before Vegas.

It's been... two months-ish?

What if this is something far, *far* worse than bad sushi?

"Fuck," I whisper, fumbling with my keys at the door. I drop them twice before I finally manage to unlock it.

Inside my apartment, I drop my bag on the counter and head straight for the bathroom. I dig through the cabinet under the sink, searching for the emergency pregnancy test I bought last year after a condom broke with a guy I met off an app for a hookup. I never needed to use it.

Not until today.

My hands shake as I read the instructions. Pee on the stick. Wait three minutes. Try not to freak out.

That last one's not actually in the instructions, but it should be. And I'm failing at it.

Three minutes feels like three years. I pace my small bathroom, checking my phone every five seconds. I just let my mind run away with all sorts of calculations and scenarios, but none of it helps.

All my thoughts end up right back in one place: Vegas.

We used protection... I think. Most of the night is still a blur, but I remember bits and pieces of what happened. Mostly things like Kasen's hands on my hips, my fingers in his hair, his mouth hot against my neck.

I know we used a condom the first time. I think I remember that much.

But did we for round two? Round three?

My head falls back and I close my eyes, praying to anyone who'll listen and begging to not let this be what I think it is.

The timer on my phone chimes, and I freeze. I can't look.

I *can't*.

If I don't look, it's not real. Nothing changes.

"Woman up, Wren. You can handle this," I mutter, forcing myself to pick up the plastic stick.

And look at that. Two lines. Clear as fucking day.

"No." The word comes out strangled because *I absolutely cannot handle this*. "No, no, no."

It could be a false positive, right? Those happen. The test is probably expired or faulty or—

I need a second opinion. A professional one.

My hands are still shaking as I call the number for Dr. Reed Walker, one of the top-rated OB/GYNs in Portland. I met him once at the re-opening of Timber after the fire last year, though we barely spoke. Yeah, he's good friends with Kasen and this could totally bite me in the ass, but if I'm going to do this, I want the best, and that's Dr. Walker.

I just have to pray doctor-patient confidentiality is really a thing.

"Portland OBGYN," a cheerful voice answers. "How can I help you?"

"I need to see Dr. Walker," I say, my voice steadier than I feel. "Today, if possible. It's an emergency."

"I'm sorry, but Dr. Walker doesn't have anything available until—"

"Tell him it's Wren Callan. I'm friends with Clover Priestly. Please tell him it's an emergency." I hate using connections, especially Kasen's sister, who I'm not exactly friends with, but desperate times and all that.

I'm friends-ish with Clover's best friend Navy, and also married to her brother even if she doesn't know it, so what the hell.

There's a pause, then, "One moment, please."

While I wait, I chew on my thumbnail, something I haven't done in years.

"Ms. Callan?" the receptionist's voice is just as cheery when she comes back on the line. "Dr. Walker says he can fit you in at four o'clock."

The rush of relief I feel is insane, followed right up with another dose of anxiety because now I have to face this *for real.* "I'll be there."

I hang up and sink onto the edge of the bathtub, letting my head fall into my hands and my phone drop to the floor. This *cannot* be happening. I have a five-year plan, a distribution empire to build, and absolutely zero room for a baby.

Especially not Kasen James's baby.

What the hell am I going to do?

5
Wren

DR. WALKER'S office is exactly what you'd expect from a high-end OB/GYN practice. The waiting room is decorated in soft, soothing colors. The chairs look comfortable, and there's somehow a distinct lack of screaming children. I mean, where do they put them all? I glance around. There's got to be a nursery or some hidden panic room or something where they force the moms with kids to wait, right? So they don't disturb everyone else?

Yes, I'm aware my train of thought is stupid, but I'm also embracing the chaos in my head right now. It's a good distraction.

Black and white photos of pregnant bellies and new families, all looking unreasonably happy about the life-altering mess they've signed up for, decorate the walls. Meanwhile, I'm coated in a layer of nervous sweat and every second spent in this place brings me closer to a panic attack.

I check in at the front desk, grateful that the waiting room is nearly empty. The fewer witnesses to this disaster, the better.

"First time with Dr. Walker?" the receptionist asks as she hands me a clipboard full of forms.

"Yep," I say, taking the paperwork.

"You'll love him. He delivered my sister's twins last year. He's the best in Portland."

"So I hear." I manage a tight smile and find a seat in the corner, as far from the other patients as possible. The forms are typical, wanting to know my medical history, insurance information, and last period.

I think we've already established it's been a while, but I check the app on my phone to get the exact date.

Oh yay, looks like that weekend in Vegas was right in my ovulation window.

I hand in the completed paperwork and try not to fidget as I wait. My phone buzzes in my purse, and I pull it out to find another text from Kasen.

> Kasen: Ignore me all you want
>
> Kasen: But it's not going away, Pink.

I stare at the screen with zero clue what to say. I'm literally sitting in the doctor's office waiting to find out if he knocked me up.

Wait.

The timing of his texts is suspect, right?

Does he know I'm here right now? How could he possibly know? Did someone see me come in here? Did Dr. Walker call Clover because I name dropped her to get this appointment?

No, I'm just losing my mind is all. He can't know. I only just found out myself. Well, actually I know nothing yet. This could totally be food poisoning and a false positive. He's just trying to get me to sign the divorce papers.

Which just brings up another question I don't want to answer: why do I keep putting him off?

My heart's racing, and another wave of nausea that has

nothing to do with morning sickness and everything to do with panic starts to build. This is a nightmare. This is—

"Wren Callan?"

I snap my head up, shoving my phone back into my purse without responding. The nurse is standing with a tablet in her hand, waiting for me to acknowledge that yes, I'm Wren Callan, and yes, I'm here because I'm probably not-maybe-definitely knocked up.

With my husband-slash-enemy's baby.

"That's me," I say, my voice shaky as hell as I rise to follow her.

The examination room is clean and clinical, with diagrams of female anatomy on the walls that make me want to look anywhere else. I'm sweating and *oh my god I can't do this*. The nurse takes my vitals, then asks a few preliminary questions.

"Dr. Walker will be with you shortly," she says with a reassuring smile before closing the door.

I try to regulate my breathing while I perch awkwardly on the edge of the examination table. The paper beneath me crinkles with every slight movement. I hate feeling this vulnerable, this exposed.

There's a soft knock on the door before Dr. Walker steps into the room. He looks like I remember him from last year, tall and lean, with his hair pulled back in a bun. He's younger and hotter than you want a man who's going to be seeing your vagina in a clinical setting to be, but he's also the best, so it is what it is.

"Ms. Callan," he says, extending his hand like we've never met before. "I'm Dr. Walker. Reed, if you prefer. It's nice to meet you officially." He grins. "Now, what can I do for you? My receptionist told me you were having some sort of emergency?"

His handshake is firm but gentle. "Call me Wren." I let his hand go, wiping my sweaty palm on my pants. "And yep, it's an emergency all right."

Reed sits on a rolling stool, opening my file. "I see from your forms that you think you might be pregnant?"

I hesitate for a second. He's friends with Kasen. He wouldn't say anything, would he? No, there's that whole doctor patient confidentiality thing, right?

And besides, how would he know Kasen's my maybe-baby daddy?

Unless Kasen said something?

Reed's watching me and I realize that it's taking me way too long to respond. Like, an awkward amount of time.

Finally, I nod, my throat suddenly dry. "You're not allowed to tell anyone what we talk about, right?"

"Not a word unless you give me your permission."

"I took a home test, and it was positive. But I wanted to be sure."

"Of course." He glances at the form. He doesn't try to tell me that this isn't really an emergency, which I appreciate. "You noted your last period was approximately eight weeks ago, and you've been experiencing nausea, fatigue, and dizziness?"

"Yes. I thought it was stress or something I ate, but..."

"But the timing lines up," he finishes for me. His manner is professional but warm, without a hint of judgment, and I find myself relaxing just a little. "We'll do a blood test to confirm. Is there anything else I should know?"

I nearly choke on the waterfall of words trying to pour out of my mouth. "It was—" I hesitate, unsure how to explain the absolute clusterfuck that is my current situation. "It was unplanned. Very unplanned. And complicated."

Reed nods, making a note in my file. "I understand. Lots of pregnancies are unplanned. Let's focus on confirming whether you're pregnant, and then we can talk about your options."

The rest of the exam passes in a blur of questions, blood draws, and a urine sample. Through it all, Reed stays calm and matter-of-fact. His bedside manner is better than I thought it'd be, considering he's one of Kasen's best friends. He helps me stay calm, which I really needed. I understand why he's so highly sought after by the women of Portland.

When we're done with the exam, Reed steps out. My phone buzzes again, but I ignore it. If it's another text from Kasen, I might spiral all the way into crazy town and I can't do that in public no matter how bad things get.

Reed returns with a tablet in hand, his expression carefully neutral. "Well, Wren, the results are in. Your blood test confirms you are indeed pregnant. Based on your last period, you're approximately eight weeks along."

Even though I was expecting it, the confirmation is like a punch in the face. I fall into the chair in the corner as my legs give out.

"Are you sure?" I ask, though I know it's a stupid question.

"I'm sure. The hCG levels in your blood are consistent with early pregnancy." He studies my face, his expression softening. "I know this might not be the news you were hoping for."

That's the understatement of the century.

"What are my options?" I ask, proud that my voice doesn't shake.

Reed leans back against the counter, crossing one long leg over the other. "You have several. You can continue with the pregnancy and parent, continue with the pregnancy and place the child for adoption, or terminate the pregnancy. Oregon law protects your right to choose any of these options."

I nod mechanically, trying to process the information through the haze of shock. "How long do I have to decide?"

"If you're considering termination, Oregon allows it up to the point of viability, which is around twenty-four weeks. But earlier is safer and less complicated." His tone remains factual, without pressure in either direction. "Whatever you decide, I'm here to provide medical care and support."

"Thank you," I say automatically, though I don't really know what I'm saying right now.

Reed hands me a folder of information. "This contains resources for all options, including prenatal care schedules if you choose to continue the pregnancy, as well as information about adoption services and termination procedures. Take some time to review it and think about what's right for you."

I take the folder, clutching it to my body like I can absorb the information through my skin if I just hold it close enough. "And if I—if I decide to continue?"

He flashes me a grin and if I wasn't... whatever I am with Kasen, I might have developed a crush on hot Dr. Walker. "Then we'd schedule your first prenatal appointment, do an ultrasound, and start you on prenatal vitamins." He pauses. "Regardless of your decision, I'd recommend you start taking them now, just to be safe."

I nod, because my mouth has forgotten how to form words.

"Do you have any questions for me?" Reed asks gently.

A thousand, but none I can articulate right now. "Not yet. I need to process."

"Of course. My nurse will give you some prenatal vitamin samples and schedule a follow-up appointment for next week. In the meantime, if you have any questions or concerns, don't hesitate to call." He stands, extending his hand again. "And Wren? Whatever you decide, it's your choice. Don't let anyone tell you otherwise."

I shake his hand, grateful for his kindness despite the circumstances. "Thank you, Dr. Walker."

"Reed," he corrects with a small smile. "And you're welcome."

The nurse gives me the promised vitamins, schedules my next appointment, and sends me on my way with a smile. I walk out of the office as I disassociate from reality. Everything looks a little off as I try to come to terms with what just happened.

Pregnant.

I'm freaking *pregnant* with Kasen James's baby.

There's a part of him inside me *right now*. *How did I let this happen?*

I'm so distracted that I nearly collide with someone in the parking garage as I walk toward my car.

"Sorry, I wasn't—Mom?" I blink in surprise, finding myself face to face with Margot Callan, her sleek gray pixie and designer glasses unmistakable even in the gloomy light in here.

"Wren?" My mother's sharp eyes scan me from head to toe, stopping on the folder in my arms, then glancing up at the sign for the medical building. "What are you doing here?"

Of all the people to run into on this day outside an OB/GYN's office, it had to be my mother, the woman who raised me on equal parts feminist theory and warnings about men who'll suck you dry and throw you away with nothing left.

Yeah, she's going to *love* the news that I went and got myself knocked up.

"I was just—it's nothing." I tuck the folder into my bag. "What are you doing here?"

"Book club meets in the coffee shop across the street. This is the closest parking garage." Her eyes narrow suspiciously. "You look pale. Are you sick?"

"No, it was just a checkup," I say, hating having to lie to her. She may be intense, but we've always been pretty close. I know she only wants the best for me.

My mother's mouth presses into a line as she watches me. She's always been able to see right through me and I try to keep any trace of my current drama off my face. "You're not taking care of yourself again." Her frown kicks up into a half-smile. "Working too many hours, I assume?"

"Guilty." I shift uncomfortably. "I learned from the best. Look, I need to go. I have a presentation to prepare for tomorrow."

"Nonsense. You look like you need a decent meal and some quality time with your mother." She links her arm through mine, leaving no room for argument. "I was headed to Verdigris for lunch. You'll join me."

It's not a question. My mother doesn't ask; she bulldozes.

Twenty minutes later, we're seated at a small table by the window, my mother sipping sparkling water while I pick at a salad I have no appetite for. She's spent the last fifteen minutes updating me on what's been going on with her. She's this badass professor and I'm so proud of everything she's built, but sometimes it's a lot.

The Margot Callan excellence that has always been an inspiration is also an impossible standard for me to live up to, and sometimes I feel like a disappointment, even though she's never said anything like that to me.

"Enough about my department politics," she says finally, setting down her glass. "Tell me what's really going on with you."

I set down my fork, abandoning the pretense of eating. "I told you, it's just work stress." No way am I about to confess anything to her before I've even had a chance to make a decision or, you know, curl up in a ball and ugly cry.

"Wren Elizabeth Callan." She fixes me with the same look that mostly kept me in line as a teenager. "I didn't raise you to lie to me."

Something about her concerned tone hits me right in the feels. It's the same mix of authority and warmth she always uses when she knows I'm bullshitting her because it always works to get me to spill everything. Before I can stop myself, tears fill my eyes.

"Oh, sweetheart." My mother's hand covers mine on the table, her voice softening. "What is it?"

I swallow hard, fighting for control. "I made a mistake, Mom."

"We all make mistakes. That's how we learn." She squeezes my hand. "Whatever it is, we'll handle it."

I almost tell her. The words are right there, just dying to be set free.

I got drunk-married in Vegas to a man I've spent the last two years hating.

And if that wasn't bad enough, *I'm pregnant.*

Single motherhood, here I come.

I know she'll be disappointed I'm repeating her mistakes, and honestly I am a little bit, too.

The words, though, they stick in my throat when I see the Pride pin on her lapel, the one she's worn since I came out as bisexual in college. The one that represents her unwavering support of my choices, even when they weren't the ones she would have made. How can I tell her I've done exactly what she warned me against— let a man derail the future I've worked so hard to build?

Not that it's his fault. I made my choices. But I don't think she'll see it that way.

"It's just business stuff," I say instead, pulling my hand away to wipe at my eyes. "A contract dispute that might get messy and it's got me really stressed."

My mother studies me for a long moment, clearly not buying it, but thankfully doesn't push. "All right. But remember what I've always told you—"

"No man is worth sacrificing your ambitions for," I recite, the mantra she's repeated since I was old enough to understand what ambition even was.

"Exactly." She nods approvingly. "Men come and go, but what you build for yourself lasts."

If only she knew how catastrophically those two things were colliding in my life right now.

"I know, Mom," I mumble. "I remember."

"And if worse comes to worst, you can always get Kieran to help out."

The rest of lunch passes with safer topics and I manage to get down enough to my salad to be convincing. By the time we part outside the restaurant, I've almost convinced myself I can handle this. Almost.

"Call me if you need anything," she says, kissing my cheek. "And for god's sake, get some rest. You look like the walking dead."

"I will," I say with a weak smile.

Two hours later, alone in my apartment, I sit cross-legged on my bed, staring at the folder from Dr. Walker. I've read through every pamphlet, every option, but I'm no closer to a decision than I was this afternoon.

Could I really *not* keep this baby?

I let my hand slowly drift down to rest on my stomach. There's a *person* in there right now growing and I wonder what they'll look like. *Who* they'll look like.

All I know is that before I decide anything, I need to tell Kasen. He deserves to know, even if the thought of telling him makes me want to throw up again.

Or maybe that's just the morning-slash-all day sickness. Hard to tell at this point.

I pull out my phone and open his text from earlier.

Before I can talk myself out of it, I type a response:

> Me: Tomorrow. 7pm. Your brewery.

His reply comes almost immediately:

> Kasen: I'll be there.

I flop back onto the bed and stare at the ceiling, wishing it held all the answers. Hell, I'd even settle for just one answer at this point.

"It's gonna be fine," I whisper to myself.

But for the first time in my life, I'm not sure I believe it.

6
Kasen

SHIT. *I'm gonna be adding another goddamn tattoo to my collection.*

That's my first thought when Wren Callan walks into my brewery at exactly seven oh one, looking like she's marching to her own execution.

It's been a habit since my mom died—marking major life shifts with permanent ink. And seeing Wren standing there, pink hair pulled back in a ponytail, gray eyes filled with something that looks a whole hell of a lot like fear, I can feel it in my bones. Whatever she's about to say is tattoo-worthy.

"Hey." My voice comes out rough and I clear my throat as I set down my pencil. The label design I've been working on—a Northwest IPA with hints of pine and citrus—is half finished on the page in front of me.

Wren doesn't say anything. She stands in the doorway, taking everything in like she's never been here before. I've been sketching beer labels at the corner table of the empty tasting room, the long wooden bar stretching along one wall, brewing tanks visible through the glass partition behind it. She studies the scattered pages of my designs, the charcoal pencils, the half-empty coffee mug beside my work, before her gaze finally lands on me. The intensity of it hits me square in the chest.

It's been both too long and not long enough since I last saw her.

I almost forgot how life-destroyingly beautiful she is.

She walks over, drops her bag on the chair across from me, and stays standing.

"We need to talk," she says, and even though I'm the one who's been texting her that exact phrase for weeks, hearing it from her lips makes my stomach clench. You know it's never a good thing when a woman says those dreaded four words.

"That's what I've been saying." I stand, wiping charcoal-stained fingers on my jeans. "Want a beer? Or—"

"No beer." She cuts me off sharply, then seems to catch herself. "I can't—I mean, no thanks."

I cock my head at her. Wren never turns down the chance to critique my brewing. Half our arguments start with her telling me what's wrong with my latest release.

"Water? Coffee?" I offer instead, gesturing toward the bar.

"I'm fine." She crosses her arms over her chest. Those perky tits that I've—

Nah, I'm not going there. I force my eyes to stay on her face and that's when I notice the shadows under her eyes, the paleness of her skin. She looks exhausted in a way I've never seen before.

"You don't look fine," I say before I can stop myself.

Her jaw tightens. "Thanks."

"That's not what I—" I exhale heavily, running a hand through my hair. "You wanted to talk. So talk."

For a second, I think she might turn around and walk out. I wouldn't blame her. We've never been good at this—the whole civil conversation thing. We're better at fighting, at pushing each other's buttons until something explosive happens.

Like in Vegas.

And that's when the memory hits me—Wren in that black dress, her pink hair loose around her shoulders, eyes bright with challenge as she debated the merits of traditional versus experimental brewing techniques. How the argument somehow turned into her pressed against the elevator wall, my hand gripping her thigh, hers in my hair, her mouth hot and desperate against mine.

"Are you even listening to me?" Wren's irritated voice snaps me back to the present.

"Sorry, what?" Shit. I was so lost in the memory that I missed whatever she just said.

She makes a frustrated sound. "I said, I saw the paperwork isn't filed yet. Why?"

Right. The divorce papers. The ones sitting on my desk at home, half-filled out and untouched for weeks.

"I've been busy," I mutter, gesturing vaguely to the brewery around us. "Trying to convince new breweries to go direct-to-bar after you locked down MacIntyre and Henderson. Not to mention poaching The Hop Yard right across the street from us."

"I didn't 'poach' anything," she fires back, and *here we fucking go*. "I made better offers. That's business."

"Whatever helps you sleep at night, Pink."

Her eyes narrow at the nickname, and I wait for the usual verbal backhand. She never lets me get away with calling her that. Normally she'd tell me exactly where I could shove my condescending nickname, maybe threaten to cut my balls off if I ever used it again. But instead, she just stands there, gripping the chair back so hard her knuckles go white.

And are her hands shaking?

Something's off. She's not fighting back like she always does, not bitching at me about how my direct-to-bar model is outdated or how my stubbornness is killing my business.

Instead, she's standing there looking like she might either throw up or run at any second.

"What's going on with you?" I ask, softer this time.

Wren takes a deep breath, squares her shoulders, and meets my eyes directly. "I'm pregnant."

Two words. Just two fucking words, and my entire world tilts sideways.

Yup, I knew I'd be getting a new tattoo.

"You're..." My brain checks all the way out while I try to process what she's just said. "With a..."

"Baby. Yes." Her voice is steady, but her hands are trembling slightly at her sides. "I'm approximately eight weeks along. Which means—"

"Vegas," I finish for her, my voice barely audible.

Suddenly I'm thrown back there, to the sheets tangled around our bodies, to her skin slick and sweaty against mine, the taste of whiskey and insanity on both of our tongues. Did we use protection? I thought we did, at least the first time. But after that, when we moved to the jacuzzi tub, then back to the bed...

"Are you sure?" I ask, even though I know it's a stupid question. Wren Callan wouldn't come to me unless she was one hundred percent.

"Blood test confirmed." She doesn't elaborate further, just watches my reaction.

I need to move. I need to do something with the burst of adrenaline coursing through my body. I pace to the small fridge, pull out a water bottle, then change my mind and close the door without taking anything, moving to the bar instead.

I need a fucking beer.

My mind is racing, spinning through implications and possibilities faster than I can track them.

A baby. With Wren. My wife. *Christ.*

"Say something," she says finally, her voice holding an edge of vulnerability I've never heard from her before.

I turn to face her and I just stare at her. No words will come. They just... aren't there.

She's the woman who's driven me to drink since the day I met her. And now she's my wife, my secret obsession, and apparently the mother of my child. I don't know how to handle this, but I do know I can't get enough air.

And why the fuck is it so hot in here?

"I'll support you," I say, the words tumbling out. "Whatever you decide. If you want to keep it, I'm all in. If you don't..." The thought is like a knife between the ribs, but I push through. "It's your choice. But I'm here."

She can't hide the surprise on her face and I don't know whether to laugh or be pissed off at how she sees me. What kind of guy does she think I am?

"I haven't decided yet," she admits. "But I thought you should know."

"Thank you." The words feel inadequate, but I mean every one of them. "For telling me."

Holy *fuck*.

An awkward silence stretches between us. There's too much to say and no easy way to say any of it. I move back to my table, needing to do something with my hands.

"I talked to Dr. Walker," she continues. "He confirmed everything."

My head snaps up. "Reed? My Reed?"

"He's the best OB/GYN in Portland," she says defensively. "And I got an emergency appointment because I mentioned knowing Clover."

"Does she know?" Panic surges through me at the thought of my sister finding out about this mess from someone other than me.

"No." Wren shakes her head. "No one knows except Dr. Walker. And now you."

Relief washes over me, followed immediately by a strange possessiveness. This is our secret. Our baby.

Our baby. The phrase echoes in my head, settling into my bones with unexpected rightness.

The door to the tasting room swings open, and Lake strolls in like my life as I knew it isn't dying a slow death at my feet. He stops short when he sees Wren, a slow smile spreading across his face.

"Well, well. Look who finally showed up." Lake looks between us, clearly enjoying the tension or drama or whatever he sees on our faces. "I was wondering when you two would finally talk after whatever happened in Vegas."

"Not now, Lake," I growl.

Wren's eyes narrow. "What exactly did you tell him?"

"Nothing," I blurt out. "I swear."

"Boss man here has been a miserable bastard for weeks," Lake says with a smirk. "Even more than usual. Plus, everyone at the Brewers Convention saw you two practically setting fire to the hotel bar with your 'argument.'" He makes air quotes around the word.

"Lake," I say, my voice dropping to a dangerous level. "Leave."

"Fine, fine. Just came to tell you Wallace called. Airport's officially off the table. They renewed with Cascade for another two years."

Of course they did. I glance at Wren, who doesn't even try to hide the smug little smile tugging at the corner of her mouth. She lifts her chin slightly, practically daring me to start with her right now.

Any other day, this news would have me seething. I'd be plotting how to get back at her, how to steal one of her accounts right from under her and convince them to go direct-to-bar like we do. Now it barely registers next to the bombshell she just dropped.

"We'll talk about it tomorrow," I tell him, my eyes not leaving Wren's face.

Lake takes the hint and fucks off backs toward the door. "Nice seeing you again, Wren. Congrats on the airport deal. And, uh, whatever else is going on here." He gestures vaguely between us before disappearing into the main brewery.

When the door closes behind him, Wren turns to me, her expression tight. "So everyone knows about Vegas."

"People saw us leave together. That's all anyone knows for sure." I hesitate, then add, "Well, and that we've been avoiding each other since."

"Fantastic," she mutters. There's no way she hasn't heard the same things from her contacts, so I don't get why she's acting surprised.

"Look, no one knows about the marriage. Or..." I gesture vaguely toward her stomach, not sure if I'm ready to say the word 'pregnancy' again just yet.

"And I'd like to keep it that way." She paces to the window, staring out at the brewing tanks visible through the glass. "This is such a mess."

"It doesn't have to be," I say, the words forming before I've fully thought them through.

She turns back to me, eyebrow raised. "How do you figure that?"

I take a deep breath, mentally preparing for the reaction I'm about to get. "What if we didn't get divorced?"

"Excuse me?" Her voice rises to that pitch only dogs can hear at the end.

"Hear me out." I hold up my hands, knowing I'm about to take a walk straight through a minefield. "We're already legally married. You're pregnant with my child. Maybe... maybe this doesn't have to be a disaster."

Wren stares at me like I've just suggested she tattoo my name across her forehead. "You can't be serious."

"I am." The certainty in my voice surprises even me. My hand slips into my pocket, and my fingers play with the wedding band I've been carrying around since Vegas. I haven't worn it, but I couldn't bring myself to toss it in a drawer either. I rub my thumb over the smooth metal, a habit I've developed these past weeks without really understanding why. "A kid needs both parents. And I don't want to miss out on anything."

"We can co-parent without being married," she says. "Plenty of people do."

"I watched my dad bail on us when we needed him most. I promised myself I'd never do that to my own kid. I want to be there. Every day."

"For the baby," she repeats flatly. "The baby that may or may not exist depending on what I decide."

I wince at the reminder that she might not keep my baby. Honestly, the thought makes me fucking sick, but it's not up to me.

And I don't bother telling her it's not just for the baby. That I think I want *her* just as much. Maybe more. There's a reason I haven't finished filling out that paperwork. "That's your choice. I meant what I said."

She starts pacing, those sharp as hell heels she always wears stabbing into the concrete. Each step looks like it could kill a man, which is probably why she wears them. "This is insane. You don't even like me. I don't like you. You've been trying to undermine my company since day one."

"That's not true," I argue. "I respect what you've built. I just don't agree with your methods."

"Oh, please." She rolls her eyes. "You literally tried to convince the airport to cut out distributors entirely and deal directly with local breweries."

"That's just business."

60

"Exactly!" She throws up her hands. "This is business, Kasen. Not some fairy tale where enemies suddenly fall in love because of an accidental pregnancy."

"I'm not talking about love," I say carefully. "I'm talking about responsibility. Partnership. Doing the right thing."

"The right thing," she repeats with a sharp laugh. "Says who? The same outdated thinking that expects women to give up their careers the minute they get knocked up?"

"I'm not trying to control you or your career," I say, keeping my voice even despite the frustration building. "You're acting like I'm asking you to become a housewife. I'm just saying we're already married, and there's a baby in the mix. Maybe we should at least try to make something work."

Wren stops pacing, something shifting in her expression. "You honestly believe we could make this work? Us? The same people who've been at each other's throats for years?"

"I don't know," I admit. "But I think we owe it to ourselves—and maybe to this kid—to find out."

She studies me, arms still crossed. "And what exactly are you proposing here? Because I'm not giving up my company or my apartment."

"I wouldn't ask you to." I lean back against the table, trying to look more relaxed than I feel. "I just think we should get to know each other. Outside of business. See if there's... I don't know, something worth building on."

"Something besides volatile chemistry and a mutual love of craft beer," she says dryly. "That I can no longer drink thanks to you and your super sperm."

I can't help the half-smile that tugs at my mouth. "Yeah. Besides that."

She's quiet for a moment, and I can almost see the wheels turning in her head. I've found Wren always approaches everything like a business problem to solve, weighing options, calculating risks.

"Which way are you leaning?" I ask quietly. "About the baby?"

The question hangs between us, and I hold my breath while she takes her sweet time thinking about what she wants to say. Wren's hand moves to her stomach, then drops back to her side when she notices what she's doing.

"I'm leaning toward keeping it," she admits, her voice barely above a whisper. "But I haven't decided for sure."

The relief that pulses through me is so intense I have to grip the edge of the table to steady myself. "Okay."

She nods, then squares her shoulders. "If—and that's a big if—I decide to keep this baby, what would your involvement look like?"

"Whatever you're comfortable with," I say. "But ideally? I'd want to be there for everything. Doctor's appointments, setting up a nursery, late-night feedings. All of it."

"And our businesses? We'd keep those separate?"

"Completely. What happens at Timber stays at Timber. What happens at Cascade stays at Cascade."

She narrows her eyes. "So if I landed another account you were after..."

"I'd be pissed, but I wouldn't bring it home." I meet her gaze steadily. "This would be about us, not business."

Easier said than done, but I'd try. For her.

For *them*.

"There is no 'us,'" she says.

"Not yet," I agree. "But maybe there could be."

Wren turns away again, her fingers fidgeting with the strap of her purse. "This is insane," she mutters, but I can tell she's considering it.

"Look," I say, taking a chance. "Before we make any major decisions, let's just... spend some time together. Get coffee. Have dinner. Talk about something besides Cascade versus Timber for once."

She glances back at me, one eyebrow raised. "You want to date?"

"I want to get to know the woman who might be raising my kid," I say, then add, "And yeah, maybe I want to know if there's more to us than what happened in Vegas."

Her cheeks flush at the mention of Vegas, and not gonna lie, it's cute as hell. "And if it turns out we still can't stand each other?"

"Then at least we tried. We'll figure out co-parenting if it comes to that." I hesitate, then ask the question that's been burning in my mind. "Do you really hate me that much?"

"I don't hate you," she admits. "You frustrate the hell out of me professionally. But I don't hate you."

It's not a declaration of affection, but it's a start.

"So, what do you say?" I ask. "Give this a shot?"

She takes a deep breath. "We can try getting to know each other," she says finally. "No promises beyond that. And I'll let you know when I've made a final decision about the baby."

Relief floods through me. "Thank you."

"Don't thank me yet," she warns. "I could still change my mind. About all of it."

I nod. "I know."

Wren adjusts her purse strap. "I should go. I have an early meeting tomorrow."

"Can I call you? Maybe we could get dinner this weekend?"

She hesitates, then nods. "Don't call, though. What are you, a psychopath?" She wrinkles her nose. "Text me like a normal human being. We'll figure something out."

My lips twitch. "Will do."

She turns toward the door, then pauses. "Kasen?"

"Yeah?"

"Breathe a word about this baby to anyone, and I'll rewire your truck so the horn plays 'It's Raining Men' at full volume every time you hit the brakes." Her tone is light, but her eyes are dead serious.

And she has the audacity to call *me* the psychopath.

I can't help but laugh. "Noted."

With a final glance, she's gone.

I sink into the booth, the full weight of what just happened crashing down on me. Wren's pregnant. With my baby. And she's agreed to try to see if there might be something between us.

Considering I haven't been able to get her out of my head for months, I'm gonna go ahead and guess there is.

Her agreement isn't the commitment I was hoping for, but it's more than I have any right to expect. And she's leaning toward keeping the baby.

My baby.

I reach for my phone and pull up Reed's contact, typing quickly before I can second-guess myself.

> Me: Need to talk.

His response comes almost immediately.

> Reed: Sure. Everything okay?

I stare at the screen, the realization suddenly hitting me. Reed. Dr. Reed Walker. The guy who examined Wren, who knew about my baby before I did. Who had her put her feet in those stirrups and checked out parts of her I've only seen in a very different context.

Something hot and uncomfortable twists in my gut. I know it's his job, completely professional, but still. Banks mentioned feeling weirdly territorial when Reed became Clover's doctor during her pregnancy with Noble. I thought he was being an idiot at the time, but now I get it.

And Reed has no idea that I'm the father of Wren's baby. No idea that the woman he examined is technically my wife.

> Me: I either need a beer or therapy after today. You're cheaper, so beer?

After he agrees, I set the phone down and turn back to my half-finished label. The design that had seemed so important a few hours ago now feels trivial compared to the seismic shift that just rocked my world.

A baby. A chance to know Wren beyond the girl I can't stand. A chance to be the father mine never was.

I've always believed actions speak louder than words.

Now it's time to prove it.

7
Wren

HOMELESS AND PREGNANT.

It has a ring to it, right?

They could totally make reality TV out of the shitshow my life has become.

I stare at the notice in my hands, reading it for the fourth time as if the words might magically rearrange themselves into something less catastrophic. The pristine letterhead of Triton Development mocks me with its understated elegance as it announces the complete demolition of my life.

"Thirty days," I mutter, dropping the notice onto my kitchen counter. "Thirty fucking days to vacate."

My apartment—the one with exposed brick and floor-to-ceiling windows that I practically sold a kidney for—is being converted into luxury condos next month. Why would it not be? I must have some shitty karma coming due or something.

God forbid Portland have one affordable living space that doesn't eventually get flipped into a yoga studio or an overpriced condo with a name like "The Arbor at Eastwick" or some equally pretentious bullshit.

I press my palms against my eyes until I see stars. I *will not* cry over this. I'm Wren Callan, for fuck's sake. I built Cascade Distribution from nothing. I was the valedictorian of my university. I can handle a housing crisis.

Even if I'm ten weeks pregnant. Even if the rental market in Portland is a nightmare. Even if my body has decided that staying awake past eight is now physically impossible.

My phone buzzes with a text from Kieran.

> Kieran: Did you call that place on Burnside?

> Me: Waiting list. 3 months minimum.

> Kieran: My couch offer still stands.

Kieran's studio apartment is basically the size of a filing cabinet. It's a studio with half a kitchen and a bathroom where you have to sit sideways on the toilet. His pullout couch doubles as his bed, and I'm *not* sharing a bed with a guy who's like my brother.

Not happening.

> Me: Your bathroom can barely fit your seventeen-step Korean skincare routine. Where would I put all my stuff?

> Kieran: Storage unit? Also it's only 12 steps now. I've streamlined.

> Me: Impressed and horrified simultaneously.

The thought of cramming my life into boxes makes me want to cry. Again. I've spent years curating this space, making it reflect exactly who I am—independent, successful, and a lover of pretty things. Now I have to dismantle it all in less than a month and even if I move everything to a new place, it won't be the same.

My phone rings, and my mother's name flashes on the screen. She has an uncanny ability to sense when my life is imploding. It's like her "my daughter is in crisis" radar goes off and she drops whatever she's doing.

"Hi, Mom," I answer, trying to sound less devastated than I feel.

"You haven't returned my calls," she says without a hello. "It's been two days. Are you avoiding me for some reason, daughter of mine?"

"I've been busy." Busy panicking, busy sleeping when I have way too much to do, busy crying over stupid laundry commercials, busy trying to figure out how to tell her she's going to be a grandmother. If I keep the baby. Which I still have decided I'm going to do. "There's a lot happening at work right now."

"Mmm." It's amazing how my mother can pack so much into a single sound. "Well, Janine's daughter works for Portland Living, and she mentioned that your building was sold to developers. I assume that's why you're avoiding me?"

Of course she already knows. This is what I get for living in a city where everyone is connected by two degrees of separation. And having a mother who keeps tabs on me like it's her favorite hobby.

"I'm not avoiding you," I lie. "And yes, my building was sold. I have thirty days to find a new place."

"In this market?" She makes a tsking sound. "You know, my guest room is always available. I have that nice desk where you could work remotely—"

"Mom." I cut her off before she can suck me in and somehow convince me moving home is a good idea. "I appreciate the offer, but I'm not moving in with you."

"There's nothing wrong with accepting help, Wren."

"I know that." I don't know that. I've spent my entire adult life proving I don't need help from anyone. The way she taught me. "But I'm twenty-seven years old. I'm not moving back in with my mother."

"Pride goeth before a fall," she quotes. My mother has a literary reference for every occasion.

"I'll figure it out," I say firmly. "I always do."

I'll say one good thing about getting kicked out of my apartment—it's given my mother something to focus on as a reason for my sketchiness.

After getting off the phone, I pull up the real estate apps I've been obsessively checking since I got the notice this morning. Every decent rental in my price range has a waiting list longer than the line at Voodoo Doughnut on a Saturday morning. Everything else is either a converted garden shed asking two thousand dollars a month or so far from the city I'd need to commute by helicopter.

I check the time. It's almost eight. I have an ultrasound with Dr. Walker in an hour. For two weeks, I've been avoiding making any permanent decisions about the pregnancy, but I've followed every one of his instructions. Prenatal vitamins, reduced caffeine, no alcohol. Acting as if I'm keeping this baby even though I haven't officially decided.

Though the fact that I'm going to this ultrasound probably says more than I'm ready to admit.

I text Kasen as I grab my purse:

> Me: Ultrasound today at 9:15.

> Me: You wanted to be involved, here's your chance.

I'm not sure why I'm inviting him. Maybe because, despite everything, he deserves to be there. Maybe because I'm tired of going through this alone. Maybe because in the two weeks since I told him about the pregnancy, he's been surprisingly... decent.

His response is immediate:

> Kasen: I'll be there.
>
> Kasen: Want me to pick you up?
>
> Me: I can drive myself. See you there.

Forty minutes later, I'm sitting in Dr. Walker's waiting room, flipping through a parenting magazine without actually reading any of it, when Kasen walks in. Honestly, the pictures freak me out a little and don't get me started on the article titles.

Kasen's traded his usual flannel for a clean black t-shirt that shows off the colorful tattoos running down both arms. The ones on his muscular, veiny forearms...

I blink a couple of times and snap my mouth shut because, for some reason, it'd fallen open. His dark hair is tucked under that stupid beanie he always wears, but he's freshly shaven, like he made an effort.

For me? For the baby? I'm not sure which possibility unnerves me more.

And okay, I kind of like it.

He spots me immediately and crosses the room, taking the seat beside me. "Hey."

"Hey." I set down the magazine. "Thanks for coming."

"Wouldn't miss it." His blue eyes scan my face with an intensity that makes my skin prickle. "You look tired."

"Thanks. Every woman loves hearing that."

"That's not what I—" He stops, runs a hand through his hair, dislodging the beanie slightly like he forgot it was there. "Sorry. I meant... are you feeling okay?"

The genuine concern in his voice catches me off guard. "I'm

fine. Just exhausted all the time. Apparently, growing a human sucks the energy out of you."

"Is that normal? The exhaustion?"

"According to the internet and Dr. Walker, yes." I pick at a loose thread on my sleeve. "Morning sickness is tapering off, but I can barely keep my eyes open past dinner time. And yesterday I cried because Kieran brought me a decaf instead of regular coffee—which I'm not supposed to have anyway."

Kasen's lips quirk up at the corners. "You cried over coffee?"

"I also cried during a truck commercial about a father and son fixing up an old Chevy." Even talking about it now makes my eyes prickle. I glare at the smirk on his face. "If you laugh, I will end you."

"Not laughing," he says, but his eyes are definitely laughing. "Hormones, huh?"

"Among other things."

"Like what?"

I hadn't meant to bring it up here, but the genuine interest in his expression breaks down a barrier I didn't realize I'd constructed. "My apartment building was sold to developers. I have thirty days to find a new place."

Kasen's expression shifts to concern. "Shit. Really?"

"Really." I stare down at my hands. "And the rental market is a nightmare right now. Everything decent has a waiting list, and everything available is either outrageously expensive or practically uninhabitable."

"That's—"

"Wren Callan?" a nurse calls, interrupting whatever Kasen was about to say.

We follow her back to an exam room, and I hop up on the table while Kasen sits in the single chair. He's stiff and has a look on his face I can't read, but whatever he's feeling, he's radiating tension and I'm not sure why. Maybe it's the whole baby thing, but maybe it's the fact that one of his best friends is my doctor and doesn't know about the baby.

Yeah, it's probably that.

Dr. Walker—Reed—walks in a few minutes later, looking down at the tablet in his hand. "Alright Wren, let's just review these initial—" He looks up, stops dead, and then a slow grin spreads across his face, replacing the absolute shock. "Kase? What the *hell* are you doing here?"

I can't help it. I get all sorts of enjoyment out of watching my doctor try to compute one of his best friends sitting awkwardly in *his* OB-GYN exam room. With *me*.

"Hey, Reed." Kasen shifts, looking so uncomfortable. I bite the inside of my cheek to keep from laughing. He tugs the edge of his beanie looking like he wishes he was anywhere but here. He gestures vaguely towards me. "Uh, yeah. I'm here with Wren." He sounds like he just got caught doing something he shouldn't.

This time I can't hold in the snort, but I catch myself and try to turn it into a cough instead of cracking up like I want to.

Reed's gaze darts between Kasen and me, then down to the tablet. His eyes widen as his head snaps back up to me and then his friend as he laughs. "Wait. You're the— Wren, he's the...?" Reed fumbles, a faint flush creeping up his neck before he visibly clamps down, forcing the doctor mask back into place. He clears his throat, adjusting his perfectly knotted tie. "Right. The father."

"Took you long enough," I say, unable to resist. What can I say? Watching Kasen squirm is fun. "Yep. He's my baby daddy."

Reed blinks, his brain clearly still processing the shock. "Okay. Wow. Okay." He takes a slow, deep breath. "This is... definitely not what I expected walking in here." He shoots Kasen a look that clearly promises an interrogation later. "Does Banks know about this?"

"No," Kasen mutters quickly, suddenly finding the pattern

on the linoleum floor intensely interesting. "We haven't told anyone."

"Uh-huh," Reed says again, and I can practically see him writing the mental note to get all the details out of Kasen later. He turns back to me, forcing a professional tone, though he still looks like he'd rather sit down and talk about what's happening here. He glances down and taps something on his tablet. "So, Wren, putting *that* aside... how have you been feeling since our last appointment?"

"Less like I'm actively trying to redecorate your office with my stomach contents," I tell him. "More like I could pass out cold at any second. And apparently, I now cry at literally everything. This morning, I teared up because I was almost out of shampoo. It's humiliating."

"Exhaustion and emotional lability are normal for ten weeks," Reed assures me, making notes on his tablet. He glances at Kasen, whose bouncing leg is practically vibrating the chair, with a shit-eating grin on his face. "Ready to see the baby, *Dad*?"

"Uh, yeah," Kasen says, his voice tight as he glares at his friend, but then he glances over at me, and his expression softens. It's still weird that he's not glaring at me, too. "Ready." Hearing him referred to as dad, accepting it so easily sends a weird burst of... something through me. Our eyes lock for a second, and I swear I feel that look all the way down to my toes before I force myself to look away.

Reed nods. "Okay, Wren, let's get you situated."

My heart's going crazy as I lie back. Kasen moves his chair closer, and I'm hyperaware of every inch of him. The clean scent of his cologne that makes him smell good enough to eat, the barely suppressed nervous energy humming off him, and the heat from his skin seeping into mine even though we're not touching.

Reed lifts my shirt a little, exposing my still-flat stomach. He tucks a papery towel thing into the top of my jeans and then he squirts some gel on my stomach. It's so cold, it makes me gasp.

"Sorry," Reed murmurs, as he flicks off the lights and then presses the ultrasound wand against my skin. "I should've warned you, the warmer's broken."

The monitor flickers to life—a swirl of grey and black, and for a while all I see is... nothing? Black and gray and white splotches that mean nothing to me. Then I see something. A tiny baby-shaped blob in the center of a big, black nothing. It's moving and rolling around and I just... have no words.

"There's your baby," Reed says. His voice is soft and almost as awed as I feel. "Right on track for ten weeks. And that flicker..." He zooms in slightly. "That's the heartbeat. It looks great. Nice and strong."

A rhythmic *whoosh-whoosh-whoosh* sound fills the small room. It's so fast. "Is that...?"

"The heartbeat, yes."

My own heart feels like it's trying to match the rhythm. That's... *ours*. Half me, half Kasen. This infuriating, complicated man beside me. The thought is staggering, and my eyes fill with tears faster than I can blink them away.

"Holy shit," Kasen breathes beside me. He sounds utterly stunned. Wrecked, even. "That little thing... that's really it?"

I risk a look at him. Gone is the grumpy guy who I can't stand. His face is completely open, stripped bare as he stares at the screen. His eyes are wide and... is that a tear? He's locked on the image of our baby like it's the only thing in the universe. I've never, ever seen him look like this.

My hand moves before I can talk myself out of it, and I grab his. His fingers immediately crush mine, a grip that's both romantic, and like a drowning man grabbing a life preserver. His hand is warm and calloused and somehow helps the overwhelm.

"The baby's heart rate is excellent," Reed continues, taking what I'm assuming are measurements. "Development looks right on schedule."

Watching Kasen watch the screen, seeing that unexpected softness on his face... the word forms in my mind before I can stop it. *Ours.* And suddenly, the decision isn't a decision at all. It's just... fact.

"I'm keeping it," I blurt out, and they both turn to look at me.

Kasen's head snaps toward me, his eyes searching mine. The hope blooming on his face is so intense it's almost painful to see. I sort of hate that it was ever a question, and it feels stupid now as my decision settles into my bones. His voice cracks when he asks, "Are you sure?"

"Yeah." I nod, meeting his stunned gaze. The rapid beat from the monitor seems to underscore the certainty settling in my chest. "Yeah, I'm sure."

Reed's smiling when he puts the wand-thing away. "Okay, I'll print these out for you both. Give me just a minute." He hands me the tissues for the gel and then he slips out, leaving Kasen and I alone.

Kasen still hasn't let go of my hand. "Pink..." he starts, then stops, just looking at me. He lifts our joined hands slightly, then seems to think better of whatever he was going to do and lets go, running his hand through his hair instead, knocking his beanie off. His hair's messy and why is that so cute?

"Don't make this weird, Kasen," I warn, needing to regain control of the situation, tugging my hand back to wipe off the gel and pull my shirt down. "This changes things, obviously, but it doesn't magically erase..." Our rivalry. Our history. The fact we barely know each other.

All the things.

"I know," he says quickly. "We'll figure it out." He sounds like he's reassuring himself as much as me.

Reed returns with the printouts and brochures, launching

back into doctor mode. He gives me a prescription for vitamins, then tells me it's important for me to rest, stay hydrated, and the big one: avoid stress.

Pshh. As if.

Like he can read my mind, he says, "Seriously, Wren," looking pointedly from me to Kasen and back again. "Stress impacts fetal development. The first trimester is crucial. Try to keep things as low stress as you can."

I let out a laugh that sounds slightly hysterical. "Excellent advice, Doc. I'll get right on that as soon as I figure out my hopeless housing situation."

Reed frowns. "You're moving?"

"Being evicted," I say. "My building's turning into luxury condos I can't afford." I shrug, trying to project nonchalance I don't feel. "Welcome to Portland."

"Okay, that's... that's major stress," Reed says carefully, his professional concern kicking up a notch. "Finding housing quickly in this market is practically a full-time job. You really need to avoid that kind of pressure right now."

Before I can tell him I'll handle it, or bite his head off for stating the obvious, Kasen speaks up. "She can stay with me."

I pivot to face him, feeling all kinds of things. So many things I can't pin them all down. "Are you high?"

"Don't be difficult," he says, ignoring my disbelief and the way I bristle at his words. He looks determined now.

Difficult? Oh, he has no idea. But challenge accepted.

"It solves the immediate problem," he presses on, bulldozing past my glare. "You need a place, *now*. I have a spare room. It's close to both our companies." He hesitates for a fraction of a second, then adds, meeting my eye, "And yeah, maybe it gives us a chance to figure out how to coexist before the baby comes. See if we can actually do this co-parenting thing without killing each other." He quickly pivots back to safer ground. "Plus, Reed *just said* you need less stress. This is less stress."

"Less stress?" My laugh is short, brittle, disbelief dripping from every syllable. "We barely tolerate each other on a good day, Kasen! You want *me*—exhausted, hormonal, probably crying over dirty dishes one minute and irrationally angry the next—invading your space? You want this," I jab a finger toward my stomach, the emphasis sharp, maybe unfair, but fueled by panic and hormones, "mess in your life twenty-four-seven? That's not *less stress*; that's a freaking sitcom pitch waiting to happen."

"It's not forever," he counters, shoving his hands in his pockets, his jaw tight. "Just until you find your own place. Look," he exhales sharply, "I'm not trying to trap you, or pull some shit with Cascade, or... whatever convoluted conspiracy you're cooking up." He meets my eyes. "You need to avoid stress, like Reed said. This helps. Let me help, Wren. For the baby."

And at those last three words, I go all gooey and melty inside and *what the fuck*.

Fuck you, hormones.

And why does he have to be so hot? Honestly, how am I supposed to keep looking at him like my nemesis when every part of my body wants to be on every part of his?

Reed clears his throat loudly, and I startle. Holy shit, I forgot he was here. "I think I'll, ah, leave you two to discuss." He hands me the ultrasound pictures, those precious grainy images of the life inside me. "Call my office for your next appointment. And Wren? Take it easy." He makes a swift exit, practically fleeing the impending explosion.

The door clicks shut, leaving Kasen and me alone in the suddenly too-small room.

"This is certifiably insane," I state flatly.

"What's insane is you trying to find an apartment in three weeks while dealing with first-trimester bullshit," he shoots back, pulling off his beanie to run a hand through his messy dark hair. "I know we drive each other crazy. But this isn't about that. This is about making sure you and..." he gestures vaguely at my stomach, "...are okay."

"How can you possibly think this could work?"

He gives me a little smirk. "Because we worked in Vegas."

I ignore the liquid heat pouring into my veins at the reminder of his body on top of mine, behind me, under...

Nope.

"We were drunk. *Blackout* drunk. And in case you've forgotten, I can't drink right now."

"I haven't forgotten." His eyes get darker before he blinks, and it's gone. "Just think about it, Pink. I've got the space, you need a place. It's simple."

"Right," I snap, suddenly feeling all kinds of overwhelmed. "Simple. It's so *easy* to uproot my entire life."

I stand up, gathering my stuff and taking a second to wipe my face because a couple of stray tears managed to escape. I hate change and *everything's* changing, and I don't know how to cope outside of crying. And maybe chocolate.

When I refuse to look at him, he steps closer so I have to tilt my chin up to hold eye contact. "Please."

The unexpected openness in his eyes when he says that single word throws me off. This isn't the Kasen James who pisses me all the way off.

This is someone else and I don't know him. Inside my head, my thoughts are at war. His house *is* convenient. It *would* solve the immediate crisis. But living with Kasen?

"I need time to think," I say finally, clutching the ultrasound photos like they'll protect me from whatever feelings are starting to take root inside of me when it comes to him. I reluctantly loosen my grip and hand him one to take.

He nods, accepting it. He tucks the photo into his back pocket with a grin. "Okay. Fair enough."

We walk out to the parking garage, the silence between us heavy and filled with so much. He's walking close enough that his fingers brush mine while our arms swing next to each other and every time his skin touches mine, I feel it as sparks between my legs.

I'm in so much trouble.

At his truck, Kasen stops.

"Hey," he says quietly, meeting my eyes. "For what it's worth... I'm happy you decided what you did. About keeping it."

I touch the pocket in my purse where all but one of the photos are safely tucked away. "Yeah," I whisper. "Me, too."

8
Wren

THREE DAYS LATER, I've looked at fifteen apartments, filled out eight applications, and been wait-listed for every single one. The few available places were either absurdly expensive or looked like they'd been the site of at least one crime scene documentary.

I'm sitting in my office at Cascade, surrounded by listings and rental applications, when Kieran walks in with coffee and an expression that tells me he has news I won't like.

"That place on Hawthorne?" he says, placing the coffee on my desk. "Just got rented to a tech bro from Seattle who offered six months' rent in advance."

I drop my head to my desk with a thud. "Of course it did."

"How are you holding up?" Kieran perches on the edge of my desk, concern clear in his voice.

"I'm fantastic," I mumble into the stack of papers.

"You know my apartment—"

"Is too small, and you know it." I lift my head. "I love you, but we're *not* sharing a bed." My nose wrinkles, and he smirks at me. "But thank you."

"Fair enough. If I told you about my hookup last night, you'd want to even less."

I shudder. "Lucky girl."

"I like to think so."

"That was sarcasm."

He shrugs, but then turns serious. "Have you considered other options?"

"Like what? Living in my car? Squatting in the warehouse?"

"Like Kasen's offer."

I sit up straight, staring at him. "How do you know about that?"

Kieran gives me a look that says I should know better. "You've been puking in the office bathroom for weeks. You burst into tears when the coffee machine was out of caramel syrup yesterday. And you fell asleep during the Orson call and I had to cover for you." He ticks off each point on his fingers.

"That doesn't explain how you know about Kasen's offer."

"You left your phone on the conference table when you ran to the bathroom." He at least has the decency to look slightly guilty. "A text from 'Beanie Boy' asking if you'd made a decision about his offer to move into his spare room popped up."

I drop my head into my hands. "God, you're annoying."

He ignores me. "You need to do it. Take it from someone who'd rather lose all my hair than knock a girl up, if he's stepping up, you should let him."

And that's how I know he means what he says. Kieran's a vain asshole when it comes to his hair.

"I don't need him to take care of me," I say, sounding defensive even to my own ears.

"No one said you do, but what about the baby?"

My head snaps up. He might've implied he knew, but he's never outright said it and I've never confirmed, so hearing him say *the baby* is weird.

I cover my face with my hands and groan. "This is a disaster."

"Is it?" Kieran's voice turns surprisingly gentle. "Look, I'm not saying marry the guy—"

I choke out a laugh because yeah, I did that already.

"—but consider the offer. Set ground rules. Whatever you need to do, but if you don't text him and accept, I'm going to do it for you. You're too pretty to live on the street."

I scoff because he's being an insensitive asshole, but that's kind of part of his charm. I stare out the window at the warehouse floor below, watching my team moving kegs and loading cases onto vans for delivery. Everything is in its place, neatly organized, exactly as I designed it. My life used to be like that, too. Now it's a chaotic jumble of pregnancy hormones and complicated feelings for the man who used to be just someone I hated.

"The best I can do right now is think about it," I say finally. All I've been doing is *thinking about it*. "And don't you dare text him or I'll shave your head myself."

The text comes that evening as I'm attempting to pack my apartment. So far, I managed to fill exactly a box and a half before collapsing on the couch, exhausted beyond anything that's normal. I barely have the energy to pick up my phone.

Kasen: Have you decided?

Straight to the point. I can appreciate that.

Me: Not yet.

Kasen: What's holding you back?

I stare at the screen, trying to articulate the tangle of reservations in my head.

> Me: So many things.
>
> Me: My independence.
>
> Me: The fact that we've spent years trying to destroy each other.

> Kasen: Slight exaggeration, but fair.

> Me: What would people think?

> Kasen: Since when do you care what people think?

He's right, and it irritates me. I've never given a damn about others' opinions.

> Kasen: Let me be clear. This is about giving our kid the best start and getting to know each other. Not about me trying to control you or your business. We can set whatever ground rules you want.

The sincerity in his text catches me off guard. Two months ago, I would have dismissed anything Kasen said as manipulation or trying to fuck me over. Now, I'm not so sure.

Before I can overthink it, I text back,

> Me: Fine. But I have conditions.

> Kasen: Name them.

I think about everything that could possibly go wrong, and just let my fingers fly across the screen without stopping to think about how wrong some of them feel. I'm not going there.

> Me: This is only until I find something else.
>
> Me: We keep separate spaces.
>
> Me: No business talk at home.
>
> Me: We're roommates, not husband and wife. No touching.

I hesitate, then add,

> Me: I pay my way. Rent, utilities, groceries—we split everything.
>
> Me: I don't need you to take care of me.

Kasen's reply is immediate:

> Kasen: Is that all, Pink?
>
> Kasen: Easy.
>
> Kasen: You've got yourself a deal.
>
> Kasen: When do you want to move in?

I look around at my half-packed (okay, barely packed) apartment, at the life I've built that's now in boxes. Maybe this isn't giving up control. Maybe it's just adapting to circumstances.

> Me: This weekend?
>
> Kasen: That works.
>
> Kasen: And Wren?
>
> Me: Yeah?
>
> Kasen: This might not be as terrible as you think.

I can almost hear the dry humor in his text, can almost see that little half-smile he gets when he's being unexpectedly charming. And that's the problem, isn't it? I'm starting to know his expressions, his tones, his moods. I'm starting to see Kasen James as a person, not just an asshole who makes me want to punch him.

> Me: Right.

I set my phone down and lean back against the couch, one hand resting on my still-flat stomach. In the span of eight weeks, I've gone from single to pregnant, accidentally married, and about to move in with a guy I can't stand.

Couldn't stand?

Whatever.

This is not the life I planned. Not even close.

But as I look at the ultrasound picture on my coffee table—our tiny bean with its fluttering heart—I can't bring myself to regret any of it.

Well, maybe the part where I agreed to move in with Kasen. I might live to regret that.

Or not.

Guess we'll find out.

9
Kasen

MY HOUSE LOOKS like I'm trying to impress the fucking Queen of England, not a pink-haired pain in my ass with an attitude problem who's carrying my baby.

"You vacuumed the ceiling vents?" Banks stares at me like I've lost my mind, which maybe I have. "Who does that?"

"Shut up." I toss the microfiber cloth I've been using to wipe down the kitchen counters for the third time into the sink. Every surface shines like it's been polished within an inch of its life. Even the copper brewing equipment I keep on display in the kitchen sparkles under the pendant lights. "She's going to be looking for reasons why this was a mistake. I'm not giving her ammunition."

Reed leans against the refrigerator, arms crossed over his chest, barely suppressing a smirk. "Just so we have the whole picture, you slept with your arch nemesis in Vegas, accidentally married her, got her pregnant, and now she's moving in. Did I miss anything?"

"Yeah, the part where you shut the fuck up and help me move this couch two inches to the left." I glare at him. Ever since he found out about Wren and me at the ultrasound appointment, he's been relentless with the teasing.

I can't even blame him. If the situations were reversed, I'd be doing the same thing.

Banks adjusts his position on said couch, which he's been sprawled across for the last hour, offering unhelpful commentary on my cleaning frenzy. "I still can't believe you kept this from us for weeks. Your own sister doesn't even know yet."

The guilt that's been festering in my chest throbs to life to remind me that it's still there. "I'll tell Clover after Wren's settled. One shitstorm at a time."

"She's going to kick your ass," Banks says, obviously happy it.

"Again, not helping." I check my watch. Wren's due here in twenty minutes. My pulse picks up. "Are those sheets I bought for the guest room out of the dryer yet?"

Reed pushes off the fridge. "I'll check. Though I'm still not clear on why you needed fifteen-hundred thread count Egyptian cotton sheets for your 'temporary roommate.'" He makes air quotes around the words, his expression saying that he's not buying my bullshit.

"They're not—it's not like that," I snap, even though the heat creeping up my neck probably gives me away. It's absolutely like that. "She's pregnant. She needs to be comfortable."

"Right." Reed's eyebrows climb toward his hairline. "Because that's definitely all this is about. Your concern for her comfort."

I flip him off as he disappears down the hallway, calling after him, "You're a shitty friend, you know that?"

His laughter drifts back to me.

Banks finally levers himself off the couch, stretching his tall frame. "You know, for someone who claimed to hate this chick's guts for the past two years, you're putting in an awful lot of effort."

I focus on straightening a stack of magazines that're already straight. "I never said I hated her."

"No, you just called her—and I quote—'a pink-haired menace determined to destroy craft brewing as we know it.'"

"That was business," I mutter. "This is different."

Banks studies me for a long moment, his expression shifting from teasing to something more serious. "You like her."

"She's carrying my kid." Yeah, that conversation with my two best friends wasn't fun. They gave me endless shit and I don't see it stopping anytime soon.

"And?"

I meet his eyes, sighing. "I don't know what I feel. Everything's happening so fast."

He nods, his expression full of understanding. "For what it's worth, as someone who also started a relationship under less-than-ideal circumstances... sometimes the messy beginnings lead to the best endings."

The memory of his and Clover's rocky start—him moving in and them trying to keep their distance because she's my sister, and then the storm—flashes through my mind. They managed to find their way through. Maybe Wren and I...

The doorbell rings, cutting off that dangerous train of thought. My heart slams against my ribs.

"Shit, she's early." I run a hand through my hair, tugging my beanie more securely into place. "You guys need to go. Now."

Banks grins. "But I was so looking forward to watching this train wreck."

"Out." I shove him toward the back door just as Reed emerges from the laundry room with his arms full of the sheets.

"The princess' bedding is ready," he says, then catches sight of my face. "What's going on?"

"Back door. Both of you." I practically push them through the kitchen and out onto the back porch. "I'll call you later."

Reed hands me the sheets. "Remember, she needs to stay calm. Stress is bad for—"

"I know." I cut him off, anxiety making me more of a dick than usual. "Go."

Banks claps me on the shoulder. "Good luck, man. You're gonna need it."

I close the door on their identical shit-eating grins and take a deep breath, squaring my shoulders like I'm heading into battle. In a way, I am. Living with Wren is going to be... challenging. In so very many ways.

I shove my hand into my pocket and touch the warm metal of my wedding ring. Yeah, that's still a thing I'm doing. We're not gonna talk about why.

The doorbell rings again, and I know I'm out of time.

"Coming!" I toss the sheets onto the kitchen counter and stride to the front door, my palms suddenly damp. For fuck's sake, it's just Wren.

Yeah, *just* Wren. Nothing complicated about her at all.

I swing open the door, and my carefully prepared greeting dies on my lips. She's standing on my porch in a cropped band t-shirt and high-waisted jeans, her pink hair pulled into a messy ponytail, a duffle bag slung over one shoulder and a box balanced on her hip. The late afternoon sunlight catches the tiny silver hoop in her nose, making it glint.

She looks like a goddamn wet dream.

My mouth goes dry.

Bone fuckin' dry.

"You planning to let me in, or should I just set up camp on your porch?" Her voice is a little snippy, but I catch the nervousness beneath it. She's as freaked out about this as I am.

"Sorry." I step back, holding the door wider. "Need help with that?"

"I've got it." She brushes past me, bringing with her the scent of something that makes my mouth water. Some girly shit I couldn't hope to describe. My brain immediately flashes to Vegas, to how that scent lingered on my skin until I forced myself to shower it off.

I clear my throat. "Is that all you brought?"

She sets the box down on the entryway table. "Kieran's bringing the rest later. Most of my stuff is in storage now, anyway." Her eyes scan the living room, and I want to ask her who the fuck *Kieran* is, but I bite my tongue.

She's taking in the rustic-modern furniture, the vintage beer advertisements framed on the walls, the bookshelf filled with brewing texts and family photos. "It's... not what I expected."

"What were you expecting?"

She shrugs, dropping her duffel bag beside the box. "I don't know. Empty pizza boxes? Beer cans everywhere? A shrine to your ego?"

"That's in the basement," I deadpan. "Right next to my collection of voodoo dolls shaped like pink-haired tyrants."

A small smile flickers across her face before she suppresses it. "Knew it."

The moment stretches between us, and it's awkward as hell. I've spent the past two days cleaning and prepping for this, but I realize now I have no idea what comes next. How do we do this? How do we live together when we can barely have a civil conversation?

"I'll show you your room." I grab the duffel bag before she can protest. "I was just about to put clean sheets on the bed. New ones, actually." I wince internally at how eager that sounds.

I'm gonna need to grab the sheets off the counter and give them to her, I guess? I doubt she'll want me in there messing with her bed now that she's here.

She follows me down the hallway, her footsteps light

behind me. I'm hyperaware of her presence, my senses tracking her like she's a predator I need to keep an eye on.

Or what she really is, which is something much more dangerous.

"This is you." I push open the door to the guest room—formerly my home office, now hastily converted into a bedroom. The desk has been pushed against one wall to make room for the queen-sized bed I bought two days ago. "Bathroom's across the hall. There are fresh towels in the cabinet. And, uh, I cleared some space in the medicine cabinet for your stuff. I'll bring the sheets up in a second."

Wren steps into the room, her gray eyes taking everything in. The neutral walls, the simple furniture, the bay window overlooking the backyard where vines climb a trellis beside the fire pit.

"You didn't have to do all this," she says quietly, running her fingers along the edge of the desk.

"It wasn't a big deal." It was. I spent hours deliberating over the perfect mattress, choosing sheets I thought she'd like, rearranging furniture to maximize the space. "The internet's good in here if you need to work from home. Password's on a sticky note on the desk."

She turns to face me, something unreadable in her expression. "Thank you. This is... really nice, Kasen."

The sound of my name on her lips reminds me of that night. "Like I said, no big deal." I set her bag down beside the bed. "You hungry? I thought I'd make dinner."

Her eyebrows shoot up. "You cook?"

"Don't sound so surprised. I'm a brewer. It's basically liquid cooking."

"That's not—" She cuts herself off, shaking her head. "Sorry. I just assumed..."

"That I'd be subsisting on takeout and beer?" I can't help the small smirk that tugs at my lips. "I'll have you know I make a mean risotto."

"Risotto?" Her lips curve into the first genuine smile I've seen from her today. "Now I'm definitely skeptical."

"Challenge accepted." I find myself smiling back, something warm and a whole lot unsettling taking root in my chest at making her even the tiniest bit happy. And where the fuck did that come from? "Get settled. Dinner's in an hour."

Back in the kitchen, I pull ingredients from the fridge, trying to ignore the fact that *my wife* is now officially living in my house. That this is real. That we're doing this.

I've started the rice, and falling into the recipe helps take my mind off everything else. When she emerges from the bedroom, she's changed into leggings and an oversized sweater, her face freshly washed. I'm surprised she feels comfortable enough to take off her armor around me, but apparently, she does. She looks softer and younger than I'm used to seeing her, and I want to say something about it, but I also like my balls attached to my body, so I keep my mouth shut.

"Need help?" she asks, hovering at the edge of the kitchen.

"You can chop these if you want." I slide a cutting board with mushrooms toward her. "Or you can just sit. You must be tired from moving."

"I'm pregnant, not helpless." She takes the knife I offer, her fingers brushing mine. I ignore the burst of heat that happens under my skin where she touches me. "Besides, I've been sitting all day while movers did most of the work. It's nice to be up and doing something."

I keep an eye on her while I stir the rice, adding broth bit by bit. She handles the knife like she has no idea how to cook, but it's fun watching her try.

"So," she says after a few minutes of surprisingly comfortable silence, "what's the deal with all the brewing books in the living room? You doing research for something, or are you just that obsessed with malt and hops?"

"Both." I add another ladle of broth to the rice. "My grandfather was a brewer before the craft scene exploded. Those older volumes were his and when my mom died, they came to me. Some of them have his notes in the margins—recipes he was developing, modifications to traditional techniques."

"That's actually pretty cool." She slides the hacked up mushrooms into the bowl I've set out. "My mom has something similar with feminist literature. Books passed down from her mother, all marked up with thoughts and arguments."

"Your mom's a professor, right?" I vaguely remember Wren mentioning it during one of our less hostile encounters at an industry event.

She nods. "English literature with a focus on feminist theory. She raised me on Virginia Woolf and bell hooks instead of bedtime stories."

"Explains a lot," I mutter, trying not to smile.

"What's that supposed to mean?" Her voice takes on that *I'm about to tear you a new asshole* tone I'm so familiar with.

"Just that you've got that whole 'take no prisoners' vibe going on. Now I know where it comes from."

She looks like she can't decide whether to be offended or flattered. "She'd like that description, actually. She's all about women claiming their power."

"What does she think about..." I gesture vaguely between us. "This situation?"

Wren's expression closes off immediately. "She doesn't know. No one does except Kieran, and that's only because he's irritatingly observant."

My teeth grind. Fucking *Kieran* again.

"Banks knows," I admit. "And Reed, but you knew that. They were here earlier, helping me clean." Although they didn't really do shit to help.

"You cleaned for me?"

"I cleaned because my house was a mess," I lie, concentrating on the risotto. "Don't read into it."

She makes a noncommittal noise, but I can feel her eyes on me, assessing. Probably seeing way too damn much.

"How are you feeling?" I ask, changing the subject. "With the pregnancy, I mean."

"Better in some ways. Worse in others." She hops up to sit on the counter beside the stove, close enough that I can smell her perfume or lotion or whatever it is about her that makes my mouth water. "The nausea isn't constant anymore, but the exhaustion is kicking my ass. And everything makes me cry. I saw a commercial for paper towels yesterday and sobbed for ten minutes because the dad and daughter were cleaning up spills together."

I can't hold back my laugh. "Seriously?"

"Don't you dare laugh at me, Kasen James." But there's a smile playing at the corners of her mouth. "This is your fault. Your genes conspiring with mine to turn me into an emotional wreck."

I don't miss the way her cheeks flush like she's thinking about something else, maybe remembering that night, but I don't call her out on it.

"Our genes, huh?" I try to keep my tone light, but something about the casual way she references our shared connection to the growing life inside her makes my chest tighten. "This poor kid doesn't stand a chance with our combined stubbornness."

"God, can you imagine? A tiny person with my ambition and your..." She gestures vaguely at me, waving her hand up and down.

"My what?"

She flushes again. "Your intensity. The way you get when you're focused on something."

"Oh." I hadn't realized she'd noticed that about me. I also

don't think that's what she was thinking about. "Yeah, that could be a dangerous combination. They might try to take over the world."

10
Kasen

THE RICE IS NEARLY DONE. I add a knob of butter, letting it melt into the creamy mixture before folding in the mushrooms and a handful of fresh herbs. The kitchen fills with the rich aroma of wine and stock and thyme.

"That smells amazing," Wren admits, leaning forward to look into the pan.

"Don't sound so shocked." I nudge her leg with my elbow and there it is again, that little spark where we touch. "I do occasionally know what I'm doing."

"Occasionally being the operative word." But there's no bite to it, just a little grin that's all trouble.

I dish up two plates, adding a sprinkle of parmesan to each. Wren slides off the counter and moves to the dining table, where I've already set water glasses and napkins.

"This feels weird," she says as we sit across from each other. "Like we're playing house or something."

"It's just dinner, Pink." I know the nickname annoys her, but it slips out anyway. I can't help it and honestly, I don't want to. Say what you want about what we're going through, but getting under her skin is still one of my favorite things. Maybe just in a different way now.

She narrows her eyes at me. "Call me that again and I'll put this risotto somewhere very uncomfortable for you."

I grin. "Noted."

She takes a bite, her eyes widening. "Holy shit, this is actually good."

"Your faith in me is overwhelming."

"Well, you've never given me reason to believe you could cook." She takes another bite. "What other hidden talents are you hiding behind that grumpy exterior?"

"If I told you, they wouldn't be hidden. And I'm not grumpy."

She rolls her eyes, but I catch the small smile she tries to hide behind her water glass. Something loosens in my chest. Maybe this won't be a complete disaster after all.

We eat in companionable silence for a few minutes, the only sounds the clink of forks against plates and the soft music playing from the speaker on the kitchen counter—one of my playlists I put on without thinking.

"So," Wren says after a while, breaking the silence. "What are the house rules? Besides the ones I already laid out."

"House rules?" I shrug. "Don't burn the place down? Clean up after yourself? I'm not big on micromanaging."

"Says the man who just deep cleaned every surface in this house." Her gaze is knowing, a little smug.

"That's different," I mutter, focusing on my plate. "I wanted to make sure you didn't have another reason to complain about living here. I'm easy to live with."

"Somehow I doubt that."

"What about you? Any roommate habits I should know about? Sleepwalking? Snoring? Secret passion for blasting death metal?"

She laughs, the sound surprising both of us. "No death

metal. I do tend to work late, though. And I'm not exactly a morning person."

"Noted. I'll try to keep the power tools to a minimum before noon."

"Power tools?"

I gesture toward the back of the house. "I have a workshop in the basement. I build furniture sometimes. When I need to think or work through things."

Her expression turns thoughtful. "Huh. I had no idea you had more to your personality than making beer. You remind me of that guy Teddy from *Brooklyn Nine-Nine* who's obsessed with Pilsners and *so* boring."

I glare at her, gritting my teeth. "I think we both know how *not* boring I can be, but if you need a reminder of all the other things I'm good at, I'd be happy to provide one."

She just grins and takes another bite of her dinner.

"Not everything's about the brewery," I feel the need to add for some reason. Why do I care that she sees there's more to me?

"Could've fooled me." She sets down her fork, her expression shifting to something more guarded. "Speaking of which, we should probably talk about how this is going to work. Professionally, I mean."

And just like that, the easy atmosphere fractures. "I thought we agreed to keep business and... this... separate."

"We did. But we're bound to run into each other. People already saw us together in Vegas. They'll talk if we're suddenly living at the same address."

I doubt anyone will even care what we do, and she's so hung up on that shit. "How would they even know? And if they did, who cares?"

She scoffs.

"What? It's nobody's business but ours what we do."

"Easy for you to say. You're not the one people will assume slept her way into—" She cuts herself off, flushing.

"Into what?" I ask as something hot and uncomfortable twists into knots in my gut. "What exactly do you think people will assume, Wren?"

"You know how this industry works. A woman sleeps with someone, she must be trying to gain some advantage. Meanwhile, the guy gets high-fives and attaboys."

"That's bullshit." My voice comes out harder than I mean for it to. "Anyone who knows you knows you've built Cascade on skill and hard work. No one's going to think—"

"Of course they will!" She pushes away from the table, irritated now. She can join the fucking club. "Do you have any idea how hard I've had to work to be taken seriously? How many times I've been patted on the head and told to leave the real decisions to the men?"

Something in her expression sets my blood on fire and not in the good way. "I never did that to you."

"No." She deflates slightly. "You didn't. You've been a pain in my ass for other reasons."

"I've always respected you professionally," I say as I try to let my anger go and relax. "Even when I wanted to strangle you after what you did with the airport."

A small smile flickers across her face. "That was a good day. Your face when you found out..."

"Don't push it."

She runs a hand through her pink hair. "Sorry. Old habits."

"Look, I get it. The industry's not always fair to women. But anyone who matters knows what you've built with Cascade. They're not going to think less of you because of..." I hesitate, not sure how to categorize what's happening between us.

"Because I got drunk-married and knocked up by some random asshole?"

"Hey." I scowl at her, but put like that, it does sound pretty bad. "We'll figure it out. Keep it private as long as possible. And when people do find out, we'll handle it."

"*We'll* handle it," she repeats, eyebrows raised. "That's a big shift from our usual dynamic."

"Yeah, well, things change." I gesture toward her stomach. "We've got more important things to think about now."

She goes quiet, her expression thoughtful. "You're really all in on this, aren't you? The baby, I mean."

"Of course I am." I meet her eyes, letting her see exactly how sure I am. I don't think she's ready to see that I don't just mean the baby. "I don't half-ass important things, Wren."

Something flickers in her gray eyes, like she's surprised I told the truth. Or maybe it's that I'm not being a complete dick. "Good to know."

The moment stretches between us, charged with things neither of us is ready to deal with. I'm the first to look away, clearing my throat. "Ice cream? I got a few options. Not sure what you're into."

She perks up. "You have ice cream? What kind?"

"Mint chip, cookie dough, and vanilla." I shrug like it's no big deal that I stocked my freezer for her. "Figured pregnancy cravings might hit, and I wanted to be prepared."

"Mint chip sounds amazing right now." Her eyes light up in a way I've never seen. I've made this woman come. Repeatedly. And that had nothing on this. Shit, she might give me a complex. "How'd you know?"

"Lucky guess." I try to play it cool, but the smile spreading across her face is lighting me up inside.

"Well, your lucky guess just earned you major points, Beanie Boy."

Later, after ice cream and a surprisingly easy conversation about everything except business and babies, Wren's energy crashes abruptly. One minute she's animated, telling me about a disastrous brewery tour she took in Belgium; the next, she's struggling to keep her eyes open.

"Hey." I nudge her foot with mine where we're sitting on opposite ends of the couch. "You should get some sleep. You look ready to pass out."

"Mmm?" She blinks slowly, like she's coming back from somewhere far away. "Sorry. It's a pregnancy thing. The sleepiness hits like a truck sometimes."

"No apologies needed." I stand, offering her a hand up. "Come on. Let me show you how to work the shower. The hot water knob's a little tricky."

She takes my hand, letting me pull her to her feet. Just like every other time, the feel of her smaller hand in mine sends an electric current up my arm. For a second, we're standing too close, her face tilted up to mine, her gray eyes dark in the dim living room lighting.

All I'd have to do is tilt my chin down a little more, and we'd be—

I drop her hand like I've been burned. "Right. Shower."

In the bathroom, I show her the counterintuitive way the shower knobs work—cold is actually on the right, despite the label—while Wren watches, arms crossed over her chest. She looks small and tired in her oversized sweater, vulnerable in a way she never lets herself be at work.

She also looks soft and sleepy, and I want to take her to bed and not to fuck.

What the hell is *that*?

"Got it?" I ask, shutting off the water.

She nods. "Think so. Left for hot, right for cold, middle lever for pressure."

"Exactly. Towels are in that cabinet. I put some of those... I don't know, bath bomb things? In there, too. Reed suggested them. Said they might help with relaxation."

Her eyebrows shoot up. "You bought me bath bombs?"

"Reed said—"

"I heard what you said." A small smile plays at the corners of her mouth. "That was thoughtful. Thank you."

The sincerity in her voice makes my chest squeeze and I tuck my hands into my pockets, immediately finding the wedding ring in my left one. "It's not a big deal."

I step back, giving her space. "I'm usually up around six, but I'll try to be quiet. Sleep as long as you need."

She nods, suddenly looking uncertain. "This is weird, right?"

"Definitely weird," I agree. "But maybe not terrible?"

"Maybe not."

"Good night, Pink."

"Night, Beanie Boy."

Back in my room, I lie awake for hours, listening to the unfamiliar sounds of another person moving through my house—the shower running, the soft pad of bare feet down the hallway, the quiet click of her bedroom door closing. The knowledge that she's sleeping just down the hall, in sheets I chose, in a room I prepared, does something to me I'm not ready to face.

Fuck.

Banks is right. I like her. Not just because she's carrying my child, though that connection between us is undeniable. I like her sharpness, her ambition, and the way she never backs down. I like the softer side I'm just beginning to glimpse beneath her professional armor.

I'm so fucked.

Rolling onto my side, I stare at the wall that separates my room from hers. I promised her boundaries. Promised I wouldn't touch her.

But lying here in the dark, with her scent lingering in my house and the memory of her smile fresh in my mind, I know those promises are going to be hard as fuck to keep.

For now, though, I'll try. Because it's what she wants.

I close my eyes, willing sleep to come. Tomorrow is day two of our bizarre living arrangement. Tomorrow, I'll figure out how to be just Wren's roommate, just the father of her child, nothing more.

Yeah, right.

Even in my own head, I don't sound convinced.

11
Kasen

SHE'S naked in my bed again. Naked and pink.

Not just her hair, but her skin where I've touched her, marked her. Dream-Wren looks up at me, intense gray eyes gone soft, and Christ, I want to drown in her. My hands grip her hips, feeling her skin hot under my palms, but every time I try to pull her closer, she slips away like smoke.

I'm yanked from sleep by a crash from the kitchen, followed by muffled cursing. My body reacts before my brain fully engages, muscles tensing as I swing my legs over the side of the bed. The red numbers on my alarm clock read one thirteen a.m.

There's another clatter and then what sounds like a cabinet door slamming shut.

I grab the baseball bat I keep beside my bed and pad silently down the hallway. The light from the refrigerator casts long shadows across the kitchen floor. A small figure is silhouetted against it, head buried deep in the freezer compartment.

"Did you find what you're looking for?" I ask, lowering the bat.

Wren yelps, jerking upright so fast she smacks her head.

"Fuck me!" She clutches the back of her head, spinning to face me. Her eyes do a slow-drag up my abs and chest before finally landing on my face. If I flex a little along the way, sue me. "What the hell, Kasen? Were you planning to beat me to death with that?"

"The thought crossed my mind." I set the bat against the wall, trying not to notice how the oversized t-shirt she's wearing barely skims the tops of her thighs. It's one of mine—black with the Timber Brewing logo faded from too many washes.

When did she grab that?

And why does seeing her in it with her messy pink hair like she just got fucked make my dick sit up and pay attention? "You were making a fuck ton of noise and I thought someone broke in."

"Well, I didn't." She rubs her head, wincing. "I'm just..." she trails off, suddenly looking embarrassed.

"Just what?"

She sighs, shoulders slumping. "I need caramel ice cream. With potato chips. Crushed up and sprinkled on top." Her expression dares me to laugh at her. "I know it sounds disgusting, but I need it right now or I might actually die."

"Ah." Understanding dawns. "The cravings have hit, huh?'

She nods miserably. "I woke up, and it was all I could think about. But all you have is that mint chip and cookie dough from earlier." She gags and I bite my cheek to keep from laughing. "No caramel." She sounds personally offended by this oversight.

I scratch the back of my neck, trying to focus on her face and not the long expanse of bare leg she's showing. Seriously, they look like they go on for miles. "Pretty sure there's a twenty-four-hour store about fifteen minutes from here."

Her eyes widen, a flash of hope quickly replaced by wariness. "It's the middle of the night. I'm not asking you to—"

"I know you're not asking." I'm already turning toward my room to grab a shirt and my shoes. "Let me grab my keys."

"Kasen, wait." Her voice stops me. When I look back, she's biting her lower lip, that tough exterior cracked just enough to let a tiny bit of vulnerability peek through. It's goddamn captivating. "You don't have to do this."

"I know I don't have to." I shrug like it's no big deal, like I'm not already calculating the fastest route to the store. "But my kid apparently wants caramel ice cream with potato chips, and who am I to argue with that?"

A small smile tugs at the corner of her mouth. "Your kid has weird taste."

"He gets that from you." I'm rewarded with that little laugh of hers, the genuine one I've only heard a couple of times.

Back in my room, I tug on a t-shirt and a pair of joggers, then grab my wallet and keys. When I return to the kitchen, Wren has moved to perch on one of the barstools, her legs swinging under her. She looks hot as fuck and for a second, I wish she'd woken up with a different craving and it was me she was straddling right now instead of that stool.

"Anything else you need while I'm out? Pickles?"

She rolls her eyes. "Just the ice cream and chips. Regular, not ridged. The ridged ones are too thick."

"Got it. Regular chips, caramel ice cream. Stay put." I grab my jacket from the hook by the door.

"Hey, Kasen?" Her voice is soft, almost hesitant. Not a tone I'm used to hearing from her.

"Yeah?"

"Thank you."

Two simple words, but for some reason they hit me hard coming from her. "No problem, Pink. Be back soon. Lock the door behind me."

The night air is cool against my face as I slide into my truck. I sit there for a minute, hands on the wheel, trying to process the surreal turn my life has taken. A couple of weeks ago, I was filling out divorce papers I couldn't bring myself to file. Now Wren's living in my house, wearing my clothes, and I'm making a middle-of-the-night ice cream run because of pregnancy cravings like it's the most natural thing in the world.

I pull out of the driveway and turn onto the empty street, streetlights casting pools of amber across the asphalt. Without really thinking about it, I hit the call button on my steering wheel.

Banks answers on the fourth ring, his voice rough with sleep. "Someone better be dying."

"I need advice."

"At—" There's a pause, presumably as he checks the time. "—one thirty in the morning? What could possibly—"

"Wren's craving caramel ice cream. With potato chips on top."

A beat of silence, then a low chuckle. "So it begins."

"What begins?"

"The cravings, man. Clover had me driving across town in the middle of the night for specific donuts from that place on Burnside. Only those would do. Nothing else."

I merge onto the main road, the truck's headlights cutting through the darkness. "You didn't warn me about this part."

"Would it have made a difference?" His voice holds a knowing edge that irritates me.

"No," I admit, turning into the parking lot of the twenty-four-hour market. Its fluorescent lights make the nearly empty lot look clinical and strange. "But a heads-up would've been nice."

"So she's all moved in?" Banks asks, sounding more awake now. "How's that going?"

"It's..." I search for the right word, finding none that adequately captures the strange tension of having Wren in my space. "Fine. Weird. I don't know. It's only been a day."

"And you're already making middle of the night food runs. That's promising."

"It's not like that," I insist, parking near the entrance. *It's totally like that.* "I'm just trying to make this easier for her. For the baby."

"Uh-huh." His skepticism is palpable even through the phone. "Keep telling yourself that, man."

"I gotta go." I kill the engine. "Thanks for nothing."

"Hey, Kase?" His tone shifts, becoming more serious. "For what it's worth, I think you're doing the right thing. Trying to make this work with her."

I stare through the windshield at the empty store, at my reflection in the glass door. "Yeah, well. One day at a time."

"One day at a time," he agrees. "Good luck with the ice cream hunt."

I end the call and head into the store, nodding at the bored cashier. The place is deserted except for a couple of night shift workers stocking shelves. I find the ice cream section easily enough, scanning the varieties until I spot a couple of different caramels. I don't know which ones she wants, so I grab them all, just in case.

In the chip aisle, I study the options. Regular, not ridged. I grab a family-size bag of plain potato chips, then on impulse, I add a bag of pretzels and one of those chocolate-covered ones too. Might as well cover all the bases.

The cashier doesn't even blink at my haul, just scans everything, yawns, and bags it up while I tap my card to pay. Ten minutes later, I'm heading back home.

Home. Where Wren is waiting.

In my t-shirt.

What's she got on under it?

The thought makes my pants tighter as my dick starts to get hard, and I adjust the rearview mirror like that's going to help me stop picturing her sprawled across my couch, my shirt riding up just enough to—

Fuck.

I grip the steering wheel harder, willing my mind and body to get it together. This is exactly why this arrangement is a terrible idea. But it's only for a little while, I remind myself. A practical solution to her housing crisis. A way to be involved in the pregnancy.

Nothing more.

I ignore how irritated the thought she'll be leaving soon makes me.

The house is quiet when I get home, the kitchen light still on, but there's no sign of Wren. I figured she'd pounce the second I stepped through the door like the feral raccoon she was acting like before I left. I set the bags on the counter and pull out the ice cream, letting it soften while I crush some chips in a bowl.

"Pink?" I call softly, heading toward the living room. "I've got your gross ice cream ready."

I find her curled up on the couch, passed out. One arm is tucked under her head, the other wrapped around her middle. My t-shirt has ridden up just enough to show off the very top of her thigh and answer my earlier question. She's got on a pair of underwear that look like tiny shorts and *fuck me.* They cling to everything.

Her face is relaxed in sleep, free from the guarded expression she usually wears.

My throat goes dry. I stand there like an idiot, just staring, while the blood in my body rushes south. I should wake her up. Or look away. Or do anything but stand here getting hard while looking at my pregnant wife passed out on my couch.

Pregnant. Wife.

Those two words tangle together in my brain, unlocking

something primitive and possessive I didn't know lived inside me.

I force myself to tear my eyes off her, rubbing the back of my neck. The ice cream's melting, I remind myself. That's a problem I can actually solve.

Back in the kitchen, I put her weird concoction together anyway—caramel ice cream in a bowl, crushed potato chips sprinkled on top—then cover it and stick it in the freezer. She can have it tomorrow. I clean up the mess from the bags, wiping down the counter where a drop of melted ice cream landed.

When I return to the living room, she hasn't moved. She's still curled up like a cat, pink hair spilling over the throw pillow.

I should wake her up. Tell her that her ice cream's ready. But I can't bring myself to disturb her when she looks so damn peaceful. So instead, I carefully slide one arm under her knees, the other around her shoulders, and lift her.

She barely weighs anything, which catches me off guard. Her body fits against mine perfectly, her head falling naturally into the curve of my shoulder. She makes a small noise in her sleep and burrows closer, her breath warm against my neck.

And yep. There goes my dick again.

Goddamnit.

It's starting to become a habit to ignore it, and instead I focus on the warm weight of her in my arms as I carry her down the hall. I nudge her bedroom door open with my foot, careful not to bang her head against the frame.

Her bed looks barely touched except for the tangled sheets she left when she got up. I lay her down as gently as I can, then stand there like an idiot, not sure if I should cover her up or just leave. Against those white sheets, she looks smaller somehow. Softer. Nothing like the sharp-tongued pain in my ass who's been driving me crazy for years.

And I want to crawl right in there with her and wrap my body around hers.

Her eyes flutter open before I can decide to do it. "Kasen?" My name in that sleepy voice does all sorts of things to me that I'm gonna have to work out with my right hand when I get back to my room.

"You passed out on the couch," I tell her, keeping my voice low. "I was just getting you to bed."

"Ice cream?" she asks, sounding like a hopeful kid.

"In the freezer."

She nods, already drifting off again. "Kay. Thanks."

"Sleep, Pink." I pull the blanket up over her, my fingers brushing her shoulder. I let them linger there a second too long, wanting to kiss her. Wanting to run them over her skin and remind myself how soft it was since I didn't get to memorize her the first time.

First time like it's going to happen again.

More like only time.

As I tuck the comforter around her, something glints in the dim light from the hallway. A thin silver chain has slipped from under my t-shirt she's wearing. And hanging from it—unmistakable even in the half-light—is a wedding band.

Her wedding band.

From when she married *me*.

I freeze, my hand suspended in mid-air. She's kept it. Not just kept it—she's wearing it around her neck, close to her heart. The sight of it knocks the wind out of me.

My fingers find their way to my pocket, closing around the warm metal I've been carrying around for weeks. My own matching ring that I can't seem to part with either, that I touch throughout the day without even realizing I'm doing it.

What the hell does this mean? That she's as confused by all this as I am? That maybe some part of her doesn't want to let go of what happened between us any more than I do?

I carefully tuck the chain back into her shirt, my calloused fingers gentle against her skin. She doesn't stir, just sighs in her sleep, completely unaware of the earthquake happening inside me.

She probably doesn't hear me. Her breathing's already evened out, lips parted slightly. I stand there watching her longer than I should, feeling something fierce and possessive tear its way through my chest.

Mine, I think. My wife. The mother of my child.

The possessiveness of that thought should scare me, but it doesn't. It settles into my bones like it's always been there.

Like she was always meant to be at the foundation of me.

I force myself to back out of the room before I do something stupid like climb into bed with her. The door closes with a soft click that sounds too final in the quiet hallway.

Back in my room, I pull the ring from my pocket and stare at it under the dim light from my bedside lamp. The matching twin to the one she keeps hidden against her skin. What the hell is happening between us?

What does she want?

I toss the ring onto my nightstand instead of putting it back in my pocket like I normally would. Sleep doesn't come easy. Every time I close my eyes, I see her—pink hair against white sheets. The vulnerable curve of her neck when she tilted her head back while dancing with me in Vegas. The way her lips parted when she whispered my name.

And that goddamn ring on the chain around her neck, marking her as mine.

I roll onto my stomach, pushing my face into the pillow like I can smother these thoughts. Six months. We agreed on six months of this torture, and we're not even through day one.

12
Kasen

I WAKE up to my alarm at five thirty, my hand smacking it silent before the noise can travel down the hall. I've been staring at the ceiling since four fifteen anyway, my brain refusing to shut off after what I found out last night.

After a quick shower that does nothing to clear my head but all kinds of things to empty my balls, I pull on jeans and a henley, running a hand through my damp hair. The routine of making coffee keeps me somewhat present in the moment, instead of letting my unhinged thoughts continue to get worse.

What's not routine is checking the fridge to make sure there's enough of that fancy creamer I bought because I remembered her drowning her coffee in it that time at the industry meeting in Seattle. Also not routine? Wondering if she'll want actual breakfast or if the pregnancy will have her reaching for that ice cream first thing.

I'm on my second cup, pretending to check emails but really just staring at the same message for ten minutes, when I hear her padding down the hallway. There's a soft yawn, then she's standing in the doorway wearing my shirt with a pair of leggings now, her pink hair piled on top of her head in a messy knot that shouldn't be as sexy as it is.

"Coffee," she mumbles, like she's sighting land after weeks at sea. "Tell me that's real coffee and not some pregnancy-approved bullshit."

"One cup a day is fine, according to Reed." I gesture toward the pot without looking up. Yes, I texted my buddy to ask about that shit. "Help yourself."

She shuffles to the cabinet where I keep the mugs, stretching up on her toes to reach. My shirt rides up with the movement, showing the bottom curve of her ass, and I bite my cheek to keep from groaning. This shit cannot be good for my circulation, having all my blood in my cock whenever she walks into the room. Or I think about her.

I force my eyes back to my laptop before I can figure out whether that chain with my ring on it is still around her neck.

"You're up early," she comments, dumping enough cream in her coffee to turn it the color of sand. She stands there for a second like she's not sure what to do, then takes the seat across from me.

"Always am, but I thought you weren't a morning person." She just shrugs as I close my laptop, knowing I haven't read a single email anyway. "How'd you sleep? After your late-night food emergency."

Her cheeks go pink. "Good. Really good, actually." She sips her coffee, eyes on me over the rim. "Did you carry me to bed last night? Or did I dream that part?"

"You were dead to the world." I try to shrug it off like it was nothing, like I haven't been thinking about how she felt in my arms since the second I put her down. "I couldn't leave you there and let you hurt your neck or your back."

"Thanks," she says, tucking a stray piece of hair behind her ear with a gesture that seems almost nervous. Not a word I'd usually associate with Wren Callan. "And thanks for the ice cream run again, even though I didn't end up eating it. That was... really great of you."

"It was nothing." I stand up, needing to move before I say something stupid. The distance helps, gives me something to focus on besides how she looks wearing my clothes in my kitchen. "You want breakfast? I can make eggs."

"You cook breakfast too?" That eyebrow of hers arches up, some of that familiar sass coming back into her voice. "Is there anything you're not good at, James?"

"I can't sing for shit," I tell her, pulling eggs and bacon from the fridge. "Banks got me banned from karaoke after I drove everyone out of the bar on his birthday."

She laughs at that—another real laugh. I think I'll become a collector of the real ones. They're so rare, I want to commit them all to memory. "That I'd pay good money to see."

"Never gonna happen." I crack eggs into a bowl, focusing on not dropping in pieces of shell instead of how that laugh hits me right in the gut. "How do you want your eggs?"

"Scrambled." She takes another drink, watching me over her mug. "I can help, you know. I'm not totally useless in the kitchen."

Uh, the mushrooms she massacred last night beg to differ. But I don't call her on it.

"I've got it." I wave her off without looking back. "Sit down. Drink your one sad cup of caffeine."

"Don't think I've forgotten it's your fault I'm spending the next eight months caffeine deprived."

I just smirk at her because I'm not sorry and she rolls her eyes.

I cook without talking, feeling her eyes on my back as I move around. It's weird how normal this feels already—her sitting there while I make food, like we've been doing this for years instead of one day.

"Oh," she says out of nowhere. "What happened to my ice cream? Did you find it?"

"It's in the freezer. Ready to go." I flip the bacon. "I don't know if I made it right, but I tried. Got you three kinds of chips, including those chocolate-covered ones, in case plain wasn't going to cut it by the time I got home."

Something changes in her face then, softens it. "You didn't have to do all that."

"I know I didn't have to." I set a plate in front of her, eggs and bacon arranged exactly how I like mine. "I wanted to."

Our eyes catch across the table, and for a second, everything else falls away. All the business bullshit, all the rivalry. All that's left is just her and me and whatever this magnetic thing is between us.

My phone rings, killing whatever moment we were having. Lake's name flashes on the screen.

"Shit," I mutter, grabbing it. "I need to take this. Lake doesn't call this early unless something's on fire."

She nods, turning back to her food like she's suddenly fascinated by scrambled eggs.

"What's wrong?" I answer, moving toward the living room.

"We've got a situation." Lake sounds stressed, which is never good. He's the chillest guy I know. "Fermenter Three sprung a leak overnight. The whole basement's flooded and the seasonal batch is totally fucked."

"Goddammit." I drag my hand through my hair. "How bad are we talking?"

"Bad enough that I'm calling you at six a.m. I need you here, boss."

I glance back at Wren, who's pretending not to listen while she pushes bacon around her plate. "I'll be there in twenty. Start cleanup and call Edwin for repairs—not that cheap asshole we tried last time."

I end the call and walk back to the kitchen, surprised by

how much I don't want to leave. Timber's been my life for years, but somehow this morning it doesn't seem as important. "I've gotta go. Shit's going down at the brewery."

She looks up, fork halfway to her mouth. "Is it serious?"

"You could say that. Some of the equipment failed. Nothing we haven't handled before, but I need to be there." I hesitate, torn between my business and this strange pull I feel to stay. "You gonna be okay here? You've got my number."

"I'll be fine, Kasen." Her mouth curls up at one corner. "Go save your precious beer. I'm a grown woman who's somehow managed to make it this far on her own."

"Right." I grab my keys and wallet from the counter while toeing into my boots. "There's more coffee... which you can't have. Sorry."

"Stop mothering me." But she doesn't sound annoyed. It almost sounds like she likes it. "I've also been feeding myself since before I met you."

I shrug my jacket on, not bothering to tell her I doubt my newfound protectiveness toward her is going to get any better. "I'll text later if I'm running late."

She tilts her head, studying me. "You don't have to check in, you know. This isn't..." She waves her hand between us. "We're not actually..."

"I know what we're not." It comes out harsher than I meant it to. "Call it roommate courtesy then."

She nods, something I can't read flashing across her face. "Fine. Go fix your crisis, Beanie Boy."

I pause at the door, looking back at her and there's that pull between us again that makes me want to say screw the brewery and spend the day figuring out what else makes her cheeks flush like that.

"See you tonight," I say finally.

"Later."

I close the door behind me and groan because why the fuck

did this have to happen today? Driving toward the brewery and whatever disaster is waiting, part of me is already counting the hours until I can come back.

Back to Wren.

I grip the steering wheel harder, finally admitting the truth I've been ignoring since Vegas. Maybe before Vegas, if I'm being honest with myself.

This "temporary arrangement" bullshit? It's going to be anything but simple. Because despite everything—our history, the boundaries we've set, my better judgment—I'm starting to think I might actually like the pink-haired menace who's turned my entire life upside down.

And that's a complication neither of us signed up for.

13
Wren

PREGNANCY HORMONES ARE A BITCH, but they've got nothing on the realization I might actually like Kasen James.

I slather cream cheese on my bagel, standing in Cascade's small kitchen, trying to pretend this morning is just like any other. Except it's not, because last night I woke up at one in the morning with a craving so intense I practically tore Kasen's kitchen apart, and then he—my mortal enemy—drove to the store just to get me caramel ice cream and potato chips.

That I didn't even eat, and he didn't get mad or even say anything about it.

And I woke up in his bed. Well, not *his* bed. The guest bed. That he made up for me. With actual high-thread-count sheets.

Then he made me breakfast.

Like, what is even *happening* right now?

And here I am, twelve hours later, still thinking about how his damp hair curled at the back of his neck after his shower and wondering how soft it is.

Oh, and then there were the inked up muscles I got an

eyeful of when he walked into the kitchen in the middle of the night without a shirt on.

"Hey," Kieran waves his hand in front of my face, startling me back to reality. Shit, I think I'm drooling. I wipe my finger across my mouth and yup. "Where'd you go? I've been talking to you for like two minutes."

"Sorry." I drop the knife into the sink with a clatter. "Just... thinking about the Henderson account."

Kieran smirks, his eyes knowing. "Uh-huh. That wasn't your business face. That was something else. And considering you've been living with James for two days now..." He lets the implication hang in the air.

My cheeks burn, which is infuriating. Humiliating, too. "Do you want to keep your job? Because speculating about my personal life is a great way to end up unemployed."

"Yeah, right," he scoffs, reaching around me to grab his mug. "You'd be lost without me and we both know it."

Unfortunately, he's right. Kieran's been with me since the beginning, when Cascade was just a half-baked business plan and a stack of rejection letters from investors who didn't think a girl with maxed out credit cards and no connections in this industry could make it.

"The Miller meeting's in thirty," he reminds me, eyeing my bagel with a raised eyebrow. "That's a lot of carbs for someone who was complaining about her pants feeling tight yesterday."

"I'm pregnant, not fat," I hiss, glancing around to make sure no one else is in earshot. "And your protein shakes give you bad breath."

"They do not."

"Oh, yes, they do. After your workouts, the first thing you should do is brush your teeth unless your goal is to repel every woman you talk to."

He watches me, then slumps. "Shit. You could've told me. I

was flirting with this smokeshow at the gym today and she wouldn't give me her number."

"I'm telling you now." And I've successfully distracted him from my little Kasen daydream. Win-win.

"Yeah, thanks for that." Kieran's expression shifts as he pulls his mug out from under the machine. "Tell me how you're really doing with everything."

I take a bite of my bagel to buy time, not wanting to admit that despite morning sickness and fatigue, I feel better than I have in weeks. Turns out decent sleep in a comfortable bed without stress-dreaming about finding a new apartment does wonders for one's overall wellbeing.

"I'm fine," I say after swallowing. "Living with Kasen is surprisingly okay."

"Details," Kieran demands, leaning against the counter and crossing his muscular arms. "Has the guy shown his true colors yet?"

"No, he's—" I stop myself, not wanting to delve into how surprisingly considerate Kasen has been. How he stocked his kitchen with food I might want. How he's just been... there for me. "He's clean. Organized, even. His house is nice."

"And?" Kieran prompts, clearly expecting more.

"And what? That's it." I take another bite, avoiding his knowing gaze. "We're coexisting. End of story."

"Sure, whatever you say." His tone makes it clear he's not buying my bullshit. "Just seems weird that you've spent two years talking about how much you can't stand the guy, and now you're getting this distant look in your eyes when you think nobody's watching."

"I do not get a 'distant look,'" I protest, complete with obnoxious air quotes. "That's ridiculous."

"Whatever you say, boss." He pushes off the counter and heads toward the door. "Ten minutes. Your office. Make sure the drool's gone."

"Make sure you brush your teeth," I counter, and he flips me off over his shoulder.

Alone in the kitchen, I let my hand drift to my stomach while I wipe at my face again. Stupid Kieran, calling me out. I can't believe it's already been twelve weeks. The first trimester's almost behind me. And somehow, impossibly, I'm living with Kasen James—the same man who once publicly declared my distribution model "the death of authentic craft beer culture."

My phone buzzes in my pocket, and I already know it's him.

> Kasen: How are you feeling?

It's the third text check-in of the day. I scroll back to see the others.

> Kasen: Fermenter disaster handled. Hope you're good.

> Kasen: Remember Reed said to stay hydrated. Are you drinking water?

My fingers hover over the screen, torn between irritation at being mothered and a strange warmth that he worries about me.

> Me: I thought you didn't micromanage.

I send it, then immediately type another.

> Me: But yes, I'm hydrated. And fine. Important meeting in 20.

His response is immediate, and I bite my lip to keep from grinning.

> Kasen: Knock 'em dead, Pink.

Yeah, it's a losing battle because I find myself smiling at the screen like an idiot before I catch myself. This is exactly what I can't afford—getting soft, getting comfortable with this arrangement. With him. It's only until I find somewhere else. Then we'll figure out how to co-parent and move on with our lives.

Our *separate* lives.

Tucking my phone away, I head back to my office as my good mood plummets at the thought of moving on, but I do my best to shake it off.

I love this space, the glass-walled corner office overlooking the warehouse floor. It's still my favorite part of Cascade—being able to see the operation I've built humming along beneath me. Forklifts moving between rows of kegs, delivery trucks being loaded, my team working with the efficiency I've drilled into them.

It's everything I hoped it'd be and also more than I even dreamed.

Kieran's already waiting in my office with the Miller file open on his tablet. "So Pacific Northwest Distribution," he says without preamble. "They've been buying up small craft operations all over the Northwest."

"Not just buying," I correct, settling behind my desk, thinking about the reports I've read and things I heard at the conference in Vegas. "Gutting. They strip away everything unique, standardize the processes, and slap the original labels on what amounts to mass-produced swill."

"Harsh but accurate." Kieran swipes through some documents. "They've acquired seven craft breweries in the last eighteen months. Last month, they approached Eastside Ales with an offer."

"Did they accept?"

"No, but rumor has it they're reconsidering after Miller

sweetened the deal. And now he's coming to us." Kieran looks up, his expression serious. "What do you think he wants?"

"To destroy everything I've built," I say without hesitation. "Cascade is the link between most of the independent craft breweries in Portland. If he folds our distribution into his control, he controls who gets tap handles and shelf space almost everywhere."

"It's a smart play," Kieran admits.

"Yes, but it doesn't mean I'm selling." I straighten a stack of papers on my desk. "Not now, not ever. I didn't build this company from nothing just to hand it over to some soulless corporate douchebag."

"Even if the number has a lot of zeros?"

"Even then." My hand moves to my stomach, then drops when I realize what I'm doing. It's a new habit I need to break before someone notices.

But Kieran sees it. Of course he does. The man misses nothing. Mercifully, though, he says nothing. "Have you talked to your new roommate about this meeting?"

"Why would I?" I tilt my head and squint at my head of operations, wondering what he's getting at. "We agreed to keep our business lives completely separate."

"Because Miller's probably talking to him too," Kieran points out. "Pacific Northwest hasn't been subtle about wanting to control the Portland craft scene. Timber would be a prime target."

The thought hadn't occurred to me, which is annoying. Kieran's right—of course Miller would approach Kasen too. Timber's built a loyal following, and their direct-to-bar model cuts out distributors like me. It's the exact kind of operation Miller would want.

"Kasen wouldn't sell," I say with a lot of confidence I hope I'm not wrong about. "He's too stubborn and too proud of what he's built."

Kieran gives me a strange look. "That almost sounded like a compliment."

"It's not. It's an observation." I stand, straightening my blazer. "I need to prep for this meeting. Make sure the conference room is ready."

"Already done." He rises too, tablet in hand. "Should I mention that the Timber team was spotted at Hopworks yesterday? From what I hear, it looked like an informal meeting. Someone matching Miller's description was there."

My stomach drops. "Why are you just telling me this now?"

"I couldn't confirm it until this morning." Kieran shrugs, but his eyes are sharp. "Thought you'd want to know before you sit down with Miller yourself."

"You're right." I grab my water bottle, all this talk of Kasen reminding me of his incessant texts about staying hydrated. "Thanks."

"That's what you pay me for." He pauses at the door. "Among other things, like snapping you out of dirty daydreams and keeping you humble."

"That happened once."

"Three times." He smirks. "So far." Then the asshole disappears down the hall.

Alone again, I sink back into my chair. My thoughts are going in a million different directions. Kasen met with Miller? It could be nothing. Or it could be everything. The idea of Kasen selling Timber makes my chest tight in a way that has nothing to do with business rivalry and everything to do with knowing how much that brewery means to him.

Not that I care. I don't. It's just—

My phone buzzes again. It's not Kasen this time, but a text from the reception desk.

> Reception: Nolan Miller is here. 15 mins early.

Yeah, that's an attempt at a power move. He's trying to make me accommodate his schedule instead of the other way around and if I was feeling like a bitch today, I'd make him wait an extra ten minutes to show him his time's no more valuable than mine.

This isn't my first rodeo.

Lucky for him, I'm not into playing games today.

> Me: Send him to the conference room. Offer coffee. I'll be there in 15.

I may not want to play games, but no way will I let him come into my territory and think he has any power or control.

It's not happening.

I take a moment to collect myself, checking my reflection in the glass wall. My hair's pulled back in a sleek ponytail, my makeup's hiding my zombie eye. Nothing about me says "knocked up by my nemesis."

I look like I've got my shit together—professional, untouchable, ready to eat corporate assholes for breakfast.

Exactly how I need to be for this meeting.

Exactly the opposite of how I feel.

The conference room's flooded with natural light when I walk in. Nolan Miller's posted up by the window like he's staring at his own kingdom instead of mine, surveying my warehouse floor. He spins around at the door click, and holy shit, that smile. It's like someone taught a snake how to grin.

"Well, if it isn't the gorgeous Wren Callan in the flesh." He glides across the room, hand extended like we're about to be best friends. "A pleasure to finally meet in person."

He's taller than I expected, with silver at his temples and the kind of tan you can only get from expensive vacations. Or a bottle. His suit is impeccably tailored, and no doubt cost thousands.

Everything about him makes my skin crawl.

"Mr. Miller." I shake his hand, making sure my grip is just as strong as his. "Welcome to Cascade."

"Please, call me Nolan." He gestures at the warehouse. "Impressive operation you've built here."

"Thanks." I claim the head of the table because fuck his power plays. "So Pacific Northwest's been on a shopping spree, I hear."

He chuckles like I've said something adorable. "Direct. I like that in a potential partner."

"We're not partners." The words come out sharper than a fresh IPA. "And Cascade isn't a brewery. So why exactly are you here?"

"You're the gatekeeper." Miller leans forward, his expression earnest in a way that immediately puts me on alert. "Many of the craft breweries in Portland go through you. That kind of influence is valuable."

"It is," I agree. "Which is why I'm not interested in selling."

He doesn't even flinch. Bastard. "I haven't made an offer yet."

"You don't need to."

Miller's smile stays plastered on, but something shifts in his eyes. "What if Cascade stayed exactly as is? You in charge with the same team and the same brand. Just with Pacific Northwest's resources backing you up."

I raise an eyebrow. "And you'd do that out of the goodness of your heart?"

"God, no." His laugh sounds like Chandler's fake work laugh from Friends. My hackles go all the way up. "I need access to breweries who'd rather chew glass than work with us directly. You're my in."

"Because you've got a reputation for destroying everything that makes craft beer special."

His smile never wavers. "I prefer to think of it as 'optimizing.' But perception matters, I understand that. Which is why

Cascade will still look independent while we pull the strings backstage. It's a win-win."

The door opens, and Kieran appears with a tray of coffee and snacks. I catch his subtle eyebrow raise and I roll my eyes. We don't need words to communicate—he just checked in and I told him this guy's full of shit.

"Thank you, Kieran." I pour myself some decaf for something to do with my hands. "Mr. Miller, Kieran Edison. He's my head of operations."

They exchange polite chit-chat that neither of them means or cares about while I death-grip my mug and try to figure out my next move. The second Kieran leaves, Miller pounces.

"Let's cut the bullshit, Wren. I'm prepared to offer twenty million for Cascade."

14
Wren

COFFEE GOES DOWN the wrong pipe. I manage not to spit out what's in my mouth, but fuck me. Twenty million dollars? For a company I started with maxed out credit cards and sheer stubbornness?

"That's..." I scramble for words that aren't 'holy fucking shit.' "Substantial."

And all I'd have to do is give up everything I've built and sit back and watch while he destroys it all and lords over me like he's my boss.

"It's what you're worth." He sips his coffee like he didn't just drop a bomb. "Plus, there's so much room to grow. Think beyond Portland. Imagine Seattle, Vancouver, San Francisco—the whole West Coast under your distribution network."

Even I can admit it's tempting. He's basically laying my ultimate dream at my feet and offering me an insane amount of money to make it happen. But the way he tells me to imagine it like I haven't already done that a million times rubs me the wrong way.

He thinks I'm some little girl who couldn't possibly have ambition that's bigger than even his.

He's offering me my dream on a silver platter. Three months ago, I'd have considered it. But now? With a baby in my belly and Kasen James somehow becoming essential to my existence? The thought of giving all of this up, of figuring out how to start over or, worse, being under Miller's thumb, makes me want to take a nap.

Throw up, *then* take a nap.

Something's off about this whole thing, too. It's too easy and too much money for a first offer.

"You know, it's funny how you're suddenly interested in my business, like you haven't been sniffing around Portland breweries for months." I watch his face carefully. "Including Timber, from what I hear."

And I think I spot the first crack in his mask. His eyes narrow just a fraction. "I see news travels fast."

"Portland may be a big city, but this is a small community." I set down my mug. "Are you making Timber an offer, too?"

"I'm exploring all opportunities." In other words, absolutely yes. "Timber has a unique approach to the market that I can appreciate."

My stomach does this weird flip thinking about Kasen across from this vulture, considering selling the brewery he built from scratch after his mom died. Which is fucked up because I shouldn't care what happens to his business.

Shouldn't.

But I do.

"Here's what I don't understand," I say, leaning forward. "Why now? Cascade's been operating for years and you've never once shown any interest in us. What's changed?"

Miller studies me, then shrugs. "Market conditions. The craft bubble is starting to contract. It's better to consolidate now, while valuations are still high."

He's lying. Or at least not telling the whole truth. Before I can call him on it, the room starts spinning. I white knuckle the edge of the table so I don't fall out of my chair.

This is why I should've had Kieran sit in on this meeting, but I couldn't let Nolan Miller think I needed a big, strong man to protect me or handle him.

"Are you alright?" Miller asks, concern creasing his brow.

"Peachy." I force a smile. "Where were we?"

"I was about to give you this." He slides a folder across the table. "It's my formal offer, along with projections for the first three years under Pacific Northwest. Take your time reviewing it. I don't expect an answer today."

I open the folder, skimming the first page. The numbers are even crazier on paper, with performance bonuses and stock options that could push the total well beyond twenty million.

"This is generous," I admit, closing the folder. "But Cascade isn't just a business to me. It's my whole life."

"I understand." Miller nods. "Which is why you'd maintain operational control. Think of it as gaining a partner, not losing your company."

Right. A partnership where he owns my ass and can destroy everything I've built.

Another wave of dizziness hits me, stronger this time. Black spots pop at the edges of my vision, and I realize I'm going to pass out if I don't get some air. Or food. Or lay down. Or all of the above.

Is this normal or should I be worried about the baby? Or maybe it's a good old-fashioned panic attack?

"Mr. Miller," I say, standing from my chair, trying not to freak out about how off I feel. "I need to step out for a minute. Kieran will show you some of our distribution data while I'm gone."

On cue, Kieran materializes at the door like the mind-reading wizard he is.

"Everything good?" he murmurs as we pass in the doorway.

"I'm about to pass out," I whisper. "Stall him."

Kieran nods, then turns to Miller with his megawatt smile. "Mr. Miller! Let me show you our Q3 projections. You're gonna love this."

I make it to my office on shaky legs, closing the door behind me before collapsing into my chair. My hands are trembling, my heart racing, and I can't tell if it's pregnancy or panic or both.

Twenty million dollars. A life-changing amount. Enough to never worry about money again, to give our baby every advantage.

But at what cost?

My phone buzzes on my desk, and Kasen's name pops up on the screen. I hesitate, then answer.

"This isn't a good time," I say instead of hello.

"What's wrong?" The concern in his voice makes my insides warm. "You sound off."

I blow out a breath. "Miller's here." I don't know why I tell him this. We agreed to keep business separate. But the words tumble out anyway. "Making an offer for Cascade."

A pause, then, "How much?"

"Twenty million. Plus incentives."

Another pause, longer this time. "That's a hell of an offer."

"Yeah." I run a hand through my hair, destroying my ponytail. "Did he approach you too? Kieran said you were meeting with him yesterday."

"He did." Kasen's voice goes flat. "He made a bullshit pitch about maintaining independence while accessing Pacific Northwest's resources."

So the exact same shit he said to me. "And?"

"And I told him to go fuck himself."

A laugh bubbles up despite everything, that ball of tension in my gut starting to loosen up. Talking to him is just... easy. "That direct, huh?"

"You know me, Pink. I'm allergic to corporate bullshit." There's a smile in his voice that I can almost see. "What're you going to do?"

"I don't know," I admit, surprising myself with my honesty. "It's a lot of money."

"It is." His tone softens. "But money isn't everything."

Coming from anyone else, it would sound like a platitude. But coming from Kasen, who rebuilt his brewery after a fire and who sells directly to bars even though others disagreed with his model, it has more impact.

"I need to get back to the meeting," I say, glancing at the clock. "I just—I'm feeling like garbage. I think it's maybe pregnancy stuff, but I don't know."

"Have you eaten?" The immediate shift to protective and worried in his voice makes everything inside of me go melty and warm all over again. *Bad Wren. What the hell are you doing?* "Low blood sugar can make you dizzy and nauseous."

"How'd you know I was dizzy?"

"Lucky guess." He pauses. "There's a protein bar in your purse. I put it there this morning while you were in the shower."

This man. "Is this gonna be a thing? You being completely overbearing?"

"Only until you start taking better care of yourself." His tone is gruff. Also, why don't I believe him? "Eat the damn bar, Wren."

"Fine." I dig through my purse and yep. It's one of those fancy bars with extra protein and vitamins that's supposed to taste like a brownie. "Anything else you hid in here I should know about?"

"Just that." He hesitates. "Call me after the meeting? Let me know how it went?"

I should say no. Should maintain the boundaries we agreed

on. But he's asking me instead of dictating orders and for some reason that's what makes me say, "Okay."

"Okay," he echoes, sounding relieved. "And Pink?"

"Yeah?"

"Trust your gut. It's gotten you this far."

He hangs up before I can respond. I stare at the phone before I set it down and unwrap the protein bar. It's actually good, and there's not a hint of cardboard.

It's not until I'm halfway done that I realize I never asked Kasen why he was calling in the first place. Guess it wasn't that important.

By the time I'm finished, the protein bar's working its magic, and the dizziness has faded enough for me to return to the meeting. I fix my ponytail, straighten my blazer, take a deep breath, and march back to that conference room, ready for war.

Miller and Kieran are bent over a tablet, but both look up when I enter.

"Everything okay?" Miller asks. He's wearing his politician's smile again, so I put on one of my own.

"Perfect." I reclaim my seat at the head of the table. "Look, Nolan. I appreciate the offer, Truly. But Cascade exists to support independent breweries, not to help corporations disguise mass production as craft."

His smile doesn't falter, but his eyes go cold. "That's a narrow view of what Pacific Northwest does."

"Maybe. But it's my view, and it's why I can't accept your offer." I slide the folder back across the table. "Cascade isn't for sale."

Miller studies me for a long moment, then nods as if he expected this. "For now," he says, tucking the folder into his briefcase. "But the market is changing, Wren. Small independents are struggling. When the craft bubble bursts—and it will—having allies with deep pockets will be the difference between survival and collapse."

"I'll take my chances," I say, feeling my resolve cement even with his vague threat. This is the right decision. "Kieran will show you out."

They leave, and I slump back in my chair. Exhausted doesn't even begin to cover how I'm feeling. The meeting took more out of me than I expected. As much as I want to pretend it isn't, this pregnancy's really kicking my ass. This kid is sapping all my energy so it can grow, but I can't be mad about it. In fact, it makes me smile just a little.

Kieran comes back a few minutes later, closing the door behind him. "That was ballsy," he says, settling into the chair Miller just vacated. "Turning down twenty million without even taking time to consider it."

"I didn't need time." I run a hand over my face. "It was never going to be a yes."

"Because of the baby?" he asks. "Or because of Kasen?"

"Because of Cascade." I sit up straighter. "This is mine. I built it. I'm not handing it over to someone who'll use it to destroy the very industry I've worked to support."

Kieran nods, his expression thoughtful. "For what it's worth, I think you made the right call. But you should probably go home. You look like shit."

"I'm fine," I say automatically, even as another wave of fatigue crashes over me.

"No, you're pregnant and stubborn as hell." He stands, holding out his hand for my laptop. "I'll handle the Orson call. Go rest or I'll call Kasen."

I know I should argue, should insist on staying, but the thought of the cloud of a bed in Kasen's guestroom is too good to pass up.

"Fine, snitch," I relent, handing over my laptop. "But call me if anything comes up with Orson. They're still waffling on the summer seasonal commitment."

"Will do, boss." Kieran gives me a little salute. "Want me to call you a car?"

"I can drive," I insist, though even as I say it, my eyelids might as well weigh a thousand pounds.

"Sure you can." He's already on his phone, ignoring me. "Car will be here in five. I'll walk you down."

The ride home passes in a blur. *Not home*, I remind myself. Kasen's house. I'm half-asleep by the time the driver pulls into the driveway of the Craftsman bungalow that feels more like coming home than my apartment ever did.

Inside, the house is quiet and empty. Kasen's still at the brewery, dealing with the fallout from whatever disaster called him away this morning. I kick off my heels in the entryway, padding in stockinged feet to the kitchen where I pour myself a glass of water.

The domesticity of it all hits me hard. Standing in Kasen's kitchen. Drinking from his glasses. Opening his freezer like I belong here and taking out the bowl of ice cream and potato chips he made me in the middle of the night. It's been two days, and already he's got me all up in my feels.

Honestly. I thought I was made of tougher stuff than this.

After my ice cream snack, I make my way to the guest room and change out of my work clothes into leggings and one of Kasen's t-shirts I snagged out of his closet. He didn't say anything to me about the one I was wearing last night, so I figure he doesn't care.

The bed calls to me, and I don't resist, crawling under the covers with a sigh of relief.

Just a quick nap, I tell myself, setting an alarm for an hour. Then I'll check in with Kieran for a debrief about the Orson call.

But as I start to drift off, it's not Cascade or Miller or million-dollar offers I'm thinking about. It's Kasen. His deep, gravelly voice on the phone. The protein bar he slipped into my purse. The way he said "trust your gut" like he actually believes in me.

The last thing I register before I set my alarm is a bizarre craving hitting me hard.

Pink Lady apples sliced thin and dipped in hot sauce. With a side of butterscotch pudding.

C'mon, even *I* know that's gross.

Like on a logical level, I mean, because my body is *not* logical with the way my mouth's watering.

I sit up in bed, rubbing my eyes and staring at my phone as my mouth waters. My stomach growls aggressively, like it's personally offended I haven't already delivered this specific combination of foods.

"Fuck my entire life," I mutter, weighing my options.

I could text Kieran. He's handled weirder requests and wouldn't ask questions. But my fingers are already typing a message to Kasen before I can talk myself out of it.

> Me: SOS. Need pink lady apples + hot sauce + butterscotch pudding. It's an emergency.

His response comes before I can even set the phone down.

> Kasen: On it. Give me 20 minutes.

I fall back against the pillows, staring at his immediate response. No questions asked. No teasing. Just "On it."

I should be irritated by how quickly he's jumping to fulfill my ridiculous cravings. I *should* be able to get up and go get them myself. Instead, I'm fighting a stupid smile I'd deny if anyone saw it. This kind of dependency wasn't part of the plan. The fact that I'm texting him instead of Kieran is a red flag I'm deliberately ignoring.

This is bad. *So* bad. I'm starting to expect his support. To count on it. To want it.

And the only thing worse than needing Kasen James? *Wanting* to need him.

15
Kasen

MY WIFE WON'T STOP STEALING my clothes.

Not that I'm complaining. There's something about seeing Wren in my clothes that does things to me. Dangerous things that make me forget all about our negotiated boundaries. Like right now, she's shuffling into the kitchen wearing my faded Timber Brewing hoodie, the fabric stretching just enough across her growing belly to make it impossible to ignore the reality of our situation.

She's sixteen weeks pregnant. With my kid. Living in my house.

And still trying to pretend we're nothing more than reluctant roommates.

"Morning," she mumbles, making a beeline for the coffeepot. Her hair is piled on top of her head in that messy knot she always wears when she's at home and there's something about her without makeup like this that just does it for me.

"Decaf's on the counter," I say, not looking up from my laptop where I've been updating my calendar with her next prenatal appointment and all the baby milestones. "I made it fresh ten minutes ago."

She grunts something that might be thanks or might be a death threat. Hard to tell with her before she's fully awake. Three weeks of living together has taught me that mornings aren't her thing.

Three weeks that have felt simultaneously like three years and three minutes. The blue balls have been no joke.

"You're up extra early," she says after her first sip of mostly creamer, leaning against the counter and eyeing me suspiciously over the rim of her mug.

"Just adding some stuff to my calendar." I close the laptop, not wanting her to see that I've been researching cribs instead of working on the new seasonal beer label like I told Lake I would. "It's a big day today."

The corner of her lips tilt up. "The ultrasound. That's why I'm up at this ungodly hour, too. I couldn't sleep anymore."

"Yeah." My stomach tightens at the reminder. "Reed said we might be able to find out the sex."

"If you want to know." She rests a hand on her belly, something she's been doing more often lately. Watching her fingers cup her belly where our baby grows makes me forget how to breathe for a second—like I'm staring at something that belongs to me in ways I never knew I wanted. "We don't have to."

"You don't want to?"

She shrugs, but I've gotten better at reading her these past weeks. The little crease between her eyebrows means she's conflicted.

"I don't know. It's just..." She searches for words, which is unusual for someone who usually has too many of them and all of which she knows exactly how to use as a weapon. "Once we know, it makes this even more real, you know?"

I do know. That's exactly why I want to find out.

"Plus," she continues, "if I know it's a boy, my mom will start sending me feminist literature on raising sons to respect women." She rolls her eyes, but there's fondness there. "And if it's a girl, I'll get twice as much."

I can't help my laugh. "Your mom sounds intense."

"You have no idea." She smiles, a real one. The corners of her eyes crinkle and her guard drops completely. Her whole face softens in a way that makes her look younger, less like the ruthless businesswoman who's been terrorizing Portland's craft beer scene. This is smile number six in my mental collection since she moved in. "Think female Bernie Sanders with better glasses and an encyclopedic knowledge of Virginia Woolf."

"That's kind of awesome."

"She'd eat you alive." Wren pushes off the counter and opens the fridge, bending to scan the contents. The hoodie slides up just enough to reveal the curve where her ass meets her thigh, and if she turned around right now, I don't think I could tear my eyes away and she'd catch me staring. My fingers itch to trace that line, to feel if her skin is as soft as I remember from Vegas.

I clear my throat, ignoring my dick, which would love nothing more than to reintroduce itself to her. "There's yogurt on the second shelf. The kind you like with the granola packets."

She straightens, shooting me a look over her shoulder. "How do you know what kind I like?"

Because I've been paying attention to everything about you, from the way you curl up in the corner of the couch when you work late to how you talk to yourself when you think I'm not listening.

Because I notice which foods make you light up and which ones make you gag.

Because I can't seem to stop cataloging every detail about you.

"Lucky guess," I say instead.

She doesn't look convinced but grabs the yogurt anyway. "You heading to the brewery today?"

"After the appointment." I get up to refill my coffee. Decaf, too, in solidarity. "Lake can handle things for a few hours."

"You don't have to come with me," she says automatically, the same thing she says every time I offer to do anything for her. "I can drive myself."

"I know I don't have to." I step closer, close enough to catch the scent of her shampoo. It's sweet and I love it, even though I'll never admit it. "I want to."

Her eyes meet mine, something flickering in their gray depths that makes my heart beat faster. For a second, I think she might actually let her guard down.

But then she blinks, and the moment's gone. "Fine. But I'm driving."

"Whatever you say, Pink."

Her eyes narrow at the nickname, but I catch the twitch of her lips. She doesn't hate it as much as she pretends to. And she's stopped calling me out on using it.

"I'm going to shower," she announces, grabbing her coffee. "Be ready by ten thirty."

I watch her go, my eyes locked on the way her ass looks in those leggings until she disappears down the hallway. Even pregnant with my kid, or maybe because of it, I want her so bad my hands shake. It takes everything I have not to follow her. Once I hear the bathroom door close, I drop my head into my hands with a groan.

Living with her is fucking killing me.

I thought it would get easier with time. That the constant awareness of her would fade into indifference. Instead, it's gotten worse. Every day I notice something new—the little humming sound she makes when she reads, the way she tucks her feet under her on the couch, how she talks to her belly when she thinks I'm not around.

And every night I lie in bed knowing she's just down the hall, remembering what it felt like to wake up with her naked in my arms in Vegas.

It's torture. Straight up torture.

I pull out my phone, checking the reminders I've set. Her prenatal vitamins. Her favorite protein bars for when she forgets to eat lunch. The shopping list for things she'll need soon. Stuff I never would've looked twice at before. Maternity clothes, body pillows, the fancy lotion Reed recommended for preventing stretch marks.

This is my life now. Planning for a baby with a woman I'm technically married to but can't touch. A woman who's determined to keep me at arm's length despite the way I catch her looking at me sometimes.

A woman I want a lot more from than just co-parenting.

That's a problem for another day. Right now, I need to focus on the appointment. On seeing our baby. On not making a complete ass of myself in front of Reed again, since he's already laughing at me on a daily basis because of my constant texts.

By the time Wren steps out of her room, dressed in jeans that look uncomfortably tight around her growing belly and one of my flannels, I've got the truck warmed up and my game face on.

"Ready?" she asks, grabbing her purse.

Not even a little bit.

Reed's office is exactly as sterile and medical as the last time we were here, but this time there's something different. There are more people in the waiting room, for one. And most of them are staring at us.

Or more specifically, at Wren's pink hair and nose ring and my tattoos.

"Everyone's staring," Wren mutters as we sign in at the reception desk.

"Let them," I say, fighting the urge to put my arm around her to shield her from all these assholes and the judgmental looks. Instead, I settle for glaring back at an older couple who are whispering behind their hands. They immediately find the carpet fascinating.

"Relax, Beanie Boy," Wren says, nudging me with her elbow as we take seats in the corner. "We're not exactly a normal-looking couple."

The word 'couple' from her lips fucks me up and I do everything I can to hide my reaction from her. Hearing her acknowledge us as something together, even accidentally, feels like winning something.

Even though I doubt she meant it the way I want her to.

"Wren Callan?" a nurse calls, and we both stand.

The exam room is the same one from before. Same posters of female anatomy that I pointedly avoid looking at. Same stirrups that I'd rather not think about Reed using on my—

No. Not going there.

Wren changes into a gown, and I try not to notice how much more her stomach has grown since the last appointment. She catches me looking anyway.

"What?" she asks, suddenly self-conscious. "Is it that obvious?"

"What?"

"The belly." She smooths a hand over it. "I had to use a hair tie to keep my jeans closed this morning."

"It's..." *Beautiful. Perfect. Proof that part of me is growing inside you.* "It's not that noticeable."

She snorts. "Liar. Kieran asked if I was sure it wasn't twins yesterday."

My teeth grind at the mention of her very jacked, very straight assistant. Before I can respond, Reed knocks and walks in, grinning at us.

"Hey," he greets us, glancing between us as the shit-eating grin on his face only grows. I flip him off where Wren can't see and he laughs.

"How's my favorite patient today? And you too, I guess, Kase."

"Hilarious," I mutter.

"I got three texts from him this morning alone," Reed tells Wren, completely ignoring me. "Did you know he's tracking your vitamin intake on a spreadsheet?"

Wren's eyebrows shoot up as she turns to me. "You're what now?"

"It's not a spreadsheet," I protest, feeling heat crawl up my neck. "It's just... a note app on my phone."

"Right," Reed says, prepping the ultrasound. "That you shared with me so I could monitor it for live updates."

"Stop. Talking," I growl, but Wren's watching me with this little smile that makes me forget why I was annoyed.

"He's been texting me constantly," Reed continues, clearly enjoying himself. "Making sure everything you're experiencing is normal." He pitches his voice lower before mocking me, "'Is it normal if she craves cereal with hot sauce?' 'How much coffee is actually safe?' 'Should I be worried that she fell asleep during a movie?'"

"If you're done embarrassing me," I say through gritted teeth, "maybe we could focus on why we're actually here?"

"Fine, fine," Reed concedes. "How are you feeling, Wren?"

"Hungry," Wren says. "All the time. And my pants don't fit."

"That's normal," Reed assures her. "The second trimester is usually the easiest now that you're past the nausea. Let's take a look at the little one."

I move to stand by Wren's head as Reed gets ready to do the ultrasound.

"This will feel a little gross," Reed warns as he squirts gel on Wren's rounded belly.

She flinches slightly, and without thinking, I reach for her hand. She looks surprised but doesn't pull away. Our fingers weave together like we've done it a thousand times.

The second our hands connect, something locks into place between us. Like every cell in my body just recognized its counterpart in hers. I don't know what it is about touching her this time versus any other accidental touches we've had over the last three weeks, but it feels different, being here with her now, about to see our baby.

The rest of the room—Reed, the machines, even the goddamn fluorescent lights—they all blur at the edges while Wren comes into sharper focus.

Her pulse races against my thumb where it rubs across her wrist, matching the chaos of my own heart. This connection between us feels like a force I couldn't fight even if I wanted to.

And I don't want to.

What I want to do is pull her closer, wrap myself around her and our baby until nothing can take them away. Until nothing can hurt them.

The need to shelter them both, to claim her as mine, burns through me with an intensity that should scare the hell out of me.

Instead, it feels like finally admitting something I've known since Vegas but was too stubborn to face.

Reed clears his throat, snapping me back to the moment. Wren looks away, too, but her cheeks are the same shade as her hair. "You two ready?" he asks, not even trying to hide his knowing smirk as he looks at our joined hands.

I nod, unable to form words as Reed positions the ultrasound wand on Wren's belly. Her grip on my hand tightens as we watch the screen.

And there's our baby. It's not the indecipherable blob from before, but something undeniably human. There's a head. A nose. Arms. Legs. It's moving and—

"Holy shit," I breathe, my grip on Wren's hand tightening. "There's really a baby in there."

"Excellent observation, dude," Reed says dryly. "Everything looks perfect. There's a strong heartbeat." He points to different parts of the screen. "Here's the head. The spine. The arms."

I can't tear my eyes away. That's my kid. My son or daughter. Moving around inside Wren even though you'd never know it from the outside.

"Do you guys want to know the sex?" Reed asks, moving the wand around.

I look down at Wren. Her eyes are glassy, like she could cry at any second, and I don't know how I ever lived without her before.

"It's up to you," I tell her, voice dropping to a whisper only she can hear.

She bites her lip, then nods once. "Yes. I want to know."

Reed moves the wand again, his face serious for once as he studies the screen. "Well..." he pauses, and for a second my heart stops completely. "Looks like I owe Banks twenty bucks. You're having a boy."

He points to something that could be literally anything on that grainy screen. "See this right here? Definitely a boy."

Holy fuck. A son. I'm having a son.

The realization lands deep in my gut, almost stealing my breath. This isn't some theoretical situation anymore—this is a little boy who'll grow up alongside Noble. Cousins close in age who'll either be best friends or mortal enemies, knowing how stubborn the James genes run.

A tiny person who'll need me to teach him everything from

tying his shoes to riding a bike to throwing a football. Who'll watch how I treat his mother and learn what it means to be a man. Who'll never know what it's like to have a father walk away when things get tough.

"A boy," Wren whispers, and I hear in her voice the same wonder vibrating through my bones. Her fingers tighten around mine, squeezing so hard it almost hurts, but I squeeze back just as hard.

Reed watches us for a moment, then quietly steps back. "I'll give you two a minute," he says, wiping the gel from Wren's stomach with more gentleness than I knew the guy possessed. "Take your time. I'll get some pictures printed for you."

The door clicks shut behind him, leaving us alone with the frozen image of our son on the screen.

Our son.

"You okay?" I ask Wren, suddenly aware that I'm still holding her hand in a death grip.

She nods, not looking at me. "It's just...real now. There's an actual person in there." Her free hand rests on her belly. "A little boy."

"Yeah." My voice comes out rougher than I intended. "A little boy."

Finally, she looks up at me, and the rawness in her eyes knocks the wind out of me. "What if I'm terrible at this? What if I screw him up?"

"You won't," I say with more confidence than I feel. "We won't."

"How do you know that?"

I squeeze her hand. "Because you're the most competent person I've ever met. Because you build things to last. Because you don't quit when things get hard." I pause, swallowing past the lump in my throat. "And because you've got me. And I'm not going anywhere."

Something shifts in her expression, a softening around the

edges that makes her even more beautiful. For a second, I think she might cry.

Instead, she pulls her hand from mine and sits up, breaking the spell.

"Reed's probably waiting to finish up," she says, straightening her gown. "And we still need to go shopping after this."

Just like that, the walls are back up. But I caught a glimpse of what's behind them, and that's enough for now.

"Right," I say, stepping back to give her space. "Shopping."

16
Kasen

THE MATERNITY STORE is a sea of pastels and pregnant mannequins without heads. They just cut off at the neck and it's creepy as fuck. I feel like a bull in a China shop with my dark jeans and tattoos, especially when a sales associate eyes my ink with all kinds of judgment.

"Can I help you find something?" she asks, directing the question to Wren while casting sidelong glances at me like I might pocket a onesie when she's not looking.

"No, thanks," Wren says, already scanning the racks with that laser focus I've seen her use to dismantle my arguments at industry panels.

"Let me know if you need anything." The woman smiles too brightly. "We have a husband waiting area with comfortable chairs, if that would be more suitable."

I narrow my eyes. "I'm good right here with my wife, thanks."

The word "wife" slips out before I can catch it. Wren's head whips around, her eyes wide, but the salesperson just nods and retreats.

"Wife?" Wren hisses once we're alone.

"It shut her up, didn't it?" I shrug, pretending it meant nothing when we both know it meant something. "Besides, it's true. You *are* my wife." I eye her, daring her to say shit, but she doesn't. And yeah, she's still got that chain tucked into the neckline of my shirt she's wearing. The one with my ring hanging on it she doesn't know I know about. "Would you rather I told her how complicated shit is?"

She rolls her eyes, but there's a hint of amusement there. "Fair point. But don't do it again."

"No promises, Pink."

She turns back to the clothes, pulling out a black dress that looks like every other black dress to me.

"What about this one?" she asks, holding it up.

"Looks like something you'd wear to a funeral."

"It's professional."

"It's boring." I scan the racks, spotting something with color. "What about this?"

I hold up a blue dress that would hug those curves that have been driving me insane for weeks.

"It'll show off too much cleavage."

"There's no such thing," I say before I can stop myself.

She rolls her eyes again, but her lips tilt up on one side. "You *would* think that. These things are ridiculous."

She looks down as she gestures to her tits and *fuck my life*.

"I need things for work, and contrary to the rumors, I've never slept with anyone in the business. Except..."

Me.

"Fine." I put the dress back, but I'm coming back for it when she's not paying attention. I need to see her in it. "But at least get something that isn't black or gray. You're having a baby, not summoning the dead."

That gets a laugh out of her,. "I didn't know you were a fashion expert."

"I'm not. But I know what looks good on you."

154

The words hang between us, too honest maybe, but I'm done fucking around. I want her to know I want her. Wren turns away, busying herself with another rack, but not before I catch the deepening blush on her cheeks.

We spend the next hour loading up a cart. Wren sticks to the practical stuff. Pants with stretchy waistbands. Tops with room for her belly. Black. Gray. Sensible.

Boring as hell.

I wouldn't hate it if she put all this shit back and just wore my shirts for the next five months, but I know she won't.

When she's busy arguing with that snobby saleswoman about whether maternity clothes need to look like shapeless sacks or whatever they're talking about, I grab that blue dress and toss it in the cart. Add a blue sweater that'll make the gray in her eyes stand out. She'll be pissed I didn't listen, but I don't really give a shit.

In the back of the store, we find ourselves in the baby section. It's still early, but we're gonna need all this shit at some point.

There are racks of tiny clothes and shoes. Onesies with ridiculous sayings that make Wren roll her eyes and me secretly smile.

"We should probably wait on this stuff," she says, but her fingers trail over a tiny flannel shirt that's clearly meant to look like mine. She thinks I don't notice, but I notice everything about her.

"Probably," I agree, but I'm already picking up a pair of miniature boots that match the ones I'm wearing. "But this is pretty damn cute."

She looks at the boots in my hand, then up at my face, something soft in her expression. "Yeah, it is."

We end up buying the boots and the flannel, along with a stuffed beer mug that makes us both laugh. Who the fuck made this for babies? It's inappropriate as hell, but whatever. It's the first thing we've chosen together for our son, and it feels significant, like we're taking a step we can't take back. I don't want to take it back.

I hope she doesn't either.

At the checkout, I pull out my credit card before Wren can reach for her wallet.

"I can pay for my own clothes," she protests.

"I know you can." I hand the card to the cashier. "But I want to."

She opens her mouth to argue, then closes it, studying me. "Why?"

Because seeing you in clothes I bought for you does something to me on a primal level.

Because you're my goddamn wife and I want to take care of you and our son.

Because it makes me feel good to do things for you.

"Because it's the right thing to do," I say instead.

She doesn't look convinced, but she lets it slide.

And look at that.

I think that counts as progress.

Back at the house, I dump the shopping bags on her bed. She can deal with her new clothes. I've got dinner to handle.

We've fallen into an unexpected routine these past weeks. I cook dinner, she tries to help me clean up and does a shitty job, but I never tell her. We watch movies on the couch with that careful space between us that feels like miles.

Tonight, it's burgers from the grill, her newest craving, except she likes them with sweet and sour sauce instead of something normal like mayo or ketchup. I flip the patties, listening to her moving around the kitchen through the open patio door. She's humming something under her breath, probably not even aware she's doing it.

It feels domestic in the very best way.

"Five minutes," I call, closing the grill lid.

"Buns are ready," she calls back. "And I made that sauce you like."

I pause, struck by how easily we've slipped into this. How natural it feels to be making dinner together, planning for our son, building a life neither of us expected.

And when this is over, I know I don't want to go back to how it was before.

I don't want her to leave.

When I bring the burgers in, she's setting the table, wearing my flannel again and a pair of the new stretchy pants. Her hair is piled on top of her head, and she's stolen my socks. Again.

"You know, you could just ask if you want to borrow my clothes," I say, setting the plate of burgers on the table.

She grins, unrepentant. "Where's the fun in that? Besides, your stuff is more comfortable than mine."

"And here I thought you were just trying to drive me crazy."

The words slip out before I can stop them, loaded with more meaning than I intended. Her eyes meet mine, and for a second, there's a flash of something that makes my pulse spike.

"Is it working?" she asks, her voice lower than before.

Heat flares in my gut and my dick perks right the hell up. "What do you think?"

The air between us crackles with the tension that's been brewing between us for months. Every second of these last four weeks feels like an eternity of wanting but not touching her. Four fucking weeks of this dance we've been doing around each other.

Four weeks of catching her eyes on my tattoos when she thinks I won't notice.

Four weeks of cold showers and jacking off with her name on my tongue as I come.

Four weeks of sleepless nights with only a wall between us.

Four weeks of dying to feel her skin under mine every second of every day.

Four weeks of pretending what we have is enough when we both know it was never going to be.

She looks away first, and I take the opportunity to adjust my dick. "The food's getting cold."

We eat in relative silence, but there's nothing silent about the way her eyes keep dropping to my mouth every time I take a bite. Nothing quiet about how my body reacts when she licks sauce from her thumb, her tongue darting out in a way that makes my jeans uncomfortably tight.

"You've got some..." I gesture to the corner of her mouth.

She swipes at it with her thumb, completely missing. "Did I get it?"

"No. Here." I reach across the table, brushing my thumb along the corner of her lips. The contact is like striking a match. Her pupils dilate, her breath catches, and something inside me snaps.

"Fuck this," I growl, standing so fast my chair crashes to the floor behind me.

"Kasen, what—"

"A month, Pink. It's been a fucking month of watching you walk around in my clothes and pretending I don't want to bend you over every goddamn surface in this house."

Her cheeks flush, but she doesn't back down. "So, what are you going to do about it?"

I'm in front of her in two strides, gripping her under her thighs and dropping her onto the table. Her plate clatters to the floor, but neither of us give a fuck. "This."

17
Kasen

MY MOUTH CLAIMS hers with a violence that she meets and matches. There's a monster inside of me that won't be satisfied until I consume her, and the taste of her on my tongue is only fueling it to take *more more more.*

She's right there with me with a monster of her own, her insanity the other half of mine as her teeth sink into my bottom lip and her tongue licks into my mouth.

This kiss is brutality and desperation. It's starvation and satisfaction. It's a craving that's been building since Vegas. Maybe before. More like since the first time she walked into the room with that pink hair and sharp mouth that cut me straight to my core.

And I never healed right.

Not until now.

She doesn't hesitate for even a fraction of a second. Her fingers dig into my biceps hard enough to bruise as she yanks me closer, dragging me half onto the table with her. The force of it knocks a glass over, water spilling across the wood, soaking into her shirt—my shirt—but neither of us stops. Her tongue pushes into my mouth, like she's trying to devour me.

I groan against her, the sound ripped from somewhere soul-deep as her teeth catch my bottom lip, biting just hard enough to feel it in my cock. Her hands are everywhere—ripping off my beanie, digging into my hair, reaching under my shirt until her nails dig into my ribs.

She's feral and unhinged and I fucking *love it.*

It's like she's been dying for this as long as I have and her eyes open while we're kissing and we stare at each other.

She dares me with those stormy eyes to keep going.

She's a hurricane I want to drown in.

A tsunami I want to destroy me.

Right now it's a goddamn battle to the death between my body and hers, my heart and hers, our souls and everything we are.

"Get up here," she demands, fingers hooking in my belt loops, yanking me forward until I almost fall on top of her. I have to catch myself so I don't crush her belly, but then she's on me again.

Her teeth sink into the underside of my jaw, her nails raking up my back, burning a path that travels straight to my dick.

Fuck, I'm so hard it hurts.

I want her.

Need her.

Would kill to be inside of her.

I grab her legs and yank them around my waist, forcing her onto her back, and she goes with a groan that's half-pain, half-pleasure, but she never lets go of me. I know she'll probably be sore in the morning, but I can't bring myself to care. Not now. Not when she's got her nails buried in my flesh, her tongue fucking into my mouth, her thighs squeezing around my waist like she's never letting me go.

There's no space between us, not even a breath, and somehow it's still not close enough.

I'm shaking, trembling on top of her, my body vibrating

with the need to be closer, to taste every inch of her, to consume her.

I'm not going to make it through this.

My hands are in her hair, fisting it at the base of her neck, yanking her head back, giving me full access to her mouth.

Her throat.

To her skin.

To the little spot where her neck meets her shoulder that makes her whimper when I bite it, sucking the skin into my mouth until there's no doubt there'll be a bruise there in the morning. My teeth rake down her throat and she shudders, her hands fisting in my hair, her legs locking around me.

I need her.

I need her more than I've ever needed anything in my entire life.

"You have no fucking clue how bad I need you," I growl against her skin, my teeth dragging along her collarbone. "I'm gonna fucking eat you alive, Pink."

She moans, the noise desperate and broken and wanting.

I drag my hand up the front of her shirt until I can get a grip on the front of it. I tear it open. Fabric rips and buttons go flying, but she's splayed out on the table, her bare tits right fucking there, and I groan.

"Shit, look at you," I say, pulling back just enough to admire her. She's flushed and panting and so fucking gorgeous I could die. I trail a hand up her ribs, brushing my thumb over her nipple. Her back arches as she whimpers, the noise going straight to my cock.

"You gonna keep staring, or are you going to do something about it?"

Goddamn that smart fucking mouth.

I smirk and dip my head, flicking my tongue over the hard peak. "You mean like this?" I ask, before sucking it into my mouth, biting down on the sensitive flesh.

Her hips shoot off the table, and a strangled moan rips from her throat.

"God," she whimpers, her fingers digging into my scalp.

"There's no god here, baby," I murmur, switching to the other breast. "Only me." I bite down again, and she cries out, her body writhing beneath me.

I reach down and grab the ring she wears on a chain around her neck, the one I'm not supposed to know about. "You know what this means?"

She shakes her head, and I pluck her nipple between my fingers.

"It means you're my fucking wife." I suck her nipple back into my mouth and her legs tighten around me. "As much as you might want to deny it, it means that you're mine, Pink."

"Kasen—"

"You need to know I don't share." I switch to the other nipple, biting it hard enough to sting before soothing the pain with my tongue. "I don't fucking share. You let me have you, and I'll kill any motherfucker who tries to touch you. I will kill him."

Yeah, I'm saying some unhinged shit, but she brings it out in me. Always has.

She moans again, and there's sauce smeared against her arm and water and lettuce in her hair. My hand shifts and a plate smashes on the floor as her fingers fumble with my belt, the button of my pants, and then she's shoving them and my boxers down just enough to free my cock.

"Tell me to stop now, Pink, because once I'm inside you, I'm never leaving." I swear to Christ, I'm about to lose my fucking mind.

My free hand works on yanking down her leggings, which is real fucking difficult considering any time I try to put space between our bodies to reach down there, she thrashes and fights to get closer.

"If you stop, I'll fill your bed with Legos and you'll never sleep again." Her hand wraps around me, stroking slowly as she stares up at me, dead serious. "Do you know how many times I've touched myself since Vegas and imagined it was you?" Her tongue darts out to lick her lips, her eyes never leaving mine.

"Fuck," I hiss, my head falling to her shoulder. "You can't just say that shit, woman." I laugh, a dark, broken sound, but it's hard to breathe, let alone laugh right now.

Her teeth sink into her bottom lip. "And I'm so sick of pretending I don't want this."

She's pumping my dick now and I grab her wrist, stopping her before I embarrass myself. "Pink—"

"What if you're right?" she whispers. "Maybe we're just crazy enough that this works."

"I'm right." I shift her arm above her head and pin her to the table with the weight of my hips. "I'm always fucking right. You should have learned that by now."

She rolls her eyes, and I grab her other hand, holding them both above her head in one of mine. I lean back and stare at her. She's splayed out on the table, dressed in only my ripped shirt with food smeared all over us both and her leggings and underwear dangling from one foot because I was too impatient to rip them all the way off.

Fucking perfect.

"Besides," I tell her, slipping my hand under her back and lifting her slightly, "I think I've earned this."

"Oh, yeah?"

I brush my thumb over the ring, and she sucks in a breath, her pupils dilating. "Yeah. I've been good to you, haven't I?"

She nods, her throat bobbing as she swallows.

"I think maybe you're the one who needs to show me how grateful you are." I drag my thumb over her bottom lip, groaning when her tongue darts out to touch my skin. "Maybe if you beg nicely, I'll give you what you want."

"I don't beg."

"Then I'm going to eat your pussy until you're about to come, and then I'm going to leave you here, high and dry, while I go fuck my hand and pretend it's you."

Her teeth sink into her bottom lip, but she doesn't give in. There's a wicked glint in her eye, the same one she gets when she's about to score a deal that'll fuck me over.

"You wouldn't dare," she says, lifting her chin in defiance. "Not if you ever want to sleep again, James."

I smirk, sliding down her body and lowering to my knees beside the table. My leg lands on top of a smashed burger, but I give no fucks. "You really are something else," I whisper, kissing my way down the swell of her stomach, my hands gripping her thighs. "We'll see how long you last."

"Maybe I'll just go find someone else to—"

I don't let her finish. I don't let her say another goddamn word, especially the one she's about to say. I'm not going to hear it. She wants to play this game? Then we're fucking playing. My mouth is on her, my teeth scraping over her clit. I slide a finger inside of her, groaning when I feel how wet she is.

So goddamn wet and hot.

She cries out, her back arching off the table as she moans my name. My name, and it's the best thing I've ever heard in my entire life.

"Kasen—"

"You're not going to find anyone else." I drag my tongue over her clit, sucking it into my mouth. "No one. Because you're married to me. You're my fucking wife, Wren." I add a second finger. "Now say what I want to hear."

"I want—"

"Say it." I flick my tongue against her, her pussy clenching around me. She's close, but I won't give it to her. I won't give her anything she wants until she gives me what I want.

"Fine. Fine, you asshole!" she gasps, writhing against me, her hips lifting, her legs trembling. "Please let me come."

I grin. "And?"

"And you were right." She's panting, her fingers fisting in my hair. "You're always fucking right."

I'm still not satisfied. I need more. I want her to admit that she feels this too, that she's just as obsessed and insane and lost as I am.

"Say you need me," I growl, curling my fingers inside her, my mouth sucking at her clit. "That you're my wife."

"I need you. Fuck, Kasen, I need you." She's shaking now, her whole body trembling as I push her to the edge. "I'm your wife."

I groan, my dick throbbing so hard it's almost painful. I want to be inside her. I need to be inside her. I'm pretty sure if I'm not, I keel right the fuck over right here on my knees on the kitchen floor.

"Yes, you fucking are," I growl, biting her clit just a little harder than necessary.

"Then fuck me like it!"

Her pussy clenches around my fingers, and she screams as she comes, her entire body convulsing on top of the table.

I stand and then I'm crawling on top of her. The table creaks underneath us, but I don't care. I'm still mostly dressed because I couldn't be bothered to take the time to strip, but my dick's out and ready to get inside her.

I drag the head of my cock through her soaking wet pussy, and she curses, still trembling, her hands gripping the back of my neck as her hips lift, trying to get me inside of her.

"Say it again," I demand, my forehead dropping to hers.

She shakes her head, and my hand tightens around her throat. I thrust against her, the head of my cock slipping inside her before I pull back out. She gasps, a shudder rolling through her body.

"Say it."

I push into her again, sinking deeper than before, but I stop when I'm halfway inside. It's heaven and hell and I'm not going to make it. Not when she's looking up at me like she wants to kill me, but also begging me with those pretty storm cloud eyes to keep going.

"No."

My teeth rake over her throat, and she whimpers, her nails sinking into my back. I pull back until I'm almost all the way out of her. "Last chance."

She doesn't say it, and I'm not even sure I want her to at this point. I want to punish her for torturing me, for making me wait, for making me insane. I need her to suffer the way I've been suffering since the moment I laid eyes on her.

But she doesn't know how to submit. She's a fighter, and that might be my favorite thing about her.

My dick has its own pulse and my balls fucking ache to unload. But I'm playing the long game, and this push and pull between us is fun as fuck.

I slide all the way out of her, and she cries out, her hips lifting, trying to get me back. I shake my head. "If you won't say it—"

"Your wife wants you to fuck her. Now." She drags me closer, her teeth sinking into the sensitive spot where my neck meets my shoulder. Pain lances through me and I curse, my hips slamming into hers. I'm buried inside of her in one brutal thrust, and I'm pretty sure I've died and gone to heaven. If not, hell wouldn't be so bad if she's there.

She's perfection.

"Kasen—" Her breath catches on a moan and she's already coming again, clamping down on me as her eyes squeeze shut and her back arches off the table.

I want her to watch. I want to see the same madness that I feel in her eyes. "Look at me."

Her eyes open and lock with mine. "You take my dick so well," I rasp as I pound into her, the table shaking beneath us. "So fucking well. It was made to be inside you, Pink. Made for your tight pussy. Do you hear me?"

She nods, her legs tightening around me. I don't stop thrusting. I don't stop thrusting into her, the table inching across the floor, plates and glasses shattering on the ground as I fuck her like I'll never get to have her again.

My shirt gets in the way and I rip it off and watch as her eyes rake down my chest and abs, and her pussy clenches around me when she does. I smirk down at her, my hand coming up to grip her jaw. "Like what you see, Pink?"

She glares up at me, but her glassy eyes ruin it. "You know I do."

I thrust harder, her head almost knocking into the wall. She has to throw her hands over her head and brace against it so I don't fucking concuss her.

That's how hard we're fucking.

I've never wanted to break someone so badly, and from the way she's clawing at me, I'm pretty sure she feels the same way.

"Fuck, you feel so fucking good. Like a goddamn dream."

It feels like I've been waiting a lifetime to have her. And I want to be so deep inside her she never gets me out.

When she starts to come again, I know I'm done. I can't take it anymore. I'm not sure how I haven't come already, but the second she squeezes around me, my balls tighten and unload.

My entire body goes rigid as my hips slam into hers, my fingers digging into her skin, my orgasm ripping through me so hard I see black spots. I'm pretty sure I'm saying her name like a prayer, and she's right there with me. Fucking her bare like this is my new favorite thing in life and I'm never going back.

Her and me? There'll never be anything between us.

Not now.

Not after this.

My chest is heaving when my vision clears, my hands braced on either side of her head as I lean over her. She's staring up at me with this look in her eyes I haven't seen before and I don't know what it is. We're a mess. There's food and broken dishes everywhere, our skin is smeared with sauce and sweat, her thighs are shaking where they're still clamped around me and my arms tremble.

I let my forehead rest against hers as we catch our breath. My dick's still inside of her and twitches with an aftershock that sends a shiver through my body.

I don't know what she's feeling, but I know I'm completely fucked.

"Wren—"

"I know."

She doesn't say anything else and neither do I. But she doesn't push me away either.

She just lifts her hand and presses it to my chest—right over my heart—and leaves it there.

18
Wren

THERE ARE FOUR BROKEN PLATES, two shattered glasses, and a whole mess of food on the floor. Oh, and we can't forget the hickey the size of Montana on my neck.

It's all damning evidence of what happens when you fuck your husband on the kitchen table.

When you finally give in to what's been building for months and things just sort of... explode.

My fingers trace the purple monstrosity at the base of my throat as I stare at myself in the bathroom mirror. I look different. My hair's a tangled pink mess, my lips are swollen, and I've got this general post-sex glow that I don't think I've ever seen on my face before.

Turns out orgasms are better than any beauty routine I've ever tried.

"Shit," I mutter, trying to tug the collar of Kasen's t-shirt higher to cover the way he marked me like I'm his property. It doesn't work. Nothing short of a turtleneck or a scarf would hide this thing.

The thought of walking into Cascade with this billboard of poor decisions on my neck makes my stomach clench. But under the low-key anxiety is something a lot more disturbing. I'm actually *happy* about this. Kasen marked me.

And I *like* it.

And it didn't happen just once. Oh, no.

Last night's boundaries-obliterating sex marathon plays on repeat in my head. The kitchen table. The shower. His bed. My god, his bed. I'm still not entirely certain how we even made it that far, considering neither of us could keep our hands off each other except when we needed to breathe.

I splash cold water on my face, which does exactly nothing for the "I've been thoroughly fucked" look I'm sporting. Everything about me screams that I just spent the night breaking every single boundary I insisted on when I moved in here. Separate spaces? Obliterated. No touching? Please. Roommates, not spouses? We literally fucked on multiple surfaces while I called him my husband.

My. Husband.

The word shouldn't make my stomach do that stupid flip thing, but here we are.

And I think it's time I finally fess up to the fact that I've never wanted anyone more in my entire life than I want Kasen James.

It's terrifying. And exhilarating. And I have no idea what happens next.

A soft knock on the bathroom door makes me jump.

"You planning on moving in there, Pink?" His voice is rough from sleep, and I hate how it makes my knees weak.

"Trying to figure out how to make myself presentable for civilization," I call back, running a hand through my tangled hair in a futile attempt to look less like I've been fucked to within an inch of my life.

"Coffee's ready when you are."

His footsteps retreat down the hall, and I blow out all the air in my lungs. How am I supposed to face him in the light of day? How do we go from dish-breaking, wall-shaking sex to casual morning coffee now that everything's changed?

I don't know how to face him now that he's seen my orgasm face. Well... again. But this time he was sober, so, yeah.

You know what? I've faced down corporate sharks and sexist brewery owners. I can handle post-sex awkwardness with my accidental husband.

Even if said husband has a body that should be illegal and knows exactly how to use it.

Even if I maybe sort of definitely want him to use it again. Immediately.

In case you're wondering, "body" definitely means dick.

Also, abs.

My phone buzzes on the counter reminding me that the real world still exists outside this house. Honestly, I kind of hate it a little.

By the time I've brushed my teeth and pulled on leggings and the least wrinkled of Kasen's shirts from my growing collection, I've almost convinced myself I can handle this like an adult. We're adults. We had sex. Earth-shattering, reality-altering, ruin-you-for-other-men sex. But still just sex.

No big deal. It'll be fine.

When I walk into the kitchen, Kasen is standing at the counter pouring coffee, his back to me. He's shirtless, because why wouldn't he be? He's only got on sweatpants that hang low on his hips and show off his ass that should have its own Instagram account. I'm actually afraid of what I'll do if I get a view of what they do for his dick.

The tattoos that cover his arms continue across his shoulders and down his spine, a canvas of colors and shapes I didn't have time to fully appreciate last night. And yep, those are scratches from me woven in with the designs, too.

It looks like I tried to claw my way inside his skin.

I press my legs together as I remember putting every single

one of them on his skin. I hope he doesn't notice how I want to jump his bones all over again right now.

Or bone. Singular.

Pregnancy hormones are a bitch, but they've got nothing on whatever this man does to my nervous system.

"Morning," I say, aiming for casual and landing somewhere in the ballpark of *hoarse because your dick was down my throat an hour ago*.

He turns, and the smile that crosses his face when he sees me knocks the air straight out of my lungs. It's warm and intimate and so genuine it hurts. It's also a little dirty at the edges. Like he's remembering how I look naked.

"Morning, Pink." He holds out a mug filled to the brim with the perfect mix of coffee and cream. "Figured you might need this after last night."

I take the coffee, careful not to let our fingers touch. One spark and we'd end up right back in his bed again, and I have a meeting in ninety minutes. "Thanks. Your coffee maker is ridiculous. It has more buttons than a spaceship."

"Worth it though." His eyes drop to the mark on my neck and then to the chain I'm still wearing around my neck, and the satisfied smirk that tugs at his mouth should piss me off. It doesn't. "Nice hickey."

I roll my eyes, but heat floods my face. "Very mature. This is going to be impossible to cover up."

"Not trying to be mature." He takes a sip of his coffee, watching me over the rim of his mug. "I like seeing my mark on you."

And there it is. The possessive caveman bullshit that should have me putting him in his place. Instead, my traitorous body responds like he just offered me chocolate-covered orgasms.

My eyes drift to the kitchen table, now cleared of broken dishes, but forever changed in my mind. I'll never be able to eat breakfast there again without remembering how he looked hovering over me, his eyes black as night, his hands gripping my thighs hard enough to bruise as he owned every inch of me.

"We should probably talk about that," I force out, meeting his gaze even though it feels like staring into the sun.

"Which part?" His tone is light, but there's weight beneath it. "The part where you begged me to fuck you? Or the part where you finally admitted you're my wife?"

"I didn't beg." The protest is automatic, even though we both know it's bullshit.

"You definitely begged." He sets his mug down and leans against the counter, crossing his arms over his chest. The movement makes his muscles flex in ways that are completely hazardous to my concentration. And vagina. "But we can argue semantics later. We need to figure out what this means."

"What this means?" I take a sip of coffee to buy time. This means I'm fucked. This means all the walls I built to keep him out are rubble at his feet. This means I actually want the thing I've been fighting against since Vegas.

"For us," he clarifies, like that makes it simpler.

"I don't know." The admission costs me, but lying feels pointless when he's already seen me at my most vulnerable. "This wasn't exactly in my five-year plan."

"Mine either." He moves closer, just one step, but suddenly the kitchen feels smaller. "But I'm not sorry it happened."

"I'm not either," I say quietly, surprising myself with the truth of it.

"Good." His eyes darken. "Because it's happening again."

It's not a question. It's a statement of fact, like the sun rising or me craving weird pregnancy foods in the middle of the night. We opened this door and there's no closing it now.

"Presumptuous much?" I say, but there's no bite to it.

"Realistic," he counters, taking another step closer. "You really think we can go back to separate bedrooms and polite small talk?"

He's close enough now that I can feel the heat radiating from his bare chest. Close enough that I can see the navy circle around the edges of his blue eyes. Close enough that all I'd have to do is lean forward and...

"No," I whisper. "We can't."

His hand comes up, fingers ghosting over the hickey that's basically a neon sign saying "Property of Kasen James." The light touch sends electricity straight to parts of me that should still be in recovery from last night.

"So, where does that leave us?"

Fucked. Completely, utterly fucked. But I can't say that, can't admit how terrified I am of wanting him this much. Of needing him. Of the way my body recognizes his like they're two pieces of the same really dysfunctional puzzle.

But before I can come up with something appropriately sarcastic to deflect with, his gaze drops to my belly where the shirt of his I'm wearing stretches across. The atmosphere shifts, softens, becomes something that makes me want to run for the hills and also never leave this kitchen.

"You're showing more," he says, his voice tinged with wonder. "When did that happen?"

I look down at the obvious bump that wasn't nearly this prominent even last week. Sixteen weeks, and there's no hiding it anymore. Not in his thin t-shirt, not in anything really.

"I don't know. It just... happened." I smooth a hand over the curve self-consciously. "None of my work clothes fit anymore."

He places his hand over mine on my belly, and the simple gesture feels more intimate than anything we did last night. "It's amazing."

"It's weird," I say, but I don't pull away. "My body doesn't feel like mine anymore."

"It's beautiful." He looks at me like I'm some kind of miracle instead of a hormonal mess with bedhead. "You're beautiful."

And damn him, he means it. I can see it in his face, in the

reverence with which he touches me. It's too much. Too real. Too close to things I'm really not ready to face yet.

"I need to get ready for work," I say, stepping back because if I don't put distance between us now, I never will.

His hand falls away, but his eyes stay locked on mine. "I know. Me too."

I turn to leave, but he catches my wrist, and just like that, I'm back in his gravitational pull.

"Wren."

The use of my actual name instead of "Pink" stops me in my tracks. He so rarely calls me that.

"What?" I ask, my voice embarrassingly breathless.

"I meant what I said last night." His thumb traces circles on the inside of my wrist, sending shivers up my arm. "About you being mine. About not sharing."

The possessive edge in his voice should irritate me. Should have me reading him the riot act about bodily autonomy and feminism and how I belong to no one but myself.

Instead, it makes me want to jump him.

Again.

"I know," I manage to say.

"And?"

"And I have a meeting in a little over an hour that I can't be late for." I pull my wrist free, but soften it with the hint of a smile. "We'll figure it out."

Disappointment flashes across his face, but he nods. "Yeah. We will."

I make it exactly halfway down the hall before I hear him behind me. Strong hands catch me by my hips and spin me around, pressing me against the wall before I can process what's happening.

"What—"

His mouth crashes into mine, cutting off whatever protest I was about to make. Not that I would have meant it anyway. His tongue pushes past my lips, tasting of coffee and mint and *Kasen*, and I melt into him, my arms winding around his neck, pulling him closer.

He kisses me like he's drowning and I'm oxygen. Like he's starving and I'm food. Like he'll die if he doesn't have me. And I kiss him back just as desperately, just as hungrily.

His hands slide under my shirt, palming the curve of my waist, the swell of my belly, before moving higher to cup my breasts. They're more sensitive now, heavier, and when his thumbs brush over my nipples, I gasp into his mouth.

"I can't stop thinking about being inside you," he murmurs against my lips, his voice a low growl that vibrates through me. "About how wet you get for me. Only for me."

God. The man's going to kill me with his dirty words. My body's already responding, already aching for him, and we literally just had this conversation about needing some space to figure out what this is and—

"Kasen," I gasp as he mouths at my throat, adding to his collection of marks. "I have to get ready—"

"You will." His hand slides down to the waistband of my leggings. "After."

I should argue. I have responsibilities. A company to run. A reputation to maintain.

But then his fingers slip beneath the elastic and find me already embarrassingly wet, and coherent thought becomes impossible.

"Fuck," he groans against my throat. "You're always so ready for me."

"Always," I admit, the word torn from somewhere deep inside me.

His fingers work magic between my legs, and my head thuds back against the wall. This is insane. I'm letting him finger me in his hallway in broad daylight like some hormone-crazed teenager.

His other hand tangles in my hair, tugging my head to the side so he can access more of my neck.

"I love seeing you like this," he says between kisses and gentle bites along my throat. "Swollen with my baby. Your body changing because of me." His fingers slide inside me, curling in just the right way to make my knees buckle. "Makes me want to keep you this way. Pregnant. Full of me."

The politically incorrect possessiveness of that statement should have me kneeing him in the balls. Instead, it sends me careening toward the edge, my hips rocking shamelessly against his hand.

"You like that," he observes, sounding entirely too pleased with himself. "You get wetter when I talk about putting another baby in you. When I tell you how fucking perfect you look carrying my son."

I whimper. Actually whimper. Who the fuck am I?

I'm beyond shame. Beyond pride. There's only his hands on me, his voice in my ear, the pleasure barreling toward the breaking point.

"That's it," he says, his fingers moving faster, harder. "Come for me, Pink. Show me how much you love being mine."

And because my body is a traitor with no loyalty whatsoever, I do. I come with his name on my lips, clenching around his fingers while he swallows my cries with his mouth. He works me through it until I'm boneless against the wall, held up mostly by his body and sheer will.

When my brain comes back online, he's watching me with a mix of pride and something deeper that I'm really starting to like.

"Better?" he asks, smirking as he pulls his hand from my leggings and sucks my juices off his fingers.

"Shut up," I mutter, but I know he doesn't take me seriously. It's hard to be mad when your bones have melted.

And why is what he's doing right now so hot?

He grins, pressing one more kiss to my lips before stepping back. "Go get ready for work. I'll make breakfast."

I smooth my shirt down over my belly, trying to regain some semblance of composure. "This doesn't solve anything, you know."

"I wasn't trying to solve anything." He shrugs, looking way too pleased with himself. "Just making sure you start your day right."

I roll my eyes, pushing off the wall. "You're impossible."

"You like it," he calls after me as I head for the shower.

The worst part is, he's right.

I do.

19
Wren

KIERAN TAKES one look at me when I stride into Cascade and immediately knows. The man has some kind of superpower when it comes to reading me, and right now I might as well have "I GOT RAILED BY KASEN JAMES" tattooed on my forehead.

"Well, well, well," he says, falling into step beside me as I head for my office. "Someone had a good night."

"Don't start." I speed up, which is pointless because his legs are longer and he's not wearing heels.

"Start what? Pointing out that you're all flushed? Or mentioning the strategic scarf placement? In summer?" He gestures to the silk scarf I grabbed at the last second in desperation. "Very pretty. Very 'hiding a hickey.'"

"I'm cold."

"You're pregnant and last week you bought that." He gestures to the extra portable AC unit I set up in the corner in my office when I was sweating through my clothes. "Don't bullshit a bullshitter."

"Did you have a point, or are you just here to be annoying?" I toss my bag onto my desk.

"Just curious what finally broke the dam." Kieran perches on the edge of my desk, arms crossed over his Tom Ford shirt. That knowing smirk makes me want to throw something at him. "Was it the midnight ice cream runs? The foot rubs? Or did he finally just bend you over something and—"

"Finish that sentence and you're fired."

"No, I'm not." He examines his watch. "You'd be lost without me and we both know it."

Damn him for being right. "Don't you have actual work to do?"

"This is more fun." He studies me with those sharp eyes that miss nothing. "But seriously, you look good. Relaxed. I haven't seen you this unbuttoned in years."

"I'm plenty buttoned." But even I can hear the lie. I'm the opposite of buttoned. I'm unbuttoned, unzipped, completely undone by Kasen James and his stupid perfect... everything.

"Sure." He's not buying it for a second. "Well, whatever happened, it's about time. I approve."

I glare at him. "I didn't ask for your approval."

"Well, you're getting it anyway." He stands, smoothing his jacket. "Henderson report's on your desk. They've agreed to expanded territory but want to haggle over tap handles."

"Of course they do." I flip open the folder, grateful for the subject change. "Set up a meeting for next week."

"Already done." He heads for the door but pauses. "Oh, and Navy called. She wants to know if you're coming to dinner at Clover's tonight."

My stomach drops. "What dinner?"

Kieran shrugs. "Apparently Clover invited you and Kasen and she wanted to make sure you're coming."

Great. That's exactly what I need—a family dinner with Kasen's sister, who still has no idea I'm carrying her brother's baby. Or that we're married. Or that we spent last night breaking furniture with our athletic fucking.

This should be fun.

"Tell her I'll call her back," I say, already dreading the conversation.

"Will do, boss." Kieran gives me an obnoxious salute. "Also, your eleven o'clock canceled, so you've got the morning clear to decompress from whatever cardio you clearly got up to last night."

"Get out."

"Going." But he stops at the door. "By the way, you might want to tell to the staff about the baby soon. That shirt's not hiding what you think it's hiding, and people are starting to notice."

I glance down at my flowy top. From my angle, I can see exactly how much it's not concealing. Fuck. "Noted."

Once he's gone, I slump in my chair. My hand automatically goes to my belly. He's right. I can't keep pretending this isn't happening. People whisper when I walk through the warehouse now. Clients do double-takes in meetings, trying to figure out if I've just been hitting the beer too hard or if there's something else going on.

It's only a matter of time before someone like Miller finds out, and I'd rather control the narrative than let rumors run wild.

And once Miller finds out...

That thought sends ice through my veins. Nolan Miller's been circling Portland's craft scene like a vulture for months, and a pregnant CEO is exactly the kind of "weakness" he'd try to exploit.

I'm pulled from this spiral of paranoia by a text message notification.

> Kasen: How's your morning going?

I stare at the screen, a smile tugging at my lips despite myself.

> Me: Fine until Kieran started interrogating me about my "glow." Thanks for that, by the way.

> Kasen: I will never apologize for making you come. But next time I'll make sure to relax you so much you don't care what he says.

Next time. The promise in those two words sends a shiver down my spine.

> Me: There won't be a next time if you keep leaving evidence.

> Kasen: Liar.

> Me: I have actual work to do, you know

> Kasen: So do I. Doesn't mean I'm not thinking about this morning. And last night. And how you taste.

My thighs clench involuntarily. This is ridiculous. I'm a grown woman, not some horny teenager sexting in class.

> Kasen: What time are you done today? Clover and Banks want us to come over for dinner.

Right. The family dinner of doom.

> Me: I know. Navy called before I got in this morning. I don't think I can make it.

> Kasen: Yes you can. It's just dinner.

> Kasen: Please?

That "please" does something to me. In all the time I've known Kasen James, I don't think I've ever heard him say that word.

> Me: Now who's begging?

Kasen: Pink.

> Me: Fine. But YOU'RE telling her everything.

Kasen: Deal. Pick you up at 6?

> Me: I can drive myself.

Kasen: I'm picking you up. It's not a negotiation.

I should argue. Should assert my independence. Remind him that just because we're fucking doesn't mean he gets to dictate my life.

I do none of those things.

> Me: Fine.

I set my phone down, wondering when exactly I started giving in to Kasen James, of all people. When his stubbornness stopped being infuriating and started being... charming? God help me.

The next hour disappears in a blur of emails and reports. I'm deep in quarterly projections when a knock on my glass door pulls me back to reality.

Kasen stands there holding a brown bag and a pint of ice cream, looking like every bad decision I've ever wanted to make. Dark jeans, a Timber Brewing hoodie with the sleeves pushed up to show off those drool worthy inked forearms, that stupid beanie that somehow works on him.

"What are you doing here?" I ask as he steps into my office, closing the door behind him.

"Bringing you lunch." He sets his offerings on my desk. "Figured you'd forget to eat."

I eye the bag suspiciously. "I'm perfectly capable of feeding myself."

"Sure you are." At this point, I think we both know I'm only fighting this because it's a habit, not because I actually mind him doing things for me.

In fact, I like it.

Don't tell him I said that.

"But would it be the grilled chicken salad Reed recommended? Or the candy bar I know you've got stashed in your top drawer?"

Fuck. How does he know about my emergency Snickers?

"Stalker."

He shrugs and shoves his hands in his pockets.

"You know, it's really annoying when you're right." He just smirks and nods toward the bag. "Thank you." I peek inside and, sure enough, there's a container of exactly what he described. "And the ice cream?"

His lips quirk up in a half-smile that does annoying things to my insides. "Phish Food. You mentioned wanting some last night before we..." He trails off, his eyes darkening at the memory. "Got distracted."

Distracted. That's one way to put it.

"You didn't have to do this."

"I know. I thought it might make up for the healthy lunch." He sinks into the chair in front of my desk, and the intensity in his eyes makes me forget about the glass walls and our potential audience. "And I wanted to see you."

The simple admission knocks me off balance. It shouldn't.

Not after everything we've done. Not after how intimate we've been. But somehow, this casual confession of wanting to see me in the middle of a workday feels more revealing than anything that's happened between us.

"You saw me this morning," I say, trying to keep my voice steady. "Pretty thoroughly."

"Not enough."

I don't know what to do with this version of Kasen. The one who brings me lunch and ice cream. The one who admits to missing me after a few hours apart. The one who looks at me like I'm something he can't get enough of instead of someone he hates.

"People are going to talk," I say, nodding toward the warehouse floor visible from here where several employees are pretending to work while obviously staring at us.

He shrugs. "Let them."

"Easy for you to say. You don't have employees questioning your judgment."

"Anyone who questions your judgment because of this," he gestures between us, "is an idiot. You're still the same badass who built this company. Being pregnant doesn't change that."

"It's not just about the baby. It's about this." I gesture between us. "Whatever this is."

"What is it?" he asks, his blue eyes intent on mine.

I open my mouth, then close it again. What is it? I don't have an answer. Not one I'm ready to say out loud, anyway.

"Complicated," I finally say.

He nods slowly. "Fair enough. But you're still my wife."

The tension between us shifts, that electrical charge that never seems to fully dissipate whenever we're in the same room. His eyes drop to my lips, and I know he's thinking about kissing me. Here. In my office. With everyone watching.

"Don't even think about it," I warn.

His smile is slow and dangerous. "Too late."

Before I can respond, a knock on the door interrupts us. Kieran pokes his head in, his eyebrows shooting up when he spots Kasen.

"Sorry to interrupt," he says, not sounding sorry at all. "But Nolan Miller just showed up without an appointment. He says it's urgent."

Every muscle in Kasen's body goes rigid. "Tell him I'm in a meeting."

"I did. He said he'll wait." Kieran glances at Kasen. "He also said it involves both Cascade and Timber."

Kasen's expression hardens. "Send him in."

"Kasen—"

"If he's here to talk about both our companies, we should both hear it." His voice leaves no room for argument.

I want to argue anyway, but he's right. Miller's been circling both of us. Whatever he wants, we're stronger together.

It doesn't matter, though, because Kieran's already gone to fetch Miller. I turn to Kasen with a glare.

"This is my office. My company. You don't get to make those decisions."

"He's trying to buy both our businesses, Pink. Whatever he has to say affects us both." He sits up straighter, suddenly every inch the businessman I've gone up against for years. "We present a united front."

Miller appears in my doorway with Kieran hovering behind him, looking about as happy as I feel.

"Miss Callan," Miller greets me with that slimy smile that never reaches his eyes, and I see Kasen tense and I wonder if it's because he wishes it was his last name attached to me. "Mr. James. What a lucky surprise to find you both here."

I seriously doubt it's a surprise at all. Miller doesn't strike me as a man who leaves anything to chance.

"What can I do for you, Nolan?" I ask, not bothering to make small talk.

"I won't take much of your time." He steps further into my office, closing the door behind him and blocking Kieran out, who flips him off behind his back. His eyes slide to Kasen, then back to me, taking in the lunch spread on my desk and likely drawing exactly the right conclusions about what's happening here. "I simply wanted to deliver some news in person, as a professional courtesy."

"What news?" Kasen asks, his voice deceptively casual.

"Pacific Northwest has acquired Eastside Ales," Miller announces. "As of this morning, they're part of our portfolio."

The statement lands like a bomb in the quiet office. Eastside is one of my biggest clients. Their beers account for nearly twenty percent of Cascade's distribution revenue.

Twenty percent of Cascade's revenue gone, just like that.

"That's interesting timing," I say, keeping my voice level despite the panic building in my chest. "Considering I have a meeting with their team in two hours to discuss expanded distribution."

Miller has the grace to look apologetic, though I doubt he feels it. "Ah, yes. They weren't at liberty to discuss our negotiations. But don't worry—we intend to honor all existing contracts, for now."

For now. The threat isn't subtle.

This asshole.

I can sense Kasen tensing and I glance at him. His hand grips the chair arm so hard I'm surprised it doesn't splinter. "And you felt the need to deliver this news in person because...?"

"Like I said, professional courtesy," Miller repeats, straightening his immaculate tie. "And to let you know my offers for both your companies still stand. In fact, given recent developments..." His gaze drops to my stomach. "I'm prepared to improve them."

"What developments would those be, exactly?" Yeah, I'm going to deny everything until I'm forced to admit it.

"Come on, Miss Callan. You know, in a sense, Portland's like a small town." His smile turns condescending. "Your situation with Mr. James has become a hot topic of discussion."

Kasen's on his feet before I can blink. "Our situation is none of your fucking business."

"Isn't it?" Miller doesn't even flinch. "Two competitors suddenly involved? A baby on the way? It changes the landscape of this business considerably, I'd say."

The casual way he discusses my pregnancy like it's a business merger makes my blood boil. I rise to stand beside Kasen. "Get out."

"I'm simply pointing out that my offer takes your new circumstances into account. A generous maternity package. Flexibility for family needs." He produces a business card like a magic trick. "When you're ready to discuss terms that work for everyone, call me."

The implication that pregnancy makes me weak, that I need his "family-friendly" accommodations, has me gripping my desk to keep from lunging at him.

"Goodbye, Nolan."

He nods, that infuriating smile never wavering, and leaves without another word.

The second the door closes, I deflate and sink back into my chair. "Fuck."

"He's playing dirty." Kasen runs a hand through his hair, dislodging his beanie. "Using your pregnancy against you."

"Against us," I correct, then freeze. When did I start thinking of us as a unit?

"He knows everything." I look through my glass walls at my employees, several of whom quickly look away. "And if he knows, everyone knows."

"Then we stop hiding," Kasen says simply. "Make an announcement. Control the narrative."

He's right. I hate that he's right, but he is. "I need to talk to my staff."

"Want me to stay?"

I consider it. Having him here would make a statement. But it might also undermine my authority or make it look like I need a man to prop me up.

"No. This is something I need to do alone."

He nods, understanding in his eyes. "I'll head out. But Wren?" He waits until I meet his gaze. "We're going to bury that fucker."

"Damn right we are."

He gathers his things, but pauses at the door. "Remember, dinner's at six. We'll talk about Eastside after. Figure out a strategy."

"I remember."

He leaves after extracting a promise that I'll eat the lunch he brought. I watch him cross the warehouse floor, several of my employees tracking his progress, then turning to look back up to me.

Kieran appears as if by magic. "Want me to assemble the troops?"

Ah, so now he's not only appearing out of thin air but also a mind reader.

"Yeah, give me ten minutes."

I spend those ten minutes stashing my ice cream and then trying to figure out what to say, how to explain that yes, I'm pregnant with Kasen James's baby, and yes, we're involved, but no, it doesn't change anything about how Cascade operates.

It sounds stupid even in my own head.

This is why I didn't want to get involved with anyone in the industry. People are going to think I'm trying to make a deal with him and sleeping with him to make it happen. Every brewery I've brought on and earned the rights to distribute for is now going to be in question.

Did she sleep with the owner to get them to sign?

Fuck, being a woman is really hard sometimes.

When I step out onto the warehouse floor where my team has gathered, I feel like my heart might pound straight out of my chest. Forty pairs of eyes watch me expectantly. Some curious, some concerned, all waiting for me to explain what's going on.

The whispered conversations die immediately.

"Thank you all for taking a few minutes for this," I begin, proud that my voice doesn't shake. "I know there have been rumors circulating and I want to address them directly."

I take a deep breath, letting my hand rest on my belly because you know what? I'm owning this shit.

"I'm pregnant," I say, the words hanging in the suddenly silent warehouse. "Sixteen weeks. And yes, Kasen James is the father."

The gasps and murmurs are exactly what I expected. What I didn't expect is how liberating it feels to say it out loud.

"This doesn't change anything about how Cascade operates. We're still committed to supporting independent craft breweries. We're still the best distribution network in Portland." I meet the eyes of my key managers. "My personal life is separate from business. But I wanted you to hear it from me, not the rumor mill."

I glance around. "Questions?"

Please don't have questions.

It's so silent all I can hear is the whooshing of blood in my ears. Then someone starts clapping. Then another. Soon the whole warehouse is applauding, and I have to blink hard against the sudden sting in my eyes. Someone yells *about time* and I laugh even though it's watery.

Fucking pregnancy hormones.

Kieran bumps his shoulder into mine and then ruffles my hair before I can swat his hand away.

"Alright, show's over. Back to work. We have beer to move."

As they disperse, Kieran leans closer so I'm the only one that hears him say, "Nicely done. Short, sweet, to the point."

"Think it was enough?"

We start back toward my office as everyone gets back to work. "For them? Yes. For explaining whatever's actually happening with you and James?" He smirks. "Not even close."

"I don't know what's happening with us," I admit.

"Bullshit." His expression softens. "You've been circling each other for years. Can you at least admit that you don't hate him?"

"I don't hate him," I say quietly, the truth of it settling deep in my bones. "I don't think I have for a while now. Maybe I never really did."

"I know." Kieran's smile turns a little wicked. "The sexual tension between you two could power the city. Vegas just gave you an excuse to act on it."

He's right. It's always been easier to frame Kasen as the enemy. The rival. The competition. It gave me somewhere to direct my frustration and a way to ignore that there might've been something else going on.

Like the fact I've maybe always been a little bit obsessed with him.

Now? Now I don't know what he is. Father of my child, for sure. Husband, technically. Lover... yeah, that happened.

But maybe also something I never expected.

Maybe also something I never knew I wanted.

"Eat your lunch," Kieran orders, moving toward the door. "I'll reschedule Eastside and confirm dinner with Navy."

"You're too good to me."

"I know. You're lucky I love you."

20
Wren

SIX O'CLOCK COMES TOO FAST. I've changed clothes three times, trying to find something that says "I'm a responsible adult you can trust with your brother" and not "I spent last night getting absolutely railed by said brother."

Kasen's truck pulls up right on time. I grab my purse, take a deep breath, and head out to face my doom.

"You look beautiful," he says when I climb in.

I glance down at my outfit—a dress that actually fits my bump, one of the only nice things I've bought so far. "I look like I swallowed a basketball."

"You look like you're carrying my son." His hand finds mine across the console. "It's the sexiest thing I've ever seen."

"You're biased."

"Definitely." He brings my hand to his lips. "Doesn't make it less true."

The drive passes too quickly. Before I know it, we're parked outside a Craftsman bungalow with toys scattered on the porch and warm light spilling from the windows.

"I can't do this," I say, my heart hammering against my ribs.

"Yes, you can." Kasen squeezes my hand. "They're going to love you."

"They're going to think I'm the enemy who trapped you with a baby."

"First of all, no one thinks that. Second, if anyone got trapped here, it's you." His thumb rubs circles on my palm. "I'm the one who couldn't keep his hands off you in Vegas."

"Pretty sure I was an active participant."

"Very active," he agrees with a grin that makes heat sink down between my thighs. "Enthusiastically active. Creatively active."

"Stop." But I'm fighting a smile now.

"Come on. Let's go face the firing squad."

The door opens before we can knock. Clover stands there with Noble on her hip, and her blue eyes—exactly like Kasen's—go comically wide when she sees my belly.

"Holy shit," she breathes, looking between Kasen and me. "You weren't kidding."

Kasen shifts beside me, his hand coming up to lightly grip the back of my neck. "Told you I wasn't."

"You're pregnant. With my brother's baby." She turns to me, and I brace myself for... something. Judgment? Hostility? Accusations?

Instead, she breaks into a massive grin. "This is amazing! Noble's going to have a cousin!" She practically vibrates with excitement. "Come in! Everyone's here. Banks is grilling. Reed brought good beer. Navy's already three drinks in and telling everyone about her latest Tinder disaster."

She ushers us inside, talking a mile a minute. The house is warm and lived-in, with that comfortable chaos that comes from actual happiness. It's everything my childhood home wasn't. It smells like grilled meat and freshly baked bread, and the sound of laughter drifts in from what must be the backyard.

"Sorry about the whirlwind," Kasen murmurs in my ear. "She's excited about being an aunt."

"It's fine." And weirdly, it is. Her enthusiasm is so genuine it's impossible to feel defensive.

The backyard is strung with lights and filled with laughter. Banks mans a grill, Reed lounges in a chair with a beer in his hands, and Navy sits cross-legged on a blanket playing with what looks like a mini-basketball hoop set up for Noble. They all look up when we step outside, and I have to fight the urge to turn and run.

This is Kasen's family. His people. And I'm the outsider who's here only because I'm carrying his child.

"Holy shit, Wren!" Navy launches herself at me, pulling me into a hug before I can react. "You didn't tell me it was this serious! I thought you hated him."

"I—we—it's complicated," I stammer, awkwardly patting her back.

"Complicated my ass. That," she points at my belly, "is pretty straightforward."

"Navy, let her breathe," Reed says, standing to offer me his chair. "She's already had a long day without you interrogating her."

"How do you know what kind of day I've had?"

"Because someone," Reed shoots Kasen a look, "has been texting me every two hours with questions about your blood pressure, stress levels, and whether you're eating enough protein."

I turn to glare at Kasen. "You've been doing what now?"

Kasen stares me dead in my eyes without a single hint of remorse. "Don't act like you don't like it."

Banks' laugh interrupts our stare off. "Welcome to the family, Wren. Fair warning—we're all up in each other's business whether you like it or not."

Family. The word hits me square in the chest. Is that what this is? What I've stumbled into?

"And speaking of your blood pressure," Reed says before I can reply to *that*. "I'm guessing it's spiking right about now, so how about we let you sit?"

Kasen's hand wraps around my waist, guiding me toward the chair Reed gave up for me. "He's right. You should sit."

"I'm fine," I protest, but I sink into the chair anyway, and bite back the groan from the relief of getting off my feet.

"Beer?" Banks offers Kasen, holding up a bottle with a Timber label.

"Thanks." Kasen takes it, then perches on the arm of my chair, his thigh brushing my shoulder. It's a casual possessiveness that doesn't escape anyone's notice, judging by the looks exchanged between the others.

Well, that and his fingers wrapped around the back of my neck again.

"So," Clover says, settling onto a nearby bench with Noble in her lap. "When are you due?"

"November," I answer. "Right around Thanksgiving."

"A boy, right?" Banks asks, flipping a burger. "Kase mentioned you're having a son."

Welp, it's my fault for telling Kasen he's in charge of telling them everything. And I guess that means *everything*.

"Yep." I still can't quite believe it myself. A son. A little boy who will hopefully have Kasen's blue eyes and not my stubborn streak. Or his.

Yeah, I'm not that lucky.

"That's perfect! Noble will have a little cousin close to his age," Clover gushes. "They'll grow up as best friends."

The way she automatically includes our baby in their family circle makes something twist in my chest. This easy acceptance isn't what I expected. I've spent so long building walls, expecting rejection, preparing for battle, that I don't quite know what to do when met with open arms instead.

"So, how exactly did this happen?" Navy asks, waving her hand between Kasen and me. "Last I saw, you two could barely stand to be in the same room together."

Kasen and I exchange a glance. How much do we share? How much do they already know?

"You know how it is in Vegas," Kasen says, taking a swig of his beer.

Reed snorts. "Yeah. But you two went from enemies to," he gestures between us, "this real quick."

"It's been an adjustment," I say, feeling defensive of our situation. Even I don't really know where we stand. And after last night, the things Kasen said... how much of that did he mean and how much was just because the sex was life-changing?

I reach up to play with the ring hanging around my neck, but at the last minute catch myself and stop.

Do I want to be Kasen's wife for real?

Uh, no. No! ...Right?

"An adjustment," Navy repeats, eyebrows raised. "That's one way to put it."

"They're living together," Clover informs her, bouncing Noble on her knee. "Kasen told me this afternoon."

"You're living together?" Navy's eyes widen. "And you didn't tell me?"

"It's only until I find something else," I say quickly. "My building was sold. I needed a place to stay."

"Uh-huh." Navy's knowing look makes me want to sink through the chair. "And how's the search going?"

Kasen's fingers tighten at the nape of my neck, and for some reason I relax into it. Just fucking melt like a popsicle on the Fourth of July. Oh, and I ignore Navy's question. The truth is I haven't even started looking.

But should I?

The conversation mercifully shifts as Banks announces the food is ready, and soon we're all seated around the table, passing dishes and filling plates. I find myself between Kasen and Clover, with Noble now in a high chair beside his mom.

It's... nice. Surprisingly so. The conversation flows easily, with none of the awkwardness I was afraid of. They tease Kasen mercilessly, share embarrassing stories that make me laugh, and somehow manage to make me feel included rather than an intruder.

By the time we're clearing plates, I realize I'm actually enjoying myself. These people—Kasen's people—are warm and funny and genuine in a way I didn't expect.

"Come help me with dessert?" Clover asks. "Navy's useless in the kitchen."

"I resent that," Navy calls. "I can make cereal!"

"Point proven," Clover laughs, then turns expectantly to me.

"Sure," I agree, following her into the kitchen.

Once we're alone, she pulls ice cream from the freezer and homemade cookies from a container. "So. You and my brother."

Here it comes. The protective sister speech. The warnings about not hurting him. The subtle, or not-so-subtle, threats. It's almost a relief. I've been waiting for it all night and finally, here it is.

"It's complicated," I say for what feels like the hundredth time today.

"Good things usually are." She hands me bowls and an ice cream scooper. "He's crazy about you, you know."

I focus on scooping ice cream instead of how my heart just went a little wild. "We're figuring things out."

"That's all any of us can do." She crumbles a cookie on top of every bowl of ice cream I scoop. "Kasen doesn't let people in easily. Not since our dad left."

I glance up, surprised by the shift in conversation. "He left?"

"Right after our mom died." Clover's expression clouds

briefly. "Kasen was in college. I was sixteen. Dad just... checked out. Started drinking, staying away for days at a time. Then one day he just didn't come back."

The information rocks everything I know about Kasen James. He's steady and solid and I can't imagine him ever running out on anyone, and now I guess I know why. I knew Kasen's mother had died—it's common knowledge in the Portland beer scene that he dropped out of college to start Timber in her memory. But I never knew about his father.

I think about Kasen—how fiercely protective he is of Clover, how determined he was to rebuild Timber after the fire, how quick he was to step up when he found out about the baby.

"He had to become the parent," she says, meeting my eyes. "When Mom died, he dropped everything to take care of me. His dreams, his plans—all of it went on hold so I wouldn't be alone. He's spent so long being the one who fixes everything for everyone else that he doesn't know how to let anyone help him."

The revelation stops me cold. Fuck. All this time, I've been treating his overprotective bullshit like it was some kind of alpha male power play, when really it's just how he learned to be there for the people he loves. I've been fighting the wrong battle. I've been reading him all wrong.

I never stopped to consider that taking care of others might be the only language of love he knows how to speak.

"I'm not trying to make excuses for him," Clover adds. "He can be stubborn as hell."

That pulls a small laugh from me. "You can say that again."

"But he's also the best man I know. And he's never looked at anyone the way he looks at you. I just want you to know where it comes from." She places a hand on my arm, her touch gentle. "He's terrified of being like our dad. Of not being there. Of letting people down."

"He won't," I say, the certainty in my voice surprising even me. "Not our son and not me."

Clover's smile is warm. "I know. And I think, deep down, he knows it too." She picks up the tray she's been stacking the bowls on. "Now, let's get this dessert out there before they riot."

As we rejoin the others in the backyard, my eyes find Kasen immediately. He's laughing at something Banks said, his head thrown back, that rare, unguarded smile lighting up his face. When he sees me, the smile shifts. It becomes something softer, more intimate.

Something just for me.

And in that moment, I understand what Clover was trying to tell me. This man—this stubborn, protective, aggravating man—has given pieces of himself to everyone he loves. His sister. His nephew. His brewery.

And now, maybe, to me.

The drive home is quiet, but it's a comfortable silence. Kasen's truck rumbles beneath us, the radio playing softly in the background. His hand rests on my thigh, thumb drawing idle patterns through my dress.

I keep stealing glances at his profile—the sharp line of his jaw, the curve of his lips, the way his eyebrows pull together slightly when he's concentrating on the road. In the dim light of passing streetlamps, he looks both familiar and new.

"Your sister's nice," I say finally, breaking the silence. "I like her."

"She likes you too." He shoots me a quick smile before returning his eyes to the road. "They all do."

"I thought she'd be more suspicious."

"She's protective of the people she cares about," Kasen says. "She's just making sure you're not going to break my heart."

The casual way he says it makes my breath catch. As if the possibility of me breaking his heart is a given. As if he's already acknowledged that I have that power.

"Is that what this is?" I ask quietly. "Something that could break hearts?"

His hand tightens on my thigh, then slides up to find mine, weaving our fingers together. "I think we both know it's not just about the baby anymore, Pink."

The admission hangs between us, neither of us ready to define it further but both acknowledging that something has shifted.

"I'm scared," I admit, the words barely audible over the engine and the music. "Of how quickly everything is changing. Of how much I want things I never thought I would."

"Like what?" His voice is gentle.

"Like this." I squeeze his hand. "Like family dinners and living together and... feeling like I belong somewhere. With someone. Letting my guard down."

He brings our joined hands to his lips, pressing a kiss to my knuckles. "You do belong, Wren. With me. With our son." He pauses. "If you want to."

The vulnerability in his voice undoes me. This is Kasen James—the man who rebuilt his brewery from ashes, who raised his sister, who never backs down from a challenge. And here he is, asking if I want to belong with him.

"I do," I whisper. "I think I have for a while now."

His exhale is shaky, his grip on my hand tightening. "Good. That's... good."

We drive the rest of the way in silence, but it's a different kind now. Charged with possibilities. With acknowledgments we both feel.

When we pull into the driveway of his house, I don't immediately move to get out. Neither does he. We just sit there in the dark, hands still joined, the engine ticking as it cools.

"I know we still have a lot to figure out," he says, turning to face me. "With the baby. With our companies. With Miller breathing down our necks."

"With us." I say. "But that's what we do, right? Fight until we win."

His smile in the darkness is warm and genuine, not the cocky smirk I'm used to. "Yeah. Except this time we're fighting on the same side."

He leans across the console and kisses me, a tender press of lips that's nothing like the wild, bruising kisses from last night. This is worse. Or better. I'm not sure which.

When he pulls back, his hand cups my cheek, his calloused thumb brushing my lower lip.

"Come on," he says. "Let's go home."

Home.

That word used to give me hives. Home meant weakness, vulnerability, a base someone could take away from you. But now?

Now it's where Kasen is. Where our son will be. Where I wake up to freshly made coffee and fall asleep knowing he's nearby and I'm safe.

For fuck's sake. When did I turn into this person?

I follow him inside anyway, because apparently this is who I am now—someone who feels more at home with Kasen James than I ever felt within four walls of my own. And you know what?

I don't hate it.

21
Kasen

I'VE ALWAYS BEEN a possessive bastard, but there's something about watching Wren sleep in my bed that makes me want to build walls around this house just to keep her from ever walking away.

Pink hair spills across my pillow and I can't imagine it any other way. She's colonized my space—stealing my shirts, my sweatshirts, my socks, and pieces of my sanity every time she bends over in front of me. I catch myself staring at her, memorizing details like they might disappear: the dip at her waist, the small sigh she makes before fully waking up, how she unconsciously rubs her stomach in her sleep.

I'm falling for her so hard and fast it scares the living shit out of me.

The moonlight filters through the blinds, casting silver stripes across her bare shoulders. She's curled on her side with one hand tucked under her cheek and the other resting on the swell of her stomach where our son grows bigger and stronger every day. I can't stop staring at her, memorizing the scatter of freckles across her shoulders that you'd never notice unless you were close enough to count them.

I've counted all nineteen of them.

I should be sleeping. It's almost two in the morning, and I've got shit to do tomorrow. But sleep feels like a waste when I could be watching her instead.

Carefully, so I don't wake her, I slip out of bed and pad down the hall to my office. The sketchbook I keep hidden in the bottom drawer calls to me. It's where I put the things that matter most—beer label designs that are too stupid or off the wall to share but have sentimental value, drawings that reveal more of me than I'm comfortable showing to anyone.

I flip through pages of half-finished sketches. There's beer shit, sure, but also the vintage Harley I've been planning to restore, designs for a custom crib I want to build in my workshop downstairs, and stupid little cartoons of Clover with Noble that I text her whenever she sounds stressed on the phone.

Then I find what I've been working on for weeks now. It's not for any beer we currently brew. It's my own project—a special batch I want to release when our son is born. My own way of marking the day everything changes.

The label doesn't have Timber's usual look. I've designed something different. It's a simple silhouette of pine trees against a night sky that lightens at the horizon. There's a constellation mapped out among the stars, the same one on Wren's shoulder scattered in freckles. At the top, I've lettered "Dawn Breaker IPA" with smaller text beneath: "Crafted for the newest James."

It's understated, nothing overtly about babies, but it still means something. The trees represent legacy, something passed down, something that outlasts us. The stars are a reminder of her, of something uniquely hers that only I would recognize. And the name, it's about endings and beginnings, about the light that comes after darkness. Our kid will break the dawn on whatever the hell comes next.

Fuck, it's sentimental garbage. The kind of soft shit I'd never put in our regular lineup. But every time I try to scrap it and start over with something edgier, I keep coming back to this design. It says things I don't know how to say out loud.

I add more detail to the stars, my pencil moving while my brain churns through the mess of my life. How did this happen? Four months ago, I was hunched over divorce papers for a woman who drove me fucking insane. Now I wake up every morning with her pink hair in my mouth, and the thought of her not being here makes my chest feel like I took a sledgehammer to the ribs.

A soft sound from the doorway makes me look up. Wren stands there in nothing but my t-shirt, hair a mess from sleep, eyes sleepy. Those long legs go on for miles, and my dick immediately perks up at the sight.

"What are you doing?" she asks, her voice husky from sleep.

I close the sketchbook quickly. "Couldn't sleep."

She tilts her head and her hair falls across one eye before she tucks it behind her ear. "So you were drawing?"

"Something like that." I set the book aside and push back from the desk, opening my arms to her. "Everything okay?"

Instead of answering, she crosses the room and settles onto my lap, her legs straddling mine in the chair. My hands automatically find her hips.

"I woke up and you weren't there." She loops her arms around my neck, fingers playing with the hair at the back of my neck. "I got cold."

"Can't have that." I pull her closer. Having her this close does things to me—makes me stupid, makes me soft in ways I never thought I could be. "Better?"

"Mmm." She nuzzles into my neck, and I feel her lips curve into a smile against my skin. "Much."

We sit like that for a minute or ten, her weight settled comfortably against me, her breath warm on my throat. It feels goddamn perfect, like she was made to fit against me.

We're also both ignoring my half-hard dick that's trying to join the party between us.

"Kasen?" She pulls back just enough to meet my eyes.

"Yeah?"

"I need something."

The way she says it, with that little catch in her voice, tells me exactly what she needs. I've learned to read her these past weeks—learned what every sigh, every shift of her body means.

"What do you need, Pink?" I slide my hands under her shirt, up the warm skin of her back.

"Pickles," she says, completely straight-faced. "The garlic dill ones. With chocolate syrup. And cheese puffs crushed on top."

I blink at her. "You're kidding me."

"Do I look like I'm kidding?" She raises one eyebrow in that way that makes me want to kiss the brat out of her until neither of us can breathe. "Your child is apparently a culinary terrorist, and he wants pickles with chocolate syrup. And cheese puffs. Can't forget those."

I can't help but laugh, the sound rumbling up from my chest. "A culinary terrorist? Jesus, Pink."

"This isn't funny, James." But she's fighting a smile now. "I'm dead serious. I need this disgusting concoction or I will actually die."

"Dramatic much?" I squeeze her hips. "Why do these cravings always hit in the middle of the night?"

"Because your son is an asshole who hates sleep. Just like his father."

"Hey." I steal a quick kiss. "I thought we established that you like his father. A lot."

She rolls her eyes. "His father is acceptable. When he brings me food."

"Only acceptable?" I slide my hand up to cup her tit, gratified when her breath hitches. "That's not what you said last night when I had my head between your—"

"Pickles, Kasen." She cuts me off, but her pupils are blown, her cheeks flushed. "Focus."

With a dramatic sigh, I lift her off my lap and set her on her feet, smirking when her eyes drop to where I'm adjusting my dick. "Fine. Garlic dill pickles, chocolate syrup, and cheese puffs. Anything else, Your Highness?"

She pretends to think about it. "Maybe some of that strawberry ice cream? The one with the chunks of actual strawberries?"

"You hate strawberry ice cream."

"I know." She grimaces. "But apparently your spawn doesn't. I've been thinking about it all day."

I shake my head, moving to the bedroom and pulling on jeans and grabbing a hoodie from the back of the door. "The things I do for you."

She catches my arm as I'm about to leave, rising on her tiptoes to press her lips to mine in a kiss that's equal parts gratitude and promise. "Thank you," she whispers against my mouth.

Fuck, the things she does to me. And not just my body, my goddamn heart. "Anything for you, Pink. You know that."

And the crazy thing is, I mean it. I'd drive across the state in the middle of rush hour if she asked. I'd probably drive across the country. I blame it on my need to make her happy.

The night air is cool against my face as I slide into my truck. The streets are empty. It's peaceful in a way Portland rarely is during the day.

As I drive, I think about how these midnight food runs have become a strange highlight of my days. There's something about doing this for her, about being the one she turns to when she needs something, that feels right in a bone-deep way I've never experienced before.

My hand drifts to my pocket, fingers brushing against the metal ring I still carry everywhere. I should probably get around to putting it on my finger one of these days, since this marriage is looking less and less like something we're going to dissolve.

The twenty-four-hour market is a fluorescent-lit oasis in the dark. The cashier barely looks up when I walk in. At this point he's probably used to seeing me on bizarre food missions.

I grab a basket and head straight for the pickle aisle, then the ice cream section, moving with the efficiency of someone who's done this too many times in recent weeks. The chocolate syrup takes a minute to find, and I grab the cheese puffs last.

Standing in the checkout line, basket filled with the strangest combination of foods imaginable, I catch my reflection in the security mirror in the corner. I'm smiling like an idiot, and I look... happy. Actually fucking happy, at two thirty in the morning, buying pickles and chocolate syrup for a woman who I used to want to launch into outer space so I wouldn't have to deal with her.

Life's fucking hilarious.

The drive home feels quicker, anticipation building as I picture the smile that's going to light up Wren's face when I walk in with her disgusting snack. She gives them to me so often now I've stopped counting. I'm turning into one of those guys who gets off on making his pregnant wife happy. Banks and Reed would give me endless shit if they knew how soft I am for her.

Then again, Banks is the same way with my sister, and if he wasn't, I'd kick his ass.

When I walk through the door, I find Wren curled up on the couch, wrapped in the throw blanket from my bed, scrolling through her phone. She looks up when she hears me, and just like I predicted, her whole face lights up.

Unfortunately, I don't know if it's for me or the food, but I'm choosing to believe it's me.

"You're back!" She makes grabby hands toward the bag. "Gimme."

"Hold your horses, woman." I kick off my shoes and head to the kitchen. "Let me at least put this nasty thing together for you."

She follows me, hovering as I unpack the groceries. "Did you get the right pickles? The garlic ones, not the sweet."

"Yes, Pink, I got the right pickles." I hold up the jar. "Give me some credit. It's not my first time."

I grab a bowl and start assembling her monstrosity—pickles sliced lengthwise, drizzled with chocolate syrup, topped with crushed cheese puffs. It looks like a really fucked up ice cream sundae.

When I hand it to her, she actually moans in anticipation, a sound that goes straight to my dick. I watch in horrified fascination as she takes the first bite.

"Oh my god," she groans, eyes closing in bliss. "This is so good."

"I'll take your word for it." I pull out the ice cream and grab a spoon. "Strawberry ice cream, as requested."

She sets down her pickle creation long enough to take the ice cream, digging in with an enthusiasm that would be cute if it wasn't for what she was eating.

"You want to try some?" She holds out a pickle dripping with chocolate.

"I'd rather lick the floor of my workshop, but thanks."

She shrugs as she takes another bite. "Your loss."

We move back to the living room, settling on the couch. She curls against my side, alternating between bites of chocolate-covered pickles with a cheese puff crust and strawberry ice cream in a combination that makes my stomach turn just watching.

Don't get me started on the way it smells.

"So," she says between bites, "I still can't believe this is my life."

"Same." I drape my arm around her shoulders, pulling her closer. "A few months ago, I would've said you were more likely to poison my beer than sleep in my bed."

She laughs, the sound soft and warm in the quiet house. "To be fair, I considered it once. After you took the last tap slot at Sun Breaks last year."

"Yeah, well, I earned it." I tug gently on a strand of her pink hair. "And if I remember right, they signed with you two months later anyway."

"Because they realized their mistake," she says primly, scooping up more ice cream.

"You know they still stock my beer."

"Okay, so not a mistake, but an... oversight, I guess."

I watch her eat and fuck, I can't get enough of her. "Can I ask you something?"

"Hmm?" She looks up, a dab of chocolate at the corner of her mouth.

Without thinking, I lean in and lick it off, earning a soft gasp from her. "Why pickles and chocolate? Of all the weird combinations?"

She sets down her bowl, considering. "Honestly? I don't know. It's like my body just decides it needs something specific and won't shut up until I get it." She rubs a hand over her belly. "I've never had cravings like this before."

"You've never been pregnant before."

"Yeah." Her voice softens. "It's strange, having my body not fully be my own anymore. Knowing he's in there, changing things, making demands."

I slide my hand over hers on her stomach. "Is it hard? The changes?"

She goes quiet, like she's really thinking about her answer. "Sometimes. My body feels... different. Not just the belly, but everything. My skin's more sensitive. My boobs hurt. I cry at all sorts of stupid shit." She looks up at me through her lashes. "And I want you pretty much all the time, which is deeply inconvenient."

That last part catches me off guard, heat spreading through me. "All the time, huh?"

"Shut up." She shoves my shoulder. "I say it all the time. Pregnancy hormones are a bitch. It's not my fault. I blame you for both the baby and being so hot. I hate it."

"Good, I'll take the blame all day, baby." I run my fingers along her arm, feeling goosebumps rise in their wake. "And you know I'm always down to help with that particular craving."

She sets aside her bowl, turning to face me more fully. "Is that right?"

"Absolutely." I wrap my fingers around her throat in a light hold that makes her body melt into me. "Any time. Day or night. In fact, I consider it my husbandly duty to take care of all your needs."

Her eyes darken at the word 'husbandly,' that same look she gets whenever I remind her of what we both already know. I've been calling her my wife since that night on the kitchen table, and while she might still dodge the label in daylight hours, her body never lies about how it affects her.

"Your husbandly duty, huh?" Her voice drops lower, taking on that husky quality that drives me wild. "That's awfully generous of you."

"I'm a giver." I tighten my fingers the tiniest bit, feeling her pulse race beneath my fingertips. "It's a burden, but someone's got to do it."

She laughs, the sound vibrating against my palm. "And here I thought you just couldn't keep your hands off me."

"That too." I pull her into my lap, settling her thighs on either side of mine. "In fact, now that you mention it, I'm having a hard time remembering why my hands aren't on you right now."

She rolls her eyes, but her body tells a different story—the way she presses against me, the flush spreading up her neck, the slight parting of her lips. The harness of her nipples where they poke against my shirt. "Maybe because I need to brush my teeth after eating that?"

"Like that would stop me." I slip my hands under her shirt, finding warm skin and the swell of her belly. "Nothing could stop me from wanting you, Pink. Not even your bad breath."

Her laugh turns into a moan when my thumbs brush the undersides of her breasts. "Kasen..."

"Yeah?" I lean in, my lips hovering just above hers. "What can I do for you, Pink?"

Her answer is to close the distance between us, her mouth hot and demanding against mine. She tastes like that unholy combination of pickles, chocolate, cheese, and strawberries, and somehow it's not terrible. Or maybe I'm just so far gone for her that I'd find anything that's part of her irresistible.

We kiss until we're both breathless, her hands fisting in my hair, my hands claiming every inch of her like I'm staking territory no other man will ever touch again. When we break apart, her eyes are half-closed, pupils blown wide.

"Bedroom," she whispers against my lips. "Now."

22
Kasen

I STAND in one fluid motion, lifting her with me. Her legs wrap around my waist as I carry her down the hall, her mouth working magic along my neck that has me stumbling into walls.

When I lay her on the bed—our bed, now since I refuse to let her go back to the guestroom—she pulls me down with her. She doesn't let me go, even for a second. Her hands are everywhere, ripping at my clothes, scraping her nails down my back, and I groan.

"I need you," she breathes, arching against me. "Need you inside me."

Those words from her lips will never get old. I strip off her shirt and take a moment just to look at her. The curve of her belly, the fullness of her tits, the flush spreading across her skin—she's the most beautiful thing I've ever seen.

"You're staring," she says, a hint of self-consciousness creeping into her voice.

"Because you're gorgeous." I run my hand over the swell of her stomach, up to cup her breast. "Fucking perfect, Pink. Carrying my baby. Looking like every fantasy I've ever had."

Her breath catches, and her eyes go soft. "Kasen..."

I crush my mouth against hers, swallowing whatever she was about to say. Not because I'm afraid of it, but because right now I need to show her rather than hear it. Words are her weapon, not mine. I speak better with my hands, my mouth, my body claiming hers until there's no question what this is between us.

I'll remind her as many times as it takes to stick.

I work my way down slowly, lingering at her tits that are big and sensitive and fucking *edible*. I can't wait to suck on them when her milk comes in and at the thought of *that,* my dick jerks. She writhes underneath me, her hands fisted in the sheets, little gasps and moans coming out of her with every touch.

"Please," she begs when I reach the curve of her belly, placing reverent kisses along the stretched skin. "Stop teasing."

"Not teasing," I murmur against her. "Appreciating."

I continue my path downward, settling between her thighs, breathing in the scent of her sweet pussy. When I finally taste her, she nearly comes off the bed, her back arching as a broken cry falls from her lips.

"Fuck, you're wet," I growl against her, addicted to the way she tastes, to the way she moves against my mouth. "So fucking wet for me."

"Only for you," she gasps, her hands finding my hair, tugging until it hurts.

Those words light something primal in me. I devour her like I haven't eaten in a week, working her with my tongue and fingers until she's shaking, hovering on the edge of release.

Just before she comes, I pull back, earning a frustrated growl. "Not yet," I tell her, tearing my own clothes off. "I want to be inside you when you come."

"Then hurry the fuck up," she demands, eyes wild, hair a pink mess around her pretty face.

I don't need to be told twice. I position myself over her,

careful not to put weight on her stomach, and slide into her in one long, slow thrust that makes us both groan.

"Christ, it's like you were built for me," I say through gritted teeth, my control hanging by a thread. "The way you take me, like your body remembers mine and welcomes me home every time."

She wraps her legs around my waist, pulling me deeper. "Move, Kasen. I need you to move."

I look down at her pink hair wild against my sheets, those eyes glazed, the way her pussy's stretched around me, and I lose my goddamn mind. I pull almost completely out before slamming back in, watching her mouth fall open as she screams.

"You fucking wreck me," I growl, establishing a rhythm that borders on punishing. "Every goddamn time, Pink. You know that?" I grip her hip hard enough to bruise, using it to angle her exactly how I want her, so I'm bottoming out and hitting her clit with every thrust. "Nobody else gets to see you like this. Nobody else gets to hear the sounds you make when I'm deep inside you."

Her nails rake down my sides, leaving trails of fire I'll feel tomorrow every time my shirt rubs against them. Good. I want the reminder.

"Tell me who you belong to," I demand, voice rough as gravel.

Her eyes lock with mine, defiant to the damn end. "Make me," she challenges, shifting her hips to take me deeper.

Something dark and possessive roars to life inside me. I lean down, teeth scraping her throat where my mark from last night still blooms purple against her skin. "I'm going to fuck you so good you forget every man who came before me," I promise against her pulse, feeling it race under my lips. "There will never be anyone for you but me."

I change my angle, hitting that spot inside her that makes

her thighs tremble. "Now come around my cock like the good girl you pretend not to be."

She does, her pussy clenching and pulling me deeper inside her body. My name's torn from her lips in a cry that I'll hear in my dreams for years to come. I follow right behind her, unable to hold back when she's squeezing me like that, when she's looking at me like I'm everything she's ever wanted.

We collapse together afterward, and I roll her to the side so I don't crush her belly. My body's wrapped around hers and I'm still inside her and I can't bring myself to put even an inch between us.

I press my face into her hair, breathing in the scent of her shampoo now mixed with sweat and sex and us. My fingers trace idle patterns on her shoulder, following that familiar constellation of freckles I've mapped a hundred times before.

For a long time, we just lay there in silence. Her breathing evens out, and I wonder if she's fallen asleep until she shifts against me.

"What were you working on earlier?" she asks, her voice still rough from screaming my name. "In your office. Before I interrupted you."

I consider blowing off the question. It's one thing to fuck her until she's incoherent, to mark her body as mine. It's another to hand over something I've created, something that shows exactly how deep this goes for me.

But what's the fucking point of hiding now? She's already seen me at my most raw.

"Don't move," I tell her, dropping a quick, hard kiss on her mouth before I slide out of her and then the bed.

My legs are still unsteady as I walk to my office. The sketchbook feels heavier than it should when I pick it up, like it's weighted with all the little pieces of me and things I've never said out loud.

Back in the bedroom, she's sitting up with the sheet tucked

loosely around her waist, not bothering to cover her tits. The sight nearly distracts me from what I was doing. Her hair's a disaster, her neck and collarbone marked by my mouth, her lips swollen from my kisses. She looks thoroughly fucked, and I want to do it all over again.

But first I need to show her this piece of me.

I sit on the edge of the bed, holding the sketchbook just out of her reach. "It's not finished," I warn her because for some reason, showing her this means a whole hell of a lot to me, and I don't know what I'll do if she laughs or gives me shit like she usually does.

Or if she blows it off.

She takes it from me with careful hands, opening to the page I've been working on. Her body goes still as she studies it.

"This is..." Her finger traces the outline of the trees, then moves to the constellation above. "For our son?"

I nod, feeling exposed in a way that has nothing to do with being naked. I don't bother to tell her it's for her, too. "Thought I'd brew it when he's born. Just a small batch."

"Dawn Breaker IPA," she reads aloud, then the line beneath it: "Crafted for the newest James."

Her voice catches on my last name, and something twists in my chest. I want her to have it, too.

"It's just an idea," I say, the words coming out gruffer than intended. "If you don't—"

"It's beautiful." She looks up at me, and the emotion in her eyes hits me hard. "It's perfect, Kasen."

Something unclenches inside me, a knot of tension I didn't even realize I was carrying. "Yeah?"

"Yeah." She sets the book carefully on the nightstand and reaches for me, pulling me back down beside her. Her fingers trace one of my tattoos, following the line of ink up my arm. "I didn't know you could draw like that."

I shrug, heat creeping up my neck. "Just beer labels and little doodles. It's not a big deal."

"No." She grabs my chin, making me look at her. "This is more than that. This is art, Kasen. You're talented."

I don't know what to do with praise like that, so I just pull her against me, burying my face in her neck where I can hide from those eyes that see too much.

We lie tangled together, her fingers tracing the lines of ink down my arm like she likes to do. My hand settles on her belly, and I wonder how long it'll be until I can feel him moving around in there.

"I'm scared," I say finally, the words rough against her skin. "About being a father."

She pulls back, surprise flashing across her face. "You are?"

"Yeah." I swallow past the tightness in my throat. "My dad... he bailed on us. After my mom died. Just checked out completely." The admission feels like glass in my mouth, but I push through it. "I don't know how to be a good father. I don't have shit to model it on."

Her hand comes up to cradle my jaw, her thumb brushing against my stubble. "You raised Clover."

"That's different."

"Is it?" Her eyes hold mine, unflinching. "You stepped up when she needed you. Put her first. Built a life for both of you." Her fingers tighten on my face like she's trying to push the truth into me. "That sounds exactly like what a good father does."

Her certainty makes my chest feel too tight. "I can't fuck this up, Pink. Not with him."

"You won't." She says it like it's a fact, immovable as stone. "We won't."

I press my forehead against hers, breathing her in. "When did you start believing in us?"

The corner of her mouth lifts. "Probably around the time

you drove across town at two in the morning for pickles and chocolate syrup without a single complaint."

I laugh, the sound rusty but real. "That's all it took? Not my devastating good looks or mind-blowing skills in bed?"

"Definitely the pickles," she says, her eyes lighting up in that way that kills me. "Though the other stuff isn't terrible."

I reach down to my discarded jeans, fishing for what I've carried for months. The metal is still warm from being in my pocket.

"I've been meaning to show you something," I say, opening my hand to reveal the wedding ring that matches the one she wears around her neck.

She goes still. "You kept it."

"I did." I meet her gaze. "Same as you. It's always on me."

Her hand goes to her neck where the chain rests. "I was hoping you were too distracted by my boobs to notice it," she says, attempting her usual snark but not quite hiding the vulnerability in her eyes.

"I notice everything about you." I take her hand, running my thumb across her knuckles. "Why'd you keep it?" The better question is probably why she never takes it off, but first things first.

She's quiet for so long, I think she might not answer. Then she takes a breath like she's diving into deep water.

"Because even when I was telling myself I hated you, I didn't." She looks down at our joined hands. "Because part of me knew Vegas wasn't just some drunk mistake. That there was something real between us, even when I couldn't admit it to myself."

Her honesty knocks the air straight out of my lungs, like someone's dropped a full keg on my chest. I run my thumb over the wedding band in my hand, then hold it up between us. "I'm putting mine on tomorrow. Just so you know."

Her eyes roam all over my face. "Are you asking me to stay married to you, Kasen James?"

"I'm asking you to consider it." I bring her hand to my mouth, pressing my lips against her knuckles. "We're good together, Pink. Better than I think either of us expected." I tighten my grip on her fingers. "It won't be easy—we're both stubborn as hell, and our businesses still put us in each other's way sometimes. But I think this thing between us is worth fighting for."

She's quiet for so long my heart starts going crazy. Then she looks down at the ring in her palm.

"I'll think about it," she says finally, meeting my eyes. "That's not a no."

"I'll take it."

Neither of us is ready to sleep after that conversation. There are too many emotions still crackling between us, too many possibilities spinning through my head.

"Want to watch a movie?" I ask, running a hand down her bare back. "I'm too wired to sleep."

She nods against my chest. "Plus, I should probably eat the rest of the snack you went out for. Wouldn't want your heroic middle of the night quest to be wasted."

I laugh, pressing a kiss to her temple. "Our kid's part vampire, I swear. Always wanting weird shit in the middle of the night. He's trying to turn us nocturnal."

"I think he probably gets that from you," she says, poking my ribs. "You're always up at strange hours working on something."

"Says the woman who'd sleep until noon every day if she could."

She flips me off and I laugh and kiss the hell out of her. Then we pull on enough clothes to be decent—boxers for me, another one of my shirts for her—and head to the living room. While she settles on the couch, I put together more of her bizarre concoction from the kitchen and grab a beer for myself.

"What are we watching?" I ask, handing her the bowl of chocolate-covered pickles that still makes my stomach turn just looking at it. I've grabbed a bottle of Timber's Winter Porter for myself - the small batch experimental one with hints of coffee and vanilla that I've been tweaking for months and finally got right.

She scrolls through options on the screen. "Something mindless. I can't handle anything that requires brain cells right now."

We settle on some action movie with explosions and a plot thin enough that it doesn't matter that we're starting it at three in the morning. I pull her against me, her back to my chest, my hand resting on her belly.

Twenty minutes in, the female lead appears on screen in some skin-tight outfit that leaves nothing to the imagination, taking down three guys twice her size.

"Damn," Wren murmurs, pausing with a pickle halfway to her mouth. "She is ridiculously hot."

I laugh, surprised. "Got a thing for badass women in leather, Pink?"

She tilts her head back to look at me, a challenge in her eyes. "I mean, I'm bisexual, so yeah. Women in leather are definitely on my list of turn-ons."

The casual admission catches me off guard, but in the best possible way. "You never mentioned that."

She shrugs. "Never came up. Does it bother you?"

"Fuck no," I say, tightening my arm around her. "Pretty sure it just makes you even hotter."

She snorts. "So predictable."

"What? Now we can appreciate hot women together."

She laughs, relaxing back against me. "Just don't expect any threesomes, James. I don't share either."

"Wouldn't dream of it." I press my lips to her neck. "I can barely handle you. Adding someone else would probably kill me."

We fall into comfortable silence, her attention back on the movie, mine split between the screen and the woman in my arms. Something about her casual revelation, the easy way she shared that piece of herself with me, makes my chest feel too full.

It's another layer of Wren I get to know, another part of her she's trusting me with. And I want all of it—every secret, every preference, every hidden corner of who she is.

My phone buzzes on the coffee table, breaking the moment. I almost ignore it, but it's four in the morning. Nobody calls at this hour unless something's wrong.

"Shit," I mutter, reaching for it. The brewery's number flashes on the screen. "I need to take this."

Wren pauses the movie, concern crossing her face as I answer.

"James."

"Kasen, it's Scott from night security." The guard's voice is tight and I go on high alert. "Someone tried to break into the brewery. The alarm scared them off, but you might want to come down here to talk to the police."

"On my way," I say, already standing. "Anyone hurt?"

"No, sir. They didn't get past the loading dock door."

I hang up, looking down at Wren. "Someone tried to break in at Timber. I need to go check it out."

She sits up immediately. "I'll come with you."

"You don't have to—"

"I'm coming," she says firmly, already heading for the bedroom to change. "Someone's messing with your brewery. I want to know who."

Ten minutes later, we're pulling up to Timber. The place is lit up, security guards and a couple of cops milling around the loading area. I spot Lake talking to an officer, his expression grim.

I don't think I've ever seen that look on his face.

"What happened?" I ask, approaching them with Wren close behind me, gripping my hand.

Lake turns, relief crossing his face. "Someone tried to force the loading dock door open. They got spooked when the alarm went off." He nods toward the security cameras. "We got decent footage, though. You're gonna want to see this."

Inside the office, Lake pulls up the feed. The video quality isn't great, but we can see two figures working on the loading dock door.

"Wait." I lean closer, focusing on the shorter guy's movements. "That's Marcus Wells. He used to work for Eastside before they sold out to Miller."

"How can you tell?" Wren asks as she leans over my shoulder to squint at the screen.

"The limp. Do you remember when he hurt his knee in that brewery softball tournament last summer? He's had it ever since." I tap the screen. "And I'd recognize that stance anywhere—he's got a specific way he leans when he's trying to take the weight off of it."

Lake nods slowly. "You're right. And didn't he just start working for Pacific Northwest after the acquisition?"

"Yes, yes, he did." My jaw tightens as the pieces click into place. "Miller's behind this."

"It gets better," Lake says grimly. "I was at Hopworks yesterday afternoon when some suits showed up. Rumor is they're being pressured to sell."

"Let me guess," Wren says. "Miller's people?"

Lake nods. "Their CFO was in a panic. He said they'd been getting equipment failures, delivery problems, all kinds of issues that are tanking their value. I think the idea is to make them desperate to sell."

"Systematic sabotage," I growl. "It's the same playbook he's trying to run on us."

"And I heard from my contact at Evergreen that they're closing their distribution contract with Cascade," Lake adds, glancing apologetically at Wren. "Sorry."

She shakes her head, her expression hardening. "It's not on you. This isn't about normal business competition. That bastard's playing dirty."

"He's trying to squeeze us from all sides," I say, the pieces falling into place. "First taking our distribution partners, now attempting what—some kind of mafia intimidation bullshit?"

"Looks like it," Lake says.

I run a hand through my hair, fury building in my chest. "We need to beef up security. We need new locks, more cameras, whatever it takes."

"Already on it," Lake assures me. "But what's his endgame here? He offered to buy you out, right? Why resort to this?"

"Because I told him to go fuck himself," I say. "And he's not used to hearing no."

Wren places a hand on my arm, her grip tight. "He's playing dirty with both of us. First taking Eastside, now trying to sabotage Timber."

I cover her hand with mine, something pissed the fuck off burning inside of me while I consider options I tossed out years ago and an idea starts to form in the back of my mind. "Well, he picked the wrong people to fuck with."

"Do you think the police will do anything with what we've told them?" she asks, glancing toward where the officers are finishing their report outside.

"Doubt it," Lake says with a frown. "We can identify Marcus, sure, but Miller will just claim he was acting on his own. Or deny any connection altogether. And it's not like he showed his face in the video. His bum leg doesn't really prove anything."

I know he's right, but the thought of Miller getting away

with this makes my blood boil. "We'll handle this ourselves. Starting with better security." I turn to Wren. "And we need to warn other local breweries. Whatever Miller's planning, it's bigger than just us."

She nods, her business face firmly in place. "I'll call a meeting tomorrow. Get everyone together."

By the time we've finished dealing with the officers and planning security upgrades, it's nearly dawn. The brewery's quiet again, the excitement over. Lake heads home to catch some sleep before his shift, leaving Wren and me in my office.

She leans against my desk, exhaustion clear in the slump of her shoulders. "You okay?"

"No," I admit, moving to stand between her legs. "I'm pissed. Someone tried to mess with my business." My hands settle on her waist. "But I'm glad you were here."

She looks up at me, her eyes serious. "We're partners in this, Kasen. Whatever Miller's up to, we'll face it together."

"Partners," I repeat, liking the sound of it more than I should.

She smiles, a tired but genuine curve of her lips. "Now take me home. I'm so tired, your cement floor is starting to look as good as your bed."

I press my forehead to hers, drawing strength from her presence.

Whatever Miller's planning, he underestimated what he's up against. He might have money and corporate power, but Wren and I? We've got something much stronger between us.

And I'm starting to think it might be love.

23
Wren

SOMEONE'S TRYING to destroy everything I've built, and my first thought is to protect Kasen. Not my company. Not my future. But him.

What the fuck is happening to me?

It's just after seven in the morning, and I'm standing in Kasen's kitchen—our kitchen?—gulping down decaf like it might magically transform into the real thing if I drink enough of it. My phone won't stop buzzing with texts from brewery owners panicking after word spread about the break-in at Timber last night.

"Evergreen just confirmed they're not renewing their contract. That's the third brewery this week," I tell Kasen as he walks in, freshly showered, his hair still damp. The sight of him makes something flip in my stomach that has no business flipping. But Kasen in nothing but low-slung jeans with a few water droplets still running down all that ink and those muscles? I never stood a chance.

I blink a few times as my brain comes back online and when my eyes finally find their way to his face, he's smirking. I, of course, ignore him.

"That motherfucker's not wasting any time, is he?" He comes up behind me and presses a kiss to my neck. His hands slide around to rest on my stomach. The little bubbles I've been feeling in there for weeks have started turning into something more as the baby gets bigger, and I don't know who's more excited for him to feel the baby for the first time, him or me. "You okay?"

Something about the way he touches me so casually sparks my need for him to life. It's not just a sexual reaction, though there's definitely that too. It's something else. Something that makes my chest tight in a way that should send me running for the hills.

Instead, I'm leaning into it. Into him. Because he's comfort and safety and protection and home and...

For fuck's sake. When did I start wanting this? Wanting him to touch me like I belong to him? Like he belongs to me?

"No," I admit, leaning back against his chest. "I've spent four years building Cascade from nothing, and this asshole thinks he can just waltz in and tear it all down."

Kasen's arms tighten around me. "We're not going to let that happen."

We. Such a simple word, and yet it undoes me. When did we become a *we* beyond the biological fact of our son growing inside me?

"The emergency meeting with all the breweries is this afternoon." I turn in his arms, needing to see his face. "Three o'clock at Cascade. We need to present a united front."

His blue eyes hold mine. "We need to talk before that meeting."

"That sounds ominous." I step out of his embrace, my defenses immediately rising. When has the phrase *we need to talk* ever been a good thing? "Are you backing out? Because if you think I'm going to face Miller alone—"

"Jesus, Pink. Of course not." He runs a hand through his

hair, messing it up in a way I refuse to find adorable right now. "It's the opposite, actually. I have an idea, but I wanted to run it by you first. In private."

"Okay..."

"Let me get coffee first." He moves around the kitchen, grabbing his mug from the cabinet. In just a few weeks, we've developed these little domestic patterns that shouldn't feel so natural, but somehow do. "You want more?" he asks, gesturing to my half-empty cup.

"I'm good."

He takes his time, and I know he's gathering his thoughts. Whatever this is, it's important enough that he's actually planning his words instead of bulldozing ahead like he usually does.

"Just spit it out, Kasen," I say finally, unable to take the suspense. "What's this big idea?"

He takes a deep breath. "I want to give Timber's distribution to Cascade."

I stare at him, sure I heard him wrong or I'm hallucinating. "You what?"

"I want Cascade to handle Timber's distribution. All of it." He meets my eyes, and he doesn't blink. "Exclusive rights, industry-standard rates, the full lineup."

"But..." I shake my head, trying to process what he's saying. "Your whole business model is direct-to-bar. You've been fighting against distributors like me for years. You've called my business model 'the death of craft beer culture' to my face."

"I know." He has the grace to look slightly remorseful. Like, the tiniest amount. "I was wrong."

Kasen James admitting he was wrong? Maybe I'm still asleep and this is some bizarre pregnancy dream. I want to call him on it, but I swallow down the instinct.

See? I can grow.

"You want to work with me?" I clarify. "Professionally? After everything?"

"Not just work with you. Partner with you." He steps closer, his expression earnest in a way that makes anything left around my heart crumble. "Miller's trying to divide and conquer. The only way we beat him is by joining forces. Completely."

"This is a big deal, Kasen." I cross my arms over my chest, trying to maintain some distance even as my mind races with the possibilities. Timber under Cascade's umbrella would be a massive win, not just financially but in terms of industry clout. And I could get him into so many places he's not in now. It would be huge for both of us and it's a smart move. "Timber is your baby. You built it from nothing."

"I know." He closes the distance between us, his hands sliding up my arms. "But that's exactly why I'm doing it. Because I know what Cascade means to you, too."

"I don't understand." And I don't. This doesn't fit with the ruthlessly competitive businessman I've spent years battling.

"It's simple." His fingers trace my cheek, tucking a strand of hair behind my ear. "I trust you. With my business. With our son." His eyes hold mine, filled with something that makes my breath catch. "With everything."

Oh.

Oh.

This isn't just a business decision. This is so, so much more.

"Is this because we're sleeping together?" I ask, needing to be sure. "Because if this is some misguided attempt to—"

"It's because I love you."

The words hit me like a cement truck to the chest. Three words I never expected to hear, especially not from Kasen James. My heart's going so crazy I'm pretty sure he can see it trying to escape through my shirt.

Love? Seriously?

Love wasn't supposed to be part of this messy equation. Sex, yes. Convenience, absolutely. A temporary solution to my housing crisis and our accidental pregnancy. But love? That's the kind of complication I've spent my entire adult life avoiding.

"You don't—" I stop, swallow, try again. "You can't—"

"I can, and I do." His voice is steady. Certain. "I'm in love with you, Wren. Have been for a while now."

"We've only been doing this for a little while," I protest weakly.

"And fighting like cats and dogs for years before that." His lips quirk up in that half-smile that does stupid things to my insides. "I think I've been falling for you since the first time you told me my IPA tasted like 'pretentious pine-scented bathroom cleaner'."

Despite everything, I laugh. We both ignore how watery it is. "It did."

"It absolutely did not." His hands frame my face. "But you were the only one brave enough to say it to my face."

I don't know what to say. My brain is short-circuiting, unable to process that Kasen James—the man I spent years convincing myself I hated—just said he loves me.

And that some part of me desperately wants to say it back.

"You don't have to say anything," he says, reading my expression so easily. "I just wanted you to know where I stand. This business decision comes from a place of trust and... yeah. The other thing."

"Love," I supply, the word feeling strange and wonderful on my tongue.

"That's the one." His thumbs brush my cheekbones as he wipes away a tear or two. "Think about the distribution offer. We can talk details later. But whatever you decide, I'm all in on us. On our family."

Family. Another word that should terrify me but somehow doesn't. Not when he says it.

"I need to think," I manage, even as my body instinctively leans toward his.

"I know." He presses a gentle kiss to my forehead. "Take your time, Pink. I'm not going anywhere."

The thing is, I believe him.

Cascade's conference room has never felt so crowded. Representatives from twelve local breweries fill the chairs around the massive table, their expressions ranging from worried to outright hostile. The energy in the room crackles with tension, and I can feel everyone's eyes on me as I take my place at the head of the table.

Beside me, Kasen stands with his arms crossed, a solid presence that somehow manages to keep me calm despite the chaos swirling around us. The murmurs die down as I clear my throat.

"Thank you all for coming on such short notice," I begin, my voice steadier than I feel. "I know rumors have been flying, so let's cut to the chase. Pacific Northwest Brewing Corp, specifically Nolan Miller, is systematically targeting independent breweries in Portland with the aim of forcing sales on his terms."

I stop to meet every single set of eyes watching me. "We've lost three distribution contracts in the past week," I continue, "and last night, someone attempted to break into Timber Brewing. We have reason to believe Miller is behind it."

This sets off a fresh wave of murmurs. Kasen steps forward.

"The security footage shows Marcus Wells, former head brewer at Eastside, now employed by Pacific Northwest." His voice is calm, but carries an undercurrent of controlled anger. Now's *really* not the time, but that tone's doing things for me, and goosebumps break out across my skin. "This is straight up sabotage."

Tom Hayes from The Hop Yard sits forward. "We've had equipment failures three times this month. Things that shouldn't break suddenly malfunctioning. I thought it was just bad luck."

"It's not," Kasen says grimly. "It's purposeful."

More voices join in, sharing similar stories of mysterious equipment failures, delivery problems, suppliers suddenly backing out of contracts. A picture starts to emerge of a coordinated attack on Portland's craft brewing scene and I get angrier with each new revelation.

"So what do we do?" asks Sarah from Evergreen, looking directly at me. "Miller offered us five million. With all these 'accidents,' we're barely staying afloat and could really use that money."

I take a deep breath. "We stand together. Miller's strategy depends on picking us off one by one. If we present a united front, he loses his leverage."

"Easy for you to say," someone mutters from the back. "Your boyfriend's brewery hasn't been targeted like the rest of us."

Kasen tenses beside me, but I place a hand on his arm. I've got this.

"First of all," I say, my voice sharp enough that a couple people flinch, "Timber was literally broken into last night, so that's factually incorrect. Second, our personal relationship has nothing to do with this discussion. And third, if you have something to say, Bill, say it to my face instead of mumbling from the back like a coward."

The room goes silent. Bill, a balding man in his fifties who's never bothered to hide his disdain for "women in the industry," flushes red.

"All I'm saying is—" he begins.

"What you're saying," Kasen cuts in, his voice a dangerous

rumble and yep, this time I can't fight off the shiver, "is that you'd rather dismiss Wren's expertise because we're together than listen to the solution that might save your brewery. That about right?"

Bill squirms uncomfortably. "I didn't mean—"

"Yes, you did." Kasen steps forward, towering over the table. "But here's what you're missing. Wren built Cascade into the most successful distribution company in Portland while facing twice the obstacles as any man in this room. She knows this industry inside and out, and if anyone can find a way through this mess, it's her." His eyes sweep the room, challenging anyone to contradict him. "So how about we shut the fuck up and listen to what she has to say?"

I should be annoyed that he's stepping in to defend me. I should tell him I can fight my own battles. Instead, I feel a rush of warmth spreading all the way down to my bones. He's not talking over me or trying to save me. He's standing beside me, acknowledging my expertise, treating me as an equal partner in this fight.

And honestly? It's hot as hell.

I clear my throat, refocusing. "Thank you, Kasen. Now, I have a proposal." I lay out the plan we've been discussing all morning—a coalition of Portland craft breweries, standing together against Miller's tactics. Shared resources, united marketing, mutual support.

"And to show our commitment," I continue, "Timber Brewing will be bringing its full distribution under Cascade's umbrella, effective immediately."

The announcement sends a shockwave through the room. Everyone knows about Kasen's staunch direct-to-bar philosophy. His willingness to abandon it speaks volumes.

And to hand it over to me? That's an even bigger middle finger to Miller.

"You're really doing this?" Sarah asks, looking between us with curiosity. "Timber's joining Cascade?"

"We are," Kasen confirms. "Because this isn't just about business anymore. It's about protecting what we've all built. And Wren's the best person to do that."

The discussion that follows is intense but productive. By the time we break two hours later, we have commitments from ten of the twelve breweries to join our coalition. Only Bill and another holdout are on the fence, and I'm not worried about them. The momentum is with us.

As the room empties, I feel a strange mix of exhaustion and exhilaration. We did it. We actually pulled this off.

"You were amazing," Kasen murmurs, wrapping me up in his arms. "The way you handled the room, laid out the strategy. I've never seen anything like it."

"*We* were amazing," I correct him, surprising myself with the admission. "Your little speech about my expertise didn't hurt either."

His lips quirk up. "Just speaking the truth."

"Well, it was..." I search for the right word. "Nice. To have someone in my corner like that."

"Always," he promises, his eyes serious despite his smile. "I've got your back, Pink. Always."

The sincerity in his voice makes something shift inside me —a wall crumbling, a door opening. I've spent so long being unflinchingly independent, fighting for respect in an industry dominated by men like Bill. I've never let myself need anyone, never let myself lean on anyone else's strength.

But maybe it's not weakness to let someone stand beside you. Maybe it's not dependence to accept support.

Maybe it's just love.

The realization hits me with startling clarity. This feeling that's been growing between us, this warmth that spreads through my chest whenever he looks at me or touches me or says something ridiculous and overprotective—it's love. I'm in *love* with Kasen James.

Holy shit.

"What's that look?" he asks, his head tilting as he stares down at me.

"Nothing." I'm not ready to say it yet. Not here, not now. "Just... processing everything."

"Why don't you finish processing at home," he suggests. "You look tired."

Home. With him. With our son growing inside me. With the man I've somehow, against all logic and expectations, fallen in love with.

"Yeah," I agree, letting him guide me toward the door. "Let's go home."

24
Wren

THE DOOR SHUTS BEHIND US, and I practically collapse against the wall to yank off my shoes. My feet are absolutely killing me after standing through that marathon meeting. Turns out growing a human while simultaneously saving your business from corporate vultures while standing in three-inch heels is exhausting. Who knew?

"Go sit," Kasen says as he gently pushes me toward the living room. "I've got you."

"I can handle sore feet, James," I roll my eyes, but I'm already making a beeline for the couch. My body betrays me, sinking into the cushions with an embarrassing groan of relief.

"Of course you can," he says, dropping onto the couch beside me and pulling my feet into his lap. "You can handle anything. Doesn't mean you have to."

Before I can argue, his thumbs press into my arches, and holy shit, it feels incredible. The man has talented hands. That's not news, but still.

"You're getting really good at that," I manage as he works a particularly painful spot.

He smirks without looking up. "I know."

We sit in comfortable silence as he continues the massage, eventually sliding his hands up to my calves where tension I didn't even realize I was carrying melts away under his touch.

"Tea?" he asks after a while, giving my ankle a gentle squeeze.

I nod, suddenly craving something warm and soothing. I never used to drink that gross leafy soup, but now for some reason I like it. "Thanks."

He disappears into the kitchen, returning minutes later with a steaming mug. He sets it on the coffee table before settling back beside me on the couch. Without thinking, I shift to lean against him, my body curling into his.

"You're not freaking out," he observes, his arm wrapping around my shoulders.

"About what?"

"Any of it. The meeting, Timber's distribution, what I said this morning..." He trails off, his fingers tracing patterns on my arm.

"I'm freaking out about all of it," I admit. "I'm just... freaking out in a different way than expected."

"Meaning?"

I sit up, needing to see his face for this. "Meaning I always thought depending on someone else would feel like weakness. Like failure. That's what my mom taught me—never need a man for anything. Always stand on your own."

His expression is patient while he waits me out.

"But this, with you..." I gesture between us. "It doesn't feel like weakness. It feels like... I don't know. Like we're stronger together than apart."

Something softens in his eyes. "We are."

"And that scared the crap out of me," I continue, the words pouring out now that I've started. "Because what if I get used to this? What if I let myself need you, want you, and then something happens?"

"Like what?"

"Like you decide this isn't what you want after all. Or you get tired of dealing with my shit. Or—" I swallow hard, my deepest fear surfacing. "Or you leave, like my father left. Like *your* father left. Like everyone leaves eventually."

His hand cups my face, his thumb brushing across my cheekbone. "Is that what you're afraid of? That I'll leave?"

I nod, unable to speak past the lump in my throat.

"Pink," he says, his voice rough. "I am never, ever leaving you or our son. Not by choice. The only way you're getting rid of me is if you kick me out yourself, and even then I'd probably camp on the lawn like a stubborn asshole."

I let out a watery laugh. "You would, too."

"Damn right." He pulls me closer, his forehead resting against mine. "I meant what I said this morning. I love you. All of you. The stubborn, competitive, brilliant, infuriating parts. The soft parts you try to hide. All of it."

I take a shaky breath. "I think I might love you, too."

He gives me one of his handsome smiles. "Yeah?"

"Yeah." I nod, the admission unlocking something inside me. "I mean, I'm pretty sure I do. Which is ridiculous and terrifying and completely unexpected, but—"

He cuts me off with a kiss, his lips capturing mine with a gentleness that makes my heart ache. It's nothing like our usual frantic, desperate kisses, but something deeper, more profound. A promise of so much more to come.

When we break apart, I'm trembling. "This is insane," I whisper.

"Then get me a straitjacket, baby," he murmurs against my lips.

Something shifts between us, the energy changing, getting intense. My hands slide up his chest, feeling the solid warmth of him under his shirt.

"I want you," I tell him, leaving no room in my tone for him to argue. Not that he would. "Now."

He sucks in a breath, but he hesitates. "You sure? After everything today, you must be exhausted."

"I am," I admit. "But I still want you."

The look he gives me is hungry, almost reverent. "Whatever you want, Pink. You know I can't say no to you."

I stand, pulling him up with me. "Good. Because right now, I want you naked and in our bed."

His eyebrows shoot up at my directness, a slow smile spreading across his face. "Our bed?"

"Do I look like I'm going back to sleeping alone?" I'm already tugging him toward the hallway. "Besides, your mattress is better."

He laughs, the sound warming me from the inside out. "Whatever you say."

In the bedroom—our bedroom, I guess, since I've officially abandoned the guest room—I turn to face him. Something switches in my brain as I look at him standing there, expectant and turned on. My body is changing daily, getting rounder, stretch marks appearing in places I never had them before. But he still looks at me like I'm the hottest thing he's ever seen, and for once, I actually feel it.

I shove him down onto the bed and I'm not gentle. The surprise on his face is gratifying as hell.

"Tonight," I tell him, yanking my top over my head, "I'm in charge."

He swallows hard, his Adam's apple bobbing. "Yes, ma'am."

I strip for him, not rushing it. His eyes track every move, and that look, the starving one, gives me a rush of power I've never felt before. When I'm naked, I don't cover up or rush to the bed. I stand there, letting him look.

"You are fucking gorgeous," he breathes, reaching for me like he can't help himself.

I step back, just out of reach. "Clothes off, James."

He practically tears them off. It would be funny if it wasn't so hot watching those muscles flex and twist as he strips. His tattoos are everywhere—arms, chest, abs, back. I'm still learning them with my fingers and mouth.

When he's naked, cock hard and ready, I climb onto the bed and straddle his thighs. His hands immediately grab for my hips, but I catch his wrists and pin them beside his head.

"No touching," I order. The flash of frustration in his eyes sends a thrill straight between my legs. "Not until I say so."

"Pink," he groans, his hips bucking while his cock slides against me. "You're fucking killing me here."

"That's the point." I grind against him, letting him feel how wet I am. The sound he makes is half-groan, half-whimper, and *god*.

Kasen James just *whimpered*.

"Fuck," he hisses through clenched teeth. "Please."

"Please what?" I lean down, my lips brushing his jaw, his throat, the spot by his collarbone that always makes him shudder. "Your turn to beg."

"Please let me touch you." His voice is strained, and he doesn't even hesitate. He doesn't make me work for it like I did to him. "I need to feel you."

"Not yet." I work my way down his body, tasting salt and skin, leaving marks of my own for once. When I reach his cock, I look up, making sure he's watching as I take him into my mouth.

The strangled noise he makes is worth it. His hands fist in the sheets, white-knuckled, all those muscles straining with the effort of not grabbing me.

I take my time, using my mouth and hands until his thighs are trembling beneath me. I pull back when he's right on the edge, and the look on his face—desperate, wrecked, needing me—is something I'm definitely keeping in my mental highlight reel.

"Christ," he pants. "Fuck me. Please."

"Since you asked so nicely." I move up his body and position myself over him. When I sink down, taking him in one slow, smooth stroke, we both make embarrassing noises at how good it feels.

"Fuck," he groans, his hands hovering near my hips, still following my rules.

"Touch me," I say, and his hands immediately grab me, guiding my movements as I ride him. This angle is killer—deeper, hitting spots inside me that make my eyes cross.

"Look what you do to me," he says, his voice a mixture of wonder and surrender. "Turn me inside out until there's nothing left but need for you."

"Do you like it?" I ask, grinding down harder.

"Fuck yes," he groans, fingers digging into my hips. "You've got no idea how hot you are right now. Fucking magnificent."

His words push me higher, make me burn hotter. I increase my pace, chasing my orgasm, watching his face get tight-jawed and intense the way it does when he's close.

"Come on me," he urges, his thumb finding my clit. "Let me feel you."

When I come, it's so intense my vision actually whites out for a second. I cry out his name, not caring how loud I am. Not caring about anything except this feeling and this man beneath me.

He follows a half-second later, his hips driving up hard, my name sounding like it's being ripped out of him as he comes.

I collapse onto his chest the best I can with my belly between us. I'm completely boneless. His arms wrap around me, holding me close while his heart races under my palm.

"I do," I whisper against his chest when I can speak again. "I do love you."

His arms tighten around me. "Say it again."

I lift my head to look at him. "I love you, you idiot."

The smile that breaks across his face is ridiculous. Gorgeous and crooked and ridiculous.

"I love you too, Pink," he says, the gruffness in his voice betraying how much this means to him. "And not just because you're currently naked with my dick inside of you."

I smack his chest, but I'm laughing. "Way to ruin the moment, James."

"Not ruined," he says, pulling me closer. "Just making it ours. Wouldn't want you thinking I've gone completely soft."

"Oh, I can confirm at least one part of you is definitely not soft," I say, and his laughter rumbles against my cheek.

As I lay there with his arms around me, feeling our baby between us, I realize I'm pretty sure Kasen James is the best damn mistake I've ever made.

25
Kasen

THERE'S a gold wedding band burning a hole in my pocket, and I can't stop thinking about putting it on.

The weight of it has become familiar these past months, constantly reminding me of what I'm waiting for. But after last night, after hearing Wren finally say she loves me too, it feels heavier somehow. More significant. Like the difference between a dream and reality.

I told her I'd put it on weeks ago, but I never did. I wasn't sure she was ready for people to know, and I didn't want to answer questions I didn't have the answers to.

Lake watches me from across the brewing floor, his eyebrows raising as I check my phone for the fifth time in twenty minutes.

"Dude. She texted you like two seconds ago saying she's fine," he says, measuring out hops for our experimental batch. "The woman survived running Cascade for four years without you hovering. Pretty sure she can handle herself."

"I'm not hovering," I snap, shoving my phone back in my pocket where my fingers brush against the ring again. "Just checking the time."

"Sure." Lake's smirk is annoying as hell. "And I'm just playing with these Citra hops because I have nothing better to do."

I flip him off, but there's no heat behind it. He's not wrong. We're prepping the specialty batch I designed for the baby months ahead of schedule. The label's already finalized with that constellation of freckles from Wren's skin, the pine trees silhouetted against the dawn sky, the simple text at the top. *Crafted for the newest James.*

"You ever think about how weird this all is?" Lake asks, dumping the hops into the scale. "You and Pink going from mortal enemies to playing house in what, six months?"

"We're not 'playing house,'" I growl, checking the malt composition for the third time. This beer has to be perfect. It's for my son, after all. "And she's not 'Pink' to you."

Lake raises both hands in surrender, but he's still grinning. "Sorry. Didn't realize the nickname was exclusive."

"It is." My tone leaves no room for argument, which only makes Lake's grin widen.

"Remember when you came back from that craft beer panel last year? The one where she called your special edition IPA 'aggressively mediocre' in front of everyone?" He chuckles, clearly enjoying my humiliation. "You were so pissed you redesigned the whole recipe because of her."

Heat creeps up my neck. "Hey, that beer won gold at regionals."

"After you spent three weeks perfecting it because of her comment," Lake points out. "Face it, man. She's been pushing your buttons for years, and you've been loving every minute of it."

"I didn't love every minute."

"Fine, but you have to admit that she makes you better."

"The new recipe was better," I mutter, refusing to acknowledge the larger point.

"It was. Because she challenged you." Lake measures out another addition with practiced precision. "Same way you challenge her. You two are like... beer and pretzels. Shouldn't work, but somehow perfect together."

"That's the worst analogy I've ever heard."

"Didn't say I was a poet." Lake shrugs. "Just calling it like I see it."

Before I can respond, the front door chimes. Banks and Reed walk in, with Noble strapped to Banks's chest in one of those baby carrier things I'll be wearing in a few months. I can't wait.

"Hey," Banks calls out, his voice carrying across the brewery. "Got time for a break?"

Reed follows behind, carrying a paper bag that probably contains lunch. The guy's always thinking about practical details, like making sure we actually eat with our drinking.

"Thought we'd stop by for lunch," Banks says, already unstrapping Noble. "Someone's been demanding his Uncle Kase all morning."

I set down my clipboard and cross the floor to them, trying not to look too eager as I reach for my nephew. Noble's gotten so big since the last time I saw him, which was only a week ago. His chubby hands immediately grab at the tattoos that crawl up my neck.

"Hey, bud," I say, taking him from Banks. Something in my chest loosens the way it always does when I hold him. "You giving your dad hell?"

"All day, every day," Banks grins, looking more tired and happy than I've ever seen him. "Sleep is for the weak."

"Where's Wren?" Reed asks.

"At Cascade," I tell him, bouncing Noble when he starts to fuss. "She's got a busy afternoon with back-to-back meetings."

"She just hit twenty-four weeks, the viability milestone,"

Reed says, like it's normal to talk about this shit over lunch. "Baby's lungs are developing surfactant now."

"Yeah, she said something about him being able to survive now if he came early," I say, shifting Noble to my other hip. "It's a relief, but it still feels surreal."

"Before you know it he'll be here," Reed says, reaching to pour himself a beer from the pitcher of Backbone IPA that Lake just dropped off at the booth we claimed as ours the first day I opened the doors.

"Not fast enough," I mutter, thinking of Miller's latest moves against local breweries. Three more have folded to his pressure in the past week alone, despite our coalition's efforts.

I hate that Wren's stressing, and that stress is so hard on the baby.

"How's the baby name situation?" Banks asks, watching me with Noble. "Still arguing over it?"

I snort. "What do you think?"

The truth is Wren and I can't agree on a single name. Everything I suggest, she hates. Everything she suggests sounds like the name of someone who'd get beaten up on a playground. We're at a standstill.

"You could always name him Banks," Banks suggests with a straight face.

"Yeah, that's not happening," I reply, making Noble bounce on my hip. His giggles are the best sound in the world, and for a second, I imagine my son making that same noise. My son. The reality of that still blows my mind.

Lake finishes with the measurements and joins us, wiping his hands on a towel. "I've got the first stage prepped. We can continue later."

"Perfect timing," Reed says, pouring Lake a glass and passing it over. "To fatherhood, and not fucking it up too badly."

We clink bottles as Lake adds a heartfelt, "fuck no," and I

take a swig while still balancing Noble on my hip. The kid's fascinated by my tattoos, his tiny fingers tracing the lines of ink down my arm.

"So," Banks says, his tone shifting to something more serious. "How are you really doing with all this? The baby. Miller. Everything."

I shrug, not quite meeting his eyes. "Fine."

Reed snorts. "That's convincing."

"What do you want me to say?" I take another sip of my beer. "That I'm terrified of screwing this up? That every time I think about holding my kid, I remember how my dad checked out when we needed him most? That I'm paranoid Miller's going to find some way to destroy everything Wren and I have built before our son even gets here?"

The room goes quiet. Noble grabs a fistful of my shirt and tugs, kicking me in the ribs.

"Well," Banks says after a moment. "At least you're not bottling anything up."

I huff out a laugh, and my shoulders relax a little. "Sorry. It's just... a lot."

"It is," Reed agrees. "But you're not your dad, Kase."

"And you're not doing this alone," Banks adds, clapping a hand on my shoulder. "You've got Wren. You've got us."

"Besides," Reed says, all business suddenly, "the fact that you're worried about it already puts you miles ahead of where your father was. Shitty parents don't generally stress about being shitty parents."

"The doctor makes a good point," Lake chimes in, spinning his beer glass between his palms.

I look down at Noble, who's now drooling contentedly on my shirt as his eyes slow blink. "I just want to get it right, you know? I want to be the father he deserves."

"You will be," Banks says with a confidence I wish I felt. "Look at you with Noble. You're a natural, dude."

"Plus, Wren will kick your ass if you screw up," Reed adds with a smirk. "She'll keep you in line."

That pulls a reluctant laugh from me. "True."

Noble starts fussing, his little face scrunching up. Yeah, a meltdown is imminent. I shift him to my other hip, swaying the way I've seen Clover do. It works, and the pride that surges through me is ridiculous.

"See?" Banks gestures toward us. "Natural."

The front door chimes again, and I turn, expecting to see Wren. Instead, a woman with a gray pixie cut and glasses stands in the entrance, her gaze sweeping the brewery.

I know exactly who she is before she speaks.

"I'm looking for Kasen James," she announces, sounding like she's about to grade my entire existence. I bet grad students shit themselves when they have to answer a question in her class. "I understand he's responsible for my daughter's current situation."

Fuck.

Margot Callan. Wren's mom. The professor who basically programmed Wren to think all men are out to ruin her career and make her a second-class citizen or something. The woman who apparently has a quote from some dead writer at the ready so she can prove her point.

And she's looking at me like I'm everything wrong with the patriarchy, condensed into human form.

No big deal.

"That would be me," I say, shifting Noble higher on my hip. The kid chooses that moment to let out an ear-piercing scream before smacking my face with a slobbery hand, which doesn't exactly help me look put together.

Margot's eyes narrow behind her glasses, taking in the tattoos, the baby on my hip, the beer in my hand. I can practically see her cataloging each detail, filing them away as evidence against me.

"I see." Her tone could ice over a volcano. "Is there somewhere we can speak privately, Mr. James? About my daughter and my grandchild?"

Banks, Reed, and Lake exchange looks that all communicate the same thing: *You're on your own, buddy.*

"My office," I say, nodding toward the back. "Lake, can you take Noble?"

Lake practically trips over himself taking my nephew, clearly eager to escape whatever showdown is about to happen. Noble immediately starts fussing at the handoff, but he should consider himself lucky he doesn't have to be a part of what's about to go down.

I lead Margot to my office, trying not to feel like I'm walking to my execution. The space isn't much—desk, couple of chairs, walls covered in beer label designs and family photos. It's cluttered but clean, at least.

She takes the seat across from my desk, spine straight, hands folded in her lap.

"Mrs. Callan—" I start.

"Doctor," she corrects immediately. "Dr. Callan."

Right. Strike one.

"Dr. Callan," I try again. "I'm guessing Wren doesn't know you're here."

"She does not." Margot's eyes are a sharp gray, just like Wren's, but lacking the warmth I've come to expect in that color. "I learned about her pregnancy through a former student who works at the Portland Tribune. Apparently, your relationship has become something of a talking point in local business circles."

Great. Exactly what Wren was afraid of.

"What exactly are your intentions with my daughter, Mr. James?" She cuts right to it, no preamble, no warming up. "Because from where I sit, this looks suspiciously like the kind of situation I've spent twenty-seven years warning Wren about."

I could bullshit her. Try to charm her with promises and reassurances. But something tells me Margot Callan has a finely tuned bullshit detector, and I'd only dig myself deeper.

So I go with honesty instead.

"I love her," I say simply. "And I'm going to be there for her and our son for as long as she'll let me, which I'm hoping is forever."

Margot's expression doesn't change. "Love is all well and good, but it doesn't pay bills or advance careers. Wren has worked incredibly hard to build Cascade from nothing. She's fought twice as hard as any man in your industry to be taken seriously. And now her reputation is being undermined by whispers that she's sleeping her way to the top."

The accusation stings, mostly because I know Wren worries about the same thing.

"Anyone who knows Wren knows she's a badass businesswoman who built Cascade without any handouts," I say, unable to keep the edge from my voice. "Her reputation isn't as fragile as you seem to think."

"Isn't it?" Margot's eyebrow arches in a gesture so familiar it momentarily throws me. Wren does the exact same thing. "Women's reputations are always more fragile than men's, Mr. James. Especially in male-dominated industries. One misstep—one perceived weakness—and everything she's built could crumble."

"This isn't a misstep," I say, my jaw tightening. "And Wren isn't weak."

"No, she isn't," Margot agrees, surprising me. "Which is why I'm concerned about the timing of all this. Pacific Northwest Brewing has been circling Portland's craft scene like a vulture for months. Suddenly my daughter is pregnant, living with... well, you, and making decisions that seem uncharacteristic, to say the least."

I lean forward, resting my forearms on the desk. "You think

what, exactly? That I got her pregnant to what, slow her down? Distract her?"

"The thought had crossed my mind," she says coolly. "Or perhaps you're using the situation to your advantage somehow. Make her dependent on you personally since you can't compete with her professionally."

Something hot and angry burns in my chest, but I force it down. Getting defensive will only confirm her suspicions. And part of me understands where she's coming from. If someone threatened Clover's happiness, I'd be ten times worse.

"If I wanted Cascade, I would have made a play for it years ago," I tell her. "I respect what Wren's built too much to ever try to take it from her. And I respect her too much to ever try to control her."

"Respect is a start," Margot allows, "but hardly a foundation for the kind of life-altering decisions she's making."

"You're right." I hold her gaze steadily. "Which is why there's also trust. And partnership. And yes, love. Wren and I are figuring this out as we go, but we're figuring it out together."

"And the aspects of your businesses that compete? How do those factor into this partnership?"

This is where it gets tricky. The news about Timber joining Cascade's distribution network isn't public yet, though the breweries in our coalition know.

"Timber is bringing its distribution under Cascade's umbrella," I say, watching her reaction carefully. "Effective immediately."

That catches her off guard. Her perfectly composed expression slips for just a second, revealing genuine surprise.

"That's... a significant concession on your part," she says slowly. "You've been loudly opposed to distributors for years."

I want to smirk, knowing Wren's talked to her mom about me apparently for years. But it's not the time.

"I've been wrong about a lot of things," I admit. "Wren's

business model. Wren herself. How much I needed someone to challenge me." I take a breath, pushing forward. "I'm not perfect, Dr. Callan. Far from it. But I'm trying to be the man Wren deserves and the father our son needs."

She studies me for a long moment, that hard glint in her eye softening the tiniest bit. "And the marriage? Wren mentioned Vegas. Was that planned?"

"No," I say with a short laugh. How the hell does she know about that? Wren must've filled her in and a little heads up might've been nice. "That was definitely not planned. But I don't regret it."

"Even though she still isn't publicly acknowledging it?"

So Wren's told her more than I thought. Interesting.

"She needed time," I say simply. "I gave it to her."

Margot uncrosses and recrosses her legs, a gesture I recognize as buying time to think. Finally, she sighs.

"Mr. James—"

"Kasen," I interrupt. "If you're going to be my mother-in-law, you might as well use my first name."

The corner of her mouth twitches in what might be the hint of a smile. "Kasen, then. My concern has always been Wren's happiness and future. I've seen too many bright young women sacrifice their potential for men who claimed to love them, only to be left picking up the pieces alone."

Yeah, like her from what Wren's told me.

"I understand that," I say. "My father walked out on us after my mom died. Left me to raise my sister alone. Well, we kind of raised each other." I huff out a laugh, but it dies fast. "I know what it's like to be abandoned when you need someone most." I meet her eyes. "I would die before I did that to Wren or our son."

Something shifts in her expression—not quite warmth, but maybe a fraction less frost.

"Well," she says after a moment. "You certainly seem convinced of your sincerity."

Before I can respond, my office door swings open. Wren stands there, belly leading the way, her expression cycling rapidly from surprise to confusion to anger when she spots her mother.

"Mom?" She looks between us, her hand going to her stomach. "What are you doing here?"

26
Kasen

"HAVING a long overdue conversation with the father of my grandchild," Margot says, rising to her feet. "Since you haven't seen fit to introduce us yourself."

Wren's cheeks flush pink. "I was going to. When the time was right."

"And when would that be? After I received a birth announcement?" Her mother's tone is sharp, but I catch the hurt beneath it. "I had to learn about my only daughter's pregnancy from Janine's girl at the Tribune, of all people."

"I'm sorry," Wren says, and I can tell she means it. "I should have told you sooner. I just... needed to figure things out first."

"And have you? Figured things out?"

Wren's eyes find mine across the room, and the look in them makes my chest feel too tight.

"Yeah," she says softly. "I think I have."

There's so much in those four words, in the way she's looking at me, that I have to grip the edge of my desk to stay seated.

Margot glances between us, her shrewd gaze clearly noting the shift in energy. "I see," she says, though her tone has softened marginally. "Well, in that case, perhaps you'd both join me for dinner this weekend. I'd like to get to know the man who's apparently going to be a permanent fixture in your life."

Wren looks as surprised by the invitation as I feel.

"We'd love to," I say before she can respond. "Sunday work for you?"

"Sunday is fine." Margot picks up her purse from where she'd set it beside the chair. "Wren knows where I live. Seven o'clock."

She moves to leave but pauses at the door. "And Kasen? If you hurt my daughter, I'll make your life a living nightmare."

She delivers the threat with her chin held high, and it takes me a second to process the words. By the time I do, she's already sweeping out of my office.

"Well," I say after a moment. "That went better than expected."

Wren shakes her head, still looking stunned. "She invited you to dinner, and she threatened your life. I don't know which I should worry about more."

"Probably the dinner invitation," I say, standing and crossing to her. "The nightmare thing isn't really a threat because I'll do everything I can not to hurt you."

A small laugh escapes her. "Fair. But still." She looks up at me. "What did you say to her? Because when she called me this morning, she was still referring to you as 'that beer man who got you into this mess'."

I shrug, pulling her closer. "Just the truth."

"Which is?"

"That I love you," I say, giving into my need to touch her by tucking a strand of pink hair behind her ear. "That I'm all in on you. That I respect what you've built too much to ever try to take it from you."

Her eyes soften, and she leans into my touch. "And she bought that?"

"I think she's reserving judgment. But the dinner invitation is probably a good sign."

Wren sighs, resting her forehead against my chest. "I'm sorry I didn't tell her sooner. I was... scared, I guess. Of her disappointment. Of having to explain how I ended up pregnant and married to the guy I spent years complaining about."

"Hey." I tip her chin up, making her look at me. "No apologies needed. Family's complicated."

Normally, I'd give her shit for admitting she talked about me for *years,* but this time I let it go. For now.

"Speaking of family," she says, glancing toward the brewery floor. "Why is Banks here with Noble? And why does Lake look like he's seen a ghost?"

I laugh. "They came by to hang out, then your mom showed up and everyone scattered like cockroaches when the light came on."

She grins, and there's that smile I can never get enough of. "Cowards."

"Can't really blame them. Your mom is terrifying."

"She grows on you," Wren assures me. "Like a fungus."

I notice her shift her weight uncomfortably. "Everything okay?"

"Just tired," she says, her hand going to her belly. "It was a long day."

"C'mere." I sit and pull her down on my lap, reaching down to rub one of her calves.

She groans as her head falls onto my shoulder. "Actually, there's something I wanted to talk to you about. I got a call from Miller on my way over here."

I tense, but then pick back up with my massage. "What did he want?"

"To set up a meeting. With both of us." She pulls out her phone, reading from the screen. "'To discuss a mutually beneficial resolution to our current situation.' Whatever that means."

"It means he's planning something," I say, already thinking through scenarios. "The coalition must be hurting him more than we thought."

"Or he's found a new angle," Wren counters. "Either way, I told him we'd meet. Tomorrow, at Cascade."

I nod slowly. "On our turf. Smart."

"I thought so." She looks up at me, her expression serious. "We need to be prepared for whatever he throws at us."

"We will be." I pull her closer and wrap myself around her as much as I can in this position. "We've got each other's backs, remember?"

"Yeah." I feel her smile against my neck. "We do."

After a few more minutes alone, we head out to rejoin the others, finding them clustered around one of the brewing tanks. Noble's happily tucked in Banks's arms again, drooling on his dad's shoulder.

"Did you survive the inquisition?" Reed asks, looking between us.

"Barely," I say. "But we've been summoned to dinner on Sunday, so the execution's been postponed."

"Meeting the parents," Lake whistles. "That's a big step."

"We're having a baby together," Wren points out dryly. "I think we're there."

Everyone laughs, and the tension from earlier dissipates. We spend the next hour catching up, sharing beers (non-alcoholic for Wren, which she wrinkles her nose at but drinks anyway), and enjoying the company of our friends. Watching Wren with Noble, the way her face softens when he grabs her finger, makes my chest ache in the best possible way.

By the time everyone heads out, it's after sunset. After I check out with my evening bar staff, Wren and I head home in comfortable silence, her hand resting on my thigh as I drive.

"So," she says as we pull into the driveway. "After all that excitement, what do you think about working on the nursery tonight? I need something normal and productive to do."

"Yeah, if you're up for it, I'm game."

When we get inside, she changes into comfortable clothes, which are more my stuff than hers. We head to the room we've designated for the nursery, which still looks more like a storage space than a baby's room.

"We should decide on a theme," Wren says, surveying the boxes we need to clear out. "Something that isn't aggressively babyish."

"What, you don't want pastel blue everywhere?" I say, already starting to move boxes.

She wrinkles her nose. "God no. I was thinking something more... I don't know. Mountain-y? Outdoorsy? To go with the whole Portland vibe."

"That could work," I agree. "Pine trees, mountains, maybe some wildlife that isn't too cutesy. Foxes or something."

"Exactly!" She looks surprised and happy that I'm on the same page. "Like the label you designed for Dawn Breaker."

This may be the first thing we've agreed on when it comes to the baby. I pause, a box half-lifted in my arms. "You want the nursery to match the beer label?"

"Is that weird?" She suddenly looks uncertain. "I just thought... it's meaningful. It represents both of us. The trees for you, the stars for me."

The weight of what she's saying settles into my bones. I set down the box and cross to her.

"That's..." I say against her hair as I pull her against me. My throat's tight as hell and I swallow a couple of times before I can finish my thought. "No, it's not weird. It's... us."

She relaxes against me, her arms sliding around my waist. "Good. Because I may have already ordered some stuff online."

I laugh, the sound rumbling through both of us. "Of course you did."

"I'm efficient." She pulls back, smiling up at me. "And I figured if I waited for us to agree on anything, this kid would be in college before his room was decorated."

Shit, at this point he might be in college before we name him, too.

"Fair point." I brush her hair out of her eyes, staring down at her just because I can. "I can build some mountain-shaped shelves that'd look good in here."

"You can?" Her eyes light up, and goddamn, I would do anything to keep that look on her face.

"I'll draw up some designs later." I drop a quick kiss on her lips. "First, let's clear this place out."

We work side by side for the next couple hours, moving boxes to the basement, sorting through old stuff, making space for our son. Wren's playlist fills the room—a mix of indie rock and 90s classics that has her singing under her breath when she thinks I'm not listening.

As I watch her arranging things, dancing around the room despite her belly and singing off-key to some Pearl Jam song, I know this is exactly where I'm supposed to be.

"Hey," I call out, grabbing a paintbrush from one of the bags. "Since we're doing this mountain thing, what if we painted an actual mountain scene on that wall?"

She turns, her hair messy from moving furniture, a smudge of dust on her cheek. "You can paint?"

"Badly," I admit. "But I can try."

Her smile starts slow, then spreads across her face. Fuck, that one right there would be the best one in my collection. "Yes, do it."

We spend the next hour arguing about the mountain range I'm trying to paint—too pointy here, not enough trees there—but it's the best kind of arguing. The kind that ends with paint on both our faces and sore abs from laughing so much.

When we finally call it quits, the nursery still looks like a disaster zone, but it's starting to come together.

"Not bad for your first try," Wren says, surveying my questionable mountain artwork.

"Shut up," I say, but I'm grinning. "Next week, I'll start on the shelves."

She leans into my side, and I wrap my arm around her shoulders automatically. "This is nice," she murmurs against my chest.

"Yeah," I agree, pressing a kiss to the top of her head. "It is."

27
Wren

THERE'S a twenty-four-week pregnant woman with swollen ankles and back pain who really needs to stop pretending she's invincible.

Unfortunately, that woman is me.

I stare at my computer screen until the numbers blur, rubbing my temple with one hand while the other rests on my belly. It's nearly nine, and I should've left the office hours ago, but these quarterly projections won't finish themselves. The baby chooses this moment to deliver a sharp kick to my ribs, making me wince.

"Yeah, I know," I mutter to him. "Your dad's going to kill me when he finds out I'm still here."

My phone buzzes. I don't need to look to know it's Kasen. The man's developed a sixth sense for when I'm pushing myself too hard.

> Kasen: You're still at work, aren't you?
>
> Kasen: Pink. It's almost 9.
>
> Kasen: At least text me back so I know you're alive.

I pick up my phone, already knowing this conversation won't end well.

> Me: Just finishing up. Be home soon.

> Kasen: Define 'soon.' Because to me, soon means now.

> Me: Soon means when I'm done. You're not my keeper.

Even as I type it, the words feel wrong. When did arguing with Kasen start feeling exhausting instead of energizing? When did coming home to him become the part of my day I look forward to most?

My door opens without a knock, and Kieran strides in, holding two cups of coffee. His designer suit is still immaculate despite the late hour, his tie perfectly knotted. The man doesn't believe in rumpled.

"One decaf with enough cream to drown a small mammal," he announces, setting a cup on my desk. "And stop giving me that look. By now you know the rules. Caffeine's off limits."

"Fine." I sigh. "Is it bad that's the thing I'm looking forward to most when this little beast pops out of me?" I rub my stomach while I take a sip.

Kieran eyes me. "Not beer or sex or, I don't know, not having a parasite leeching off of you?"

I roll my eyes. "I mean, all of those things, too."

"And why are you still here?"

"The Henderson contract needs to be finalized by tomorrow morning, and I still need to review the—"

"No," Kieran interrupts, dropping into the chair across from me. "You've been here since seven this morning. Go home. The contracts will still be here tomorrow."

I open my mouth to argue, then close it. The truth is, I've

been staying late more often lately, but not for the reasons Kieran thinks.

Working has always been my safe space, my way of maintaining control. But now, going home means facing how much I've let Kasen become integral to my life, and that terrifies me almost as much as I need it.

Yeah, I'm still trying to come to terms with a lifetime of issues and it's not always easy.

"It's not about the work," I admit finally.

Kieran watches me like he already knows. "Then what's it about?"

I trace the rim of my coffee cup, organizing my thoughts. "Remember when Kasen and I first started this whole thing? How I kept insisting it was nothing? Just until I found a place, and then just until we figured out the baby thing?"

"I remember you making very detailed lists of reasons why you two were completely incompatible," Kieran says as he sips his non-decaf coffee that I definitely don't glare at him for. "Something about him being an 'infuriating, stubborn brewery tyrant with terrible taste in beanies.'"

"I may have been slightly dramatic," I concede. "But the point is, I had rules. Boundaries. I knew exactly what this was and what it wasn't. And now..."

"Now?"

"Now I look forward to coming home to whatever amazing thing he's cooked. I get excited when I hear his truck in the driveway. I wake up reaching for him when he's not there." The admission feels like stripping naked in public. "He's become essential. Something I can't live without. And as much as I love him, it still scares the shit out of me."

Kieran leans back in his chair, studying me. "You know what I think?"

"That I've lost my mind?"

"I think you've finally stopped fighting something that's

been obvious to everyone else for months." He brushes a piece of lint off the sleeve of his jacket. "Including, probably, yourself."

I shake my head, frustrated. "It's not that simple. I've spent my entire adult life being independent. Making my own decisions, relying on no one. My mom raised me to never need a man for anything."

"There's a difference between needing someone and choosing someone," Kieran points out. "You didn't need Kasen to save you from Miller or fix your housing situation. You chose to let him in. That's not weakness, Wren. That's trust."

"When did you become so wise?"

"When I started watching my boss fall in love with her mortal enemy," he grins. "It's been quite the show."

Before I can respond, my phone rings. Not a text this time—an actual call. Kasen's name flashes on the screen.

"You better answer that," Kieran says, standing. "Before he shows up here with your dinner and that famous scowl."

I accept the call as Kieran heads for the door.

"Before you start," I begin, "I know I'm still at work, and I know you wanted me to be home by seven, and I know you're probably already planning all the ways you're going to punish me because you think I'm pushing myself too hard—"

"Are you okay?" Kasen interrupts. His voice is tight, like he's worried. It's not angry like I expected.

"I... yes? Why?"

"Because your last text was over half an hour ago, and you always respond faster than that when you're okay. Are you having contractions? Is he moving? Do I need to call Reed?"

The concern in his voice makes my heart hurt a little. "I'm fine. Really. Just lost in spreadsheets."

"That's what you said last week when you almost passed out during a call."

I frown at my computer screen. "How do you know about that?"

"Kieran texted me. At least *he* fills me in on what's going on with you."

"That little snitch," I mutter even as my gut twists with guilt because I *do* hide things from him so he doesn't overreact. Actually, knowing that Kieran and Kasen have formed some kind of alliance to take care of me feels... not terrible.

Huh.

"Come home, Pink," Kasen says, his voice softening. "I made lasagna."

"Did you actually follow a recipe this time?"

"I did, though it might be a little crispy on the edges because I got distracted by an idea in my workshop."

"Of course you did," I say, already gathering my things. "Is it edible?"

"Absolutely. Get your ass home before I eat all the good corner pieces."

Despite everything, I laugh. "You're ridiculous."

"And you love me anyway," he says, and I can hear the smile in his voice. "See you in thirty?"

"Twenty," I promise, already saving my spreadsheet. "And Kasen?"

"Yeah?"

"Save me the crispiest edge piece. Those are my favorite."

"I'm eating it if you're a minute late."

After hanging up, I gather my stuff, trying to ignore how eager I am to get home to him. To sit together at the table while he watches me eat with those light blue eyes, making sure I'm getting enough protein. To hear him tell me about his day, about Lake's latest dating disaster or the new experimental batch they're brewing.

I'm almost to the door when it swings open again. This time, it's not Kieran.

"Working late again?" My mother stands in the threshold, not a hair out of place even though it's late. She's smiling at me, despite her words. I know how much she values hard work. "Some things never change."

Damn, he's definitely going to eat my lasagna now.

"Mom." I set my bag down, already bracing for the lecture. "What are you doing here?"

"I had a faculty meeting that ran late. Thought I'd stop by." She surveys my office, her gaze lingering on the ultrasound photos I've taped to my monitor. "Though I'm surprised to find you still here. I assumed you'd be rushing home to prepare dinner for your husband."

The way she says 'husband' makes it clear what she thinks about the situation. I straighten my shoulders. "I don't make his dinner. We cook together. Or more accurately, I sit and critique while he makes the food."

"Hmm." She takes the seat Kieran just vacated. "And how is domestic life treating you? Living under a man's roof, depending on him?"

"It's not his roof, it's our house," I snap before I can stop myself. God, how did I buy into all her bullshit before? "And I don't depend on anyone. We have a partnership."

In so many ways.

My mother's eyebrows arch—the same gesture I use when I'm skeptical. It's unsettling to see my mannerisms reflected back at me.

"A partnership," she repeats. "Is that what you're calling it now?"

"What would you call it?" I challenge, crossing my arms. "Because I'm getting tired of defending my relationship to everyone, including you. You're supposed to be on my side."

"I'm not attacking your relationship, Wren. And I'm always on your side. But I'm concerned about how quickly you've thrown away everything I taught you about independence."

"I haven't thrown away anything," I say, frustration building.

"I'm still running Cascade. I'm still making my own decisions. I'm still the same person I was before—"

"Are you?" She leans against the wall, folding her arms across her chest. "Because the daughter I raised wouldn't move in with a man after knowing him for mere months. Wouldn't let herself become emotionally dependent on someone who could leave at any moment."

Her words strike a nerve because they touch on my deepest fears. But then I think about Kasen's face when he looks at me, the way he holds my hand during ultrasounds, how he regularly goes out at all hours for my cravings without a single complaint.

"You're right," I say slowly. "I'm not the same person. I'm pregnant. I'm married. I'm letting someone take care of me for the first time in my life, and you know what?" I stand, gathering my things again. "It doesn't make me weak. It makes me brave."

My mother blinks, clearly not expecting that response.

"I spent years building walls because of what you taught me," I continue, slinging my bag over my shoulder. "Proving I didn't need anyone, fighting for respect in this industry. And yes, maybe I've let those walls down faster than either of us expected. But Kasen earned that trust, Mom. Every day, in a hundred small ways."

"And when he disappoints you?" she asks quietly. "When the novelty wears off, and he realizes he's tied to a woman with a screaming infant and stretch marks?"

The vulnerability in her voice stops me. For the first time, I hear the old wounds beneath her words. Her own disappointments, her own fears.

"Then I'll deal with it," I say, softer now. "But I can't live my life waiting for people to leave. And I can't base my choices on your past experiences with men who weren't worth your time."

She's quiet for a long moment. "I just want you to be happy, sweetheart. And safe."

"I am." I really, *really* am. "You'll see at dinner Sunday. You'll get to meet him the right way, not in his office where you're trying to intimidate him. Let him show you who he really is."

My mother sighs, some of the tension leaving her shoulders. "Okay. But if he serves beer with dinner, I'm putting my foot down."

I laugh, feeling lighter than I have in weeks. "Deal."

My mother hugs me and leaves while I say goodbye to Kieran and finally leave. Yeah, I'm definitely not getting the crispiest square. To be honest, I'm surprised Kasen isn't blowing up my phone with how late I am.

I'm almost to the parking garage when a sharp pain doubles me over. *Shit shit shit.* This is different from the mild Braxton Hicks I've been having this last week. It's stronger, more focused in my lower abdomen. I lean against the elevator wall, breathing through it.

When it passes, I check my phone again. *And there it is.* Three missed calls from Kasen. Before I can call him back, another wave of pain hits, harder this time, and my heart starts to really race.

I dial his number with shaking hands. He answers on the first ring.

"Baby or not baby?" No hello, no preamble, just straight to identifying why I'm even later than I said I'd be.

"I don't know," I manage, gritting my teeth while I try to catch my breath. "Something's... wrong, I think. It," I gasp, "hurts."

28
Wren

"WHERE ARE YOU?"

"Still at the office. In the parking garage elevator." Well, sort of. I waddle toward my car as we talk.

"Stay right there. I'm calling Reed, and I'll be there in five minutes."

The call ends, and another cramp hits. This one makes me cry out. When my phone rings again, it's Reed.

"Wren, Kasen just called. Tell me what's happening."

"Contractions, I think," I gasp. "Stronger than the Braxton Hicks. They really hurt."

"How long has this been going on?"

"The last fifteen minutes, maybe? They were mild before, but now..."

"When Kasen gets there, I need you two to meet me at the hospital," Reed says, his professional calm somehow more frightening than panic would be. "At twenty-four weeks, we don't mess around with regular contractions. I'll meet you there."

I hang up and slide down the side of my car until I'm sitting on the concrete. The garage is cold, the fluorescent lights flickering overhead, and for the first time since this all began, I'm truly scared.

Twenty-four weeks. That's barely viable if something goes wrong. That's a baby who needs months more time to develop, who isn't ready for the world yet.

"Please," I whisper to my belly. "Please be okay."

I don't know how long I sit there before I hear Kasen's truck roaring through the garage. He screeches to a stop beside me, and then he's there, pulling me up into his arms.

"I've got you," he murmurs against my hair. "Everything's going to be fine."

"What if it's not?" The words come out strangled as I grip his flannel shirt so hard my knuckles turn white. "What if I've been pushing too hard? What if I've hurt him?"

"Hey." Kasen cups my face, making me look at him. "This is not your fault. You've been taking care of yourself. Sometimes these things just happen. And it's probably nothing."

"I can't lose him," I whisper, tears threatening. "I can't lose him, Kasen."

"We won't." His voice is fierce, certain. "I won't let you. Nothing's going to happen."

He helps me into his truck, buckling me in, and we speed toward the hospital. I grip his hand, trying to breathe through the fear, trying to ignore the way my back aches and my stomach feels tight.

"Talk to me," Kasen says, his thumb rubbing circles on my palm. "Tell me what you're feeling."

"Scared," I admit. "More scared than I've ever been."

"Physical symptoms, Pink."

I check in with myself. "Back pain. The contractions are coming every four or five minutes now. He's moving, though. I can feel him between them."

"Good. That's good." Kasen's jaw is tight, but his voice stays calm. "Reed's the best. If anyone can handle this, it's him."

"Why were you being even more over the top than usual today? How'd you know?"

"Because you've been working longer hours, and when you get stressed, you react differently now. I've been watching and fucking worried." He glances at me. "I had a feeling something was off today."

The simple fact that he knows me this well, that he's been paying such close attention, makes warm little grasshoppers hop around in my stomach.

"Thank you," I whisper. "For taking care of me."

"Always," he says simply and squeezes my hand.

At the hospital, everything becomes a blur of monitors and nurses and Reed in full professional mode, examining me while Kasen doesn't move an inch from my side and never once lets go of my hand.

"Everything looks good," Reed announces after what feels like forever. "All your tests are normal. The baby's heartbeat is strong and regular. What you're experiencing appears to be pre-term labor that's resolved on its own, likely triggered by stress and fatigue. We'll monitor you for a few hours to make sure everything stays quiet, but I think you and the little guy are going to be just fine."

The relief is so intense I start crying. Not pretty tears, but ugly, exhausted sobs that seem to come from somewhere deep inside me.

"Hey," Kasen murmurs, wiping my face with his thumbs. "You're both okay."

"I was so scared," I hiccup into his chest after he sits on the bed next to me and wraps his arms around me. "I thought... if something happened because I was being stubborn about work..."

"Nothing happened," he says firmly. "And from now on, you're listening to your body and to me when I tell you to take it easy."

"Yes, sir," I manage, half-laughing through my tears.

Reed clears his throat. "I'm recommending modified bed rest for the next week. No long hours at the office, no late nights, and lots of rest. And Wren?" He waits until I look at him. "Let him take care of you." He smirks. "Doctor's orders."

Hours later, after they release me, Kasen drives us home in silence. I'm exhausted, emotionally drained, but there's something settled inside me that wasn't there before.

At home, he helps me into bed, messing with the pillows and blankets until I'm comfortable. I watch as he strips down to his boxers and crawls in behind me, his body curving around mine. His arm slides around my waist, his hand coming to rest on my belly where our son moves around like he's trying to kickbox his way out of my stomach.

"This okay?" he murmurs against my neck.

"So okay," I tell him, already feeling safer with his warmth against my back. I can let go and all my muscles relax while I melt into his strong body.

I study our joined hands in the dim light, the way his tattooed fingers spread protectively over my stomach. This man who called my doctor because he noticed I was working too much, who held my hand through every contraction and test tonight without question, who's now cradling us both like we're his whole world.

"I love you," I say, and for the first time, there's no fear in it. No hedging or qualifying. Just truth.

He leans up and over until his eyes find mine. "I love you too, Pink."

"I want this to be real," I continue, the words tumbling out easier in the dark. "Not just for the baby. I want us to be real."

"We are real," he says, his thumb tracing patterns on my palm. "We have been for a while now."

"Yeah." I take a deep breath. "And I'm sorry I've been

working so late. It wasn't about the work. It was about being scared of how much I need you."

His expression softens. "You don't need me, Wren. You're the strongest person I know. But that doesn't mean it's wrong to want me."

"Very wise words, James."

"I have my moments." He leans down, pressing a gentle kiss to my lips. "Now, how about that lasagna?"

"It's midnight," I point out.

"So?"

I laugh, feeling lighter than I have in weeks. "So bring on the lasagna. And then you're telling me everything about your day, including how you ended up trading texts with my assistant."

"It's not a big deal," he admits with a grin. "Kieran and I have a group chat. Reed's in it too."

"You're all ridiculous," I say, but I'm smiling.

"And you love us anyway."

"Yeah," I agree, settling back against the pillows as he heads for the kitchen. "I really do."

As I lie there, listening to Kasen moving around downstairs, I realize something fundamental has shifted. Not just in how I feel about him, but in how I see myself. I'm still Wren Callan, CEO of Cascade Craft Distribution. I'm still independent, driven, capable of anything I set my mind to.

But now I'm also a woman who's chosen to let someone in. Who's building a family with a man I never expected to love. Who's discovered that trust isn't weakness, and partnership isn't surrender.

When Kasen returns with two plates of something that smells *amazing*, I'm ready for all of it. The uncertainty, the joy, the terrifying beauty of sharing my life with someone else.

"Verdict?" he asks, watching me take a bite.

"Delicious," I admit, moaning around the perfect blend of cheese and sauce. "You nailed it this time."

"This time?" He smirks. "I nail it every time, Pink. You just love to make me work for it."

"Humble as always," I tease, but I'm already going back for another bite. And he brought me a crispy corner square because he's the best.

As we eat together in bed, talking and laughing, our son rolling and kicking between us, I think about Kieran's words from earlier. There's a difference between needing someone and choosing someone.

I choose Kasen. And for the first time in my life, that choice doesn't feel like giving up anything.

It feels like coming home.

My phone buzzes on the nightstand, and I reach for it automatically. Miller's name appears on the screen with a text.

> Miller: Heard you had some excitement tonight. Stress is so dangerous for expectant mothers. Hope you're reconsidering our offer.

I go cold. "Kasen."

He looks up from his plate, immediately reading my expression. "What's wrong?"

I show him the text. His face darkens to something murderous.

"He wouldn't," I whisper. "Would he? Seriously try to take advantage of my health issue? In the middle of the night?"

"Forward that to me," Kasen says, his voice deadly calm. "And text that coalition group chat. Emergency meeting tomorrow morning. Miller just fucked with the wrong people."

"Whatever he's planning," I say, setting my phone aside after sending the text, "we'll stop him."

"Damn right we will," Kasen agrees, pulling me closer. "Nobody threatens my family and gets away with it."

Family. The word settles around us like a promise, like a battle cry, like the thing I've been afraid to want my whole life.

But as I let Kasen wrap me up in his arms, I'm not afraid anymore.

I'm furious.

And god help Nolan Miller, because a pregnant woman with a protective husband and a righteous anger is not someone he wants to fuck with.

He's about to enter his find out era.

29
Kasen

I'VE NEVER FELT MORE like breaking someone's face than when Nolan Miller walks into Cascade's conference room with that smug fucking smile. He's in an expensive suit and looks like he thinks he's won.

Well, fuck that.

My fingers curl into fists. Wren sits beside me at the head of the table, shoulders back, chin up. Anyone else would miss the tension in her jaw, but I've memorized every expression she makes. She's furious.

"Mr. James. Miss Callan." Miller settles into the chair across from us, placing a leather portfolio on the table. "Thank you for agreeing to meet. I trust you're feeling better?" His eyes drop pointedly to Wren's belly.

"Cut the shit," I growl before Wren can answer. "We know what you're doing."

"And what might that be?" His smile is slimy as fuck and doesn't reach his eyes.

Wren slides a folder across the table. "Attempted industrial sabotage. Targeted harassment of our partner breweries. Using my medical incident to try to pressure me into selling." Her voice is ice cold. "Should I keep going?"

Miller barely glances at the folder. "Those are some strong accusations. I assume you have proof?"

"We have Marcus Wells on video trying to break into Timber," I say, leaning forward. "The same Marcus Wells who now works for you. And a dozen breweries with similar stories of equipment failures, distribution problems, and mystery issues."

"One disgruntled employee acting on his own hardly constitutes a pattern," Miller dismisses with a wave of his hand.

Wren's smile reminds me of a shark who smells blood in the water. "Maybe not. But a dozen breweries all experiencing the same problems after refusing your offers? *That's* a pattern."

"And the text you sent me after my hospital visit?" she continues. "That was a nice touch. Very concerned. Very threatening."

"I merely expressed concern for your wellbeing," Miller replies smoothly. "Pregnancy can be so stressful."

My blood *burns* with the need for violence, but I feel Wren's hand on my thigh, her fingers digging in to steady me.

"Here's what's going to happen," she says, her voice deceptively calm. "You're going to back off. All of our partner breweries. All of our distribution routes. Us. All of it."

Miller laughs. "Or what?"

"Or we release everything." I pull out my phone, displaying the document Clover helped us compile. "Every complaint from every brewery. Every instance of suspicious timing. Every piece of evidence suggesting a pattern of intimidation and sabotage."

"To whom? The trade magazines?" Miller looks unimpressed. "Hardly world-changing."

"To the Securities and Exchange Commission," Wren says quietly. "And the Department of Justice."

The color drains from Miller's face. "You're bluffing."

"Pacific Northwest has been acquiring breweries at below-market values after systematic efforts to damage their operations and profitability," she continues. "That's not just unethical. It's potentially illegal."

"My lawyer thinks the SEC would be very interested in the way you go about acquiring businesses," I add.

Miller's eyes dart between us. "You have nothing concrete."

"Maybe not yet," Wren agrees. "But an investigation would tie up Pacific Northwest for months, maybe years. And the professional investigators would really dig into every little crack and shadow. I can't imagine your shareholders would like that."

"Not to mention what it would do to your stock price," I add. "News of a federal investigation tends to make investors nervous."

Miller's jaw tightens. For the first time since I've met him, he looks shaken.

"What do you want?" he asks finally.

"A public statement that Pacific Northwest is withdrawing from the Portland craft market," Wren says immediately. "And legally binding agreements not to approach any of our partner breweries for at least five years."

"That's ridiculous."

"Is it?" I lean back, crossing my arms. "Seems like a small price to pay to avoid a federal investigation."

The silence stretches between us. Miller stares at the folder, his bullshit facade cracking.

"I'll need to consult with our legal team," he says finally.

"You have twenty-four hours," Wren states. "After that, we go public."

The meeting ends shortly after. When Miller leaves, Wren waits until the door closes before sagging in her chair.

"You think he'll back off?" she asks, looking up at me and I get up and start rubbing her shoulders.

"He'd be stupid not to." I pull her to her feet, hands resting on her shoulders. "You were incredible."

She leans into me, her head on my chest. "We were incredible."

And just like that, another wall between us crumbles. The industry rival I spent years trying to outmaneuver is now my partner in every sense—business, life, family. The woman who's carrying my son stood beside me today, and together we faced down a corporate giant.

And I think there's a good chance we won.

"Let's go home," I say, pressing a kiss to her forehead. "You're supposed to be on bed rest."

She looks up at me with those stormy eyes that I've been lost in for months. "Lead the way."

The next day, I'm sitting in Banks's kitchen, trying to convince my best friend that I'm not completely losing my mind.

"You want to propose to a woman you're already married to?" Banks asks, adjusting Noble in his lap while we sit in his kitchen. The kid's gnawing on a teething ring, drooling everywhere. "That's like... what's that called?"

"Fucking romantic," I mutter, grabbing another beer from his fridge. "It's called being romantic, asshole."

"No, really, though." He shifts Noble to his other knee. "Why not just make the Vegas thing official? Put the ring on your finger and call it good?"

I pour myself a beer, staring into the amber liquid like it'll give me answers. "Because she deserves a real proposal. Not some drunk Elvis bullshit we can't even remember."

Banks watches me as I stand up and start to pace his

kitchen for a minute before he sets Noble in his high chair. "Alright, sit down. You're making me nervous."

I drop into the chair across from him, dragging a hand through my hair. "I've got it all planned out. Dinner at a fancy restaurant. Get down on one knee with the ring. The whole thing."

"Uh-huh." Banks sips his own beer. "And how's that working out for you?"

"What do you mean?"

"I mean, you've been planning this for three weeks, and every time you're about to do it, you chicken out." His grin pisses me off. "Remember last Tuesday when you had reservations for dinner?"

"She had a sudden craving for tacos," I mutter. "Not just any tacos. Fish tacos from that truck on Southeast Division that's only open until eight."

"Right. And when you had those sunset cruise tickets?"

"Kieran called with an emergency. Someone accidentally shipped a shit ton of beer to the wrong brewery." I take a long pull from my beer. "It was actually an emergency, but still..."

"I think the universe is telling you something," Banks says, trying not to laugh. "Maybe she doesn't want the whole fancy restaurant, one-knee thing. Maybe that's not her style."

"Of course it's not her style," I snap. "She'd probably roll her eyes and ask if I practiced my speech in the mirror while she laughs at me. But I don't have a better idea."

Banks erupts into laughter, nearly spilling his beer, and Noble squawks and then shrieks at the sound. "Dude. Look at you. You've gone from the guy who told me Wren Callan was a 'pink-haired menace who'd destroy craft beer as we know it' to the guy who drives across town for special tacos."

"Shut up." But I'm fighting a grin. "She's changed."

"No, she hasn't. You have." Banks becomes serious. "You've

fallen for her hard, man. Which is why you need to stop overthinking this. When have you ever planned grand gestures?"

"Never."

"Exactly. You're not that guy. You're the guy who rebuilt his brewery from ashes. Who raised his teenage sister after their mom died. Who builds furniture for fun in his spare time. Who makes the best goddamn IPA in Portland." He points his beer at me. "Be that guy. The direct, no-bullshit guy she fell in love with."

Noble chooses that moment to throw his teething ring across the room, letting out an indignant wail.

"Smart move, buddy," I say, getting up to retrieve the ring. "Sometimes you gotta chuck the whole thing and start over."

Banks grins, tossing me a kitchen towel. "Look, you want my advice? Stop planning. Next time you feel it, just ask. Doesn't matter where or when. Just be real."

I wipe down the teething ring and hand it back to Noble, who immediately sticks it in his mouth. "What if she says no?"

"She won't." Banks's certainty is annoying and comforting at the same time. "You know how I know?"

"Enlighten me."

"Because when I mentioned making a guys' poker night next week when her, Clover, and Navy were here, she immediately asked what I was planning to feed you. Then went on about how you always skip lunch when you're stressed and just drink coffee all day." He smirks. "That's not what someone who doesn't care does, brother."

A warmth spreads through my chest that has nothing to do with the beer. "She knows that?"

"She knows everything about you, man. And she cares. Now go home to your wife and stop being a pussy about this."

Noble claps his hands in agreement, drool smeared across his face.

"Thanks for the pep talk, you two." I finish my beer and grab my keys. "Wish me luck."

"You don't need luck," Banks calls after me. "She's already yours."

30
Kasen

THE DRIVE HOME feels different somehow. Like the universe is shifting, realigning itself around the decision I haven't made yet, but know I'm going to. The wedding ring in my pocket feels heavier than usual, warming against my thigh.

I pull into the driveway to find Wren's car already there. The house is lit up, warm golden light spilling from the windows. For a second, I just sit there, engine off, staring at our home.

The front door opens before I can reach for the handle. Wren stands there in one of my flannels—the blue one that makes her eyes look more blue than gray—and leggings I itch to peel off of her.

"You're late," she says.

"Banks was giving me life advice."

"God help us all." She steps back to let me in. "How's Noble?"

"Wise beyond his years. He made some excellent points about overthinking." I hang up my jacket, catching her scent as I brush past her and I greedily suck it down into my lungs.

"Are you going to share these excellent points?" She follows me to the kitchen.

"Later maybe." I drop the shopping bag I grabbed on the way home onto the counter. "I grabbed us dinner."

She peers into the bag. "The Thai place on Morrison?" "Your favorite."

"My favorite tonight. Next week, it'll be that Hawaiian place on Hawthorne. I can already feel it."

"And I'll go there too," I say, pulling containers from the bag. "Because your weird pregnancy cravings are somehow cute instead of annoying."

"Yeah, right."

"They are." I set down the pad Thai and meet her gaze. "And you look beautiful, by the way. Just like this, barefoot in my flannel, stealing my food."

"It's just some mango sticky rice. I think you'll survive without it," she says, but she's fighting a smile now.

"Whatever. That's why I got extra, because you're always taking my food," I say, pulling another container of rice out of the bag.

I pretend she didn't just say something that fucks me up a little bit more over her. "Just like you've taken my hoodies, my side of the bed, and most of my sanity."

Her eyes narrow. "You're being weird."

"Am I?"

"You've been weird for weeks. Jumpy. You stare at me when you think I'm not looking. And you've been really helpful lately. Like, suspiciously helpful." She props her hands on her hips, which makes the flannel pull tight against her tits, which have gotten so much bigger these past few months. My mouth waters and not for dinner. "What's going on?"

Before I can answer, she gasps and grabs my arm. "He's kicking."

I drop everything and put my hands on her belly, feeling the movements beneath my palms. "Holy shit."

"Yeah." Her voice softens. "He gets really active around dinner time. Like clockwork."

We stand there for endless seconds, my hands on her stomach, feeling our son move. The weight of it nearly knocks me on my ass. I take a second to commit every bit of this right here to memory. I never want to forget this feeling.

"We need to talk about names," I say, because suddenly I can't think about anything else.

"Not this again." She groans, but she's leaning into me now.

"We can't keep calling him 'him' forever."

"Why not? It's working so far." She captures my hands, pressing them firmer against her belly. "Feel that? That's his version of disagreeing with you."

"Smart kid." I rest my chin on her shoulder. "What about James?"

"For the baby who's going to be James James?"

"James Kasen James has a nice ring to it. We can call him JJ."

She turns in my arms to face me and glares at me. "Not a chance in hell. And I *will* die on this hill."

"What about—"

"Kasen." She cuts me off, her hands sliding up my chest. "Let's eat dinner first, then we can argue about names. I'm starving."

"When aren't you starving?"

"Shut up and feed me." But she's grinning as she grabs plates from the cabinet.

We settle at the table with our Thai food, the conversation flowing easier than it ever has. She tells me about her day, about how Kieran accidentally ordered 'premium matte finish' business cards that cost three times the budget but look incredible. "Worth every penny," she laughs, "but he was panicking about how bad my wrath was going to be."

I watch her talk, animated and passionate, gesturing with her fork. There's pad Thai sauce at the corner of her mouth, and her hair is literally falling out of its bun. She's beautiful and ridiculous and mine.

The ring in my pocket feels like it's burning through my jeans.

"What?" she asks, catching me staring.

"Nothing." I clear my throat and change the subject. "What about Theodore? We could call him Teddy."

She makes a face. "He sounds like a professor who corrects people's grammar at dinner parties."

"Oliver?"

"Too trendy."

"Sebastian?"

"Too pretentious."

"For fuck's sake, Pink. You hate everything I suggest."

"Because your suggestions are terrible." She steals one of my spring rolls. "What about something outdoorsy? To go with the nursery theme?"

"Like Forrest? River?"

"No." She pauses, chewing thoughtfully. "Although..."

"Although what?"

"What about Summit? Like a mountain peak. It's strong." She spins her fork. "And it's not as pretentious as naming him Mount Rainier or something."

I consider it. "Summit James." I test it out loud. "I think I like it."

"Holy shit, we actually agreed on something." She looks genuinely shocked. "Quick, get your phone out. Document this moment."

"Don't get cocky. We still haven't talked middle names."

"One miracle at a time." She pushes her empty plate away. "I'm exhausted."

"Want an early night?"

"Mmm." She stands, stretching, one hand automatically going to the small of her back. "Come to bed with me?"

It's not really a question, and I'm already following her down the hall.

In the bedroom, she strips out of my flannel and her leggings, climbing into bed in just her underwear and my t-shirt. I follow, turning off the lights before joining her.

She curls into me, the way she's been doing for weeks now. Like it's the most natural thing in the world. Like her body can't help but gravitate toward mine.

"Your turn to pick a middle name," she murmurs against my chest.

"William. After my grandfather."

"The one who built the original bar at Timber?"

"You remember that?"

"I remember everything about your brewery. Had to, for reconnaissance purposes."

I snort. "For reconnaissance?"

"Know thy enemy." But there's no edge to it anymore. Just warmth and sleepiness.

"And now?"

"Now you're not my enemy." Her hand finds mine on her belly. "You're so much more."

My heart flips over. The ring is still in my jeans pocket, but my jeans are on the floor. This isn't the right time. There's no candlelight, no fancy restaurant. It's just us in the dark.

But Banks was right. I'm not a grand gesture kind of guy.

"Wren."

"Hmm?"

"I need to ask you something."

She tucks herself closer into me, her face buried against my neck so I can feel her breath on my skin. It goes straight to my dick, but with my nerves, it doesn't get fully hard. "If this is about baby names again—"

"It's not." I pull the elastic out of her hair and run my fingers through it. "I want you to stay married to me."

She goes still. "That wasn't a question."

"We're Vegas married. Drunk married." I take a breath. "I want you to be *really* married to me. Because you want to be, not because we got hammered and Elvis pronounced us man and wife."

"Kasen..."

"You're right, that wasn't a question." I shift so I can see her face in the dim light. "Wren Callan, will you stay my wife?"

She blinks up at me but says nothing, so I keep going.

"I know this isn't romantic. We're in bed about to fall asleep and you're wearing your underwear and there's probably still pad Thai in your teeth." She lets out a surprised laugh. "But this is us. This is real. And I love this version of us more than any of the stupid proposals I've been planning for weeks."

"You've been planning a proposal?"

"Elaborate, stupid proposals that keep getting derailed because life keeps happening." I shift so I can see her face in the dim light. "But you know what? Life happens. With us. Every day. The good and the messy and the shitty. And I don't want to stop."

She's quiet for so long, I start to panic. Then I feel wetness against my neck.

"You're crying?"

"Shut up." But she's smiling through her tears. "You're being sweet and it's freaking me out."

"Pink—"

"Yes."

"Yes, what?"

"Yes, I'll stay married to you, you idiot." She sniffles. "Only because you're right. This is us. And somehow it's everything."

Relief floods through me, followed immediately by something deeper. Something that feels like finally coming home after being lost for years.

"Really?"

"Really." She leans up to kiss me, and it's soft and sweet and tastes like tears and Thai food. "I love you, Kasen James. Even when you overthink things and bring home new beers for me to critique when I can't even drink them and leave your sketchbooks all over my clean kitchen counters."

"I love you too." I pull her closer, feeling our son push against me. "You and our son and this whole ridiculous life we're building."

"Summit William James," she murmurs against my neck. "Has a nice ring to it."

"Better than James James."

"Uh, just a little." She laughs, the sound vibrating through both of us. "We should probably tell people we're married, huh?"

"I think a lot of people already know. Your mom does, Reed, Banks, Kieran. Everyone else can wait until tomorrow," I say, already sliding down her body to kiss her neck. "Right now, I want to show my wife how much I appreciate her saying yes."

"Technically, I said yes months ago. I just didn't remember it."

"Semantics." My mouth finds that spot behind her ear that makes her shiver. "You're saying yes now, and that's what matters."

"Kasen."

"Yeah?"

"Shut up."

I do. And as I strip her underwear off and settle between her thighs, this beautiful, infuriating woman who's somehow become everything to me, I realize something profound:

Somehow, the biggest mistake of my life turned out to be the only thing I've ever gotten completely right.

"I love you," I whisper against her skin as she sighs my name.

"I love you too," she breathes back. "Now less talking, more doing."

I laugh. "Yes, ma'am."

And as I lose myself in her, I know with absolute certainty that whatever challenges await with a newborn and two businesses—we're ready.

Because what started as the dumbest mistake of my life has become the smartest thing I've ever done.

Even if I was too drunk to remember it at the time.

Later, as Wren sleeps beside me, her hand resting on her belly and our son moving beneath her skin, I finally dig the ring out of my jeans pocket. In the moonlight filtering through our bedroom window, I slip it onto my finger where it belongs.

Where it's always belonged.

Tomorrow I'll put her ring back where it belongs too. But tonight, I just want to lie here with my wife, listening to her dream, feeling like the luckiest bastard in Portland.

31
Kasen

I WAKE to find Wren already up, standing at the window in our bedroom with a mug of her cream with a splash of coffee. She's wearing my Timber Brewing hoodie, the one she's claimed as her own, and her pink hair looks almost neon in the early morning light.

"Morning," I say, my voice rough with sleep.

"Morning." She turns, and that's when I notice the tears in her eyes. "Kasen?"

"What's wrong?" I'm out of bed in seconds.

"Nothing's wrong." She laughs, wiping at her eyes. "I just—I want to do this right. The proposal. I know we already talked last night, but I want to ask you properly."

"Pink—"

"No, let me." She sets down her coffee and takes my hands. "I've spent my whole life being afraid of needing anyone. Afraid of depending on someone who might leave. My mom taught me that independence was the only safety, that men were just distractions from what really mattered."

I open my mouth to speak, but she squeezes my hands.

"But you've shown me something different. You haven't

distracted me from what matters—you've become what matters. You and Summit and this life we're building. You've never tried to dim my ambition or control my choices. You've just... supported them. Even when they went against your own interests."

Her voice cracks slightly, and I reach up to brush the tears from her cheek.

"So I'm asking you, Kasen James, will you marry me? Really marry me? Be my husband and Summit's father and my partner in all the terrifying, wonderful chaos that's coming?"

I can't speak for a minute. This woman, who once called my beer "aggressively mediocre" in a room full of industry professionals, is standing in my hoodie, asking me to be hers forever.

"Are you sure about this?" I finally manage. "Because I'm not easy to live with. I leave my socks everywhere and get obsessive about beer recipes and sometimes I'd rather work on my motorcycle than talk about feelings—"

"Stop." She laughs, more tears spilling over. "I don't want easy. I want you."

"Then yes." I frame her face with my hands. "Yes. Fuck yes. You know I'm yours. Have been since Vegas. I told you that last night. I'll marry you, Pink. Today, tomorrow, whenever you want."

"How about right now?" she whispers.

"What?"

"Our rings. Let's put them on now." She grins through her tears. "Make it official. No Elvis this time."

I stare at her, then laugh. "You want to exchange rings on a Wednesday morning while we both have morning breath and before I've had coffee?"

"I want to start wearing my ring on my finger instead of around my neck. I want to see yours on your hand every day." She reaches for the chain at her neck and slips it over her head. "I want to start being your wife officially. Is that so crazy?"

"It's the least crazy thing we've done since Vegas." I pull her against me, feeling her belly press into my stomach. I think it grew some more overnight. "Let's do it."

"Really?"

"Really." I kiss her forehead, her nose, finally her mouth. "I'll get dressed. You call Kieran and tell him we won't be in until this afternoon."

"Why Kieran?"

"Well, because he'll need to run things for the rest of the day. But also because I'm pretty sure he and Lake have a bet going about when we'd finally stop pretending we're not all-in on this marriage."

She laughs, the sound bright and free. "Fine. But you're buying breakfast after. The fancy place with the Belgian waffles."

"Deal." I'm already moving toward the closet. "Mrs. James."

"That's going to take some getting used to."

"We've got time." I grab jeans and a t-shirt, watching her across the room as she calls Kieran. "Forever, actually."

As I get dressed, I listen to her explain to Kieran that she won't be in today. "Family stuff," she says, and the way she says "family" makes something warm spread through my chest.

Banks was right. Sometimes the best moments happen when you stop planning and just let life work itself out.

And sometimes the woman who drives you crazy is also the woman who saves you.

She slips the ring off the chain and hands it to me. Her fingers shake, but she gives me her brightest smile. I take her left hand in mine, and I've never been more nervous about getting something right.

"I, Kasen Jessie James, take you, Wren Eleanor Callan..." I slide the ring onto her finger, where it belongs.

"Are you seriously doing vows right now?" she interrupts, but she's grinning through fresh tears.

"Shut up. I'm trying to be official." I finish sliding the ring on her finger. "There. Perfect."

She takes my ring from my hand after I dug it out of my jeans pocket. "Your turn." She slides it onto my finger, her touch sending electricity up my arm. "There. Proof that we're stuck with each other."

"You really know how to make a guy feel wanted."

"You love it." She rises on her toes to kiss me. "Now let's go get waffles. Your son is hungry."

"Sure, blame it on the kid." I grab my wallet and keys.

Twenty minutes later, we're settled in a corner booth at the fancy waffle place downtown, her hand in mine on the table, our rings catching the morning light.

"You know," she says as she drowns her waffle in syrup, "my mom's going to have a field day with this."

"Let her." I lift her hand to my lips. "It's not like she didn't know about Vegas. Nothing she says can touch this."

"You say that now. Wait until she starts quoting Virginia Woolf at you. 'A woman must have money and a room of her own if she is to write fiction...or run her own company.'"

I squeeze her hand, feeling the weight of my wedding ring pressing into my skin. "I've got more important things to focus on right now."

"Like what?"

"Like making sure my wife gets those Belgian waffles she's craving."

"And then?"

I grin, leaning closer. "And then I'm going to take you home and spend the rest of the day showing you exactly how much I appreciate you marrying me. Twice."

"I like this plan." She spears a piece of waffle dripping with syrup. "And for the record, I expect this level of service for all my cravings from now on, Mr. James."

"Already on it, Mrs. James."

As we eat breakfast together, I get lost in my thoughts.

This is how love stories should begin. Not with grand gestures or perfect moments, but with two people deciding to choose each other. Over and over. In big ways and small.

In drunken Vegas chapels and morning waffle dates. In midnight food runs and argued over baby names. In shared clothes and stolen sticky rice and the quiet space between sleeping and waking when the rest of the world falls away.

And if our story started with a mistake?

Well, I've never been happier to be wrong about anything in my life.

32
Wren

Three months later...

THE MOST ANNOYING thing about being thirty-six weeks pregnant isn't the swollen ankles, or the constant bathroom trips, or even the backaches that keep me up at night. It's the fact that Kasen James was right about absolutely everything, and now I'll never hear the end of it.

"I told you we'd be amazing together," he murmurs against my ear, his hand resting possessively on my hip as we watch the crowd mingle in Timber's packed tasting room. "Both in business and in bed."

"Way to be subtle," I mutter, even as I lean into his touch. "Half of Portland's craft beer scene can see you."

"Let them see." His breath is warm against my neck, sending an embarrassing shiver down my spine. "I'm not the one who insisted we keep our relationship professional in public."

I roll my eyes but can't stop the corners of my mouth from twitching upward. "That was before I looked like I swallowed a beach ball and everyone could do the math."

He chuckles, the sound vibrating through me in a way that makes my toes curl inside my ugly as hell flats. But swollen feet are no joke.

The joint Timber-Cascade celebration is in full swing. Portland's beer snobs are out in force, pretending they've always supported us while secretly wondering how the hell Kasen James and I ended up married with a baby on the way. If they only knew about Vegas and Elvis and tequila shots...

God, all this standing is killing my feet. These might be the world's most comfortable flats, according to the sales girl, but she clearly wasn't hauling around an extra thirty pounds and a tiny human who thinks my bladder is a punching bag.

Kasen's hand splays across my stomach, his tattooed fingers making my skin tingle even through the fabric of my dress. The blue one he insisted on buying after I rejected it at that maternity store months ago. "It makes me want to rip it off you," he'd said, and I'd rolled my eyes so hard I nearly gave myself a headache. But damn him, he was right again. Not that I'd ever tell him that. The man's ego barely fits in this brewery as it is.

But I look amazing in it.

I scan the room, spotting Kieran deep in conversation with the Seattle distribution guys. Three months ago, I'd have been right there, closing deals and making connections in that take-no-prisoners way that built Cascade from nothing.

Now? I'm weirdly content just watching from the sidelines as Summit practices what feels like an entire MMA fighting routine in my belly. Kasen's hovering beside me like I might suddenly get the vapors if he steps away for two seconds. It should irritate me. It would have driven me insane three months ago. But somehow I'm actually... enjoying it?

I've said it before and I'll say it again: Pregnancy hormones are a bitch.

But also, so is falling in love because now I've become *this*.

So sappy with all these feelings and ugh.

"Did Miller's lawyers ever respond to that cease and desist?" Kasen asks, nodding toward the Eugene brewers who've recently jumped ship to our distribution network.

"Yep." I can't help the smug grin that spreads across my face. "Full retreat from the Portland market, just like we demanded. Kieran framed the letter and hung it in my office."

"Of course he did." Kasen laughs, and *god* that sound does all sorts of things to my insides. "What about those other contracts?"

"Another brewery signed yesterday," I tell him, not bothering to hide my pride. "The Henderson account expanded to include their seasonal line, and we've got meetings with two new microbreweries next week who are practically begging to join our network."

"And Timber's revenue is up eighteen percent since bringing distribution under Cascade." His fingers trace distracting patterns on my back. "We make a good team, Pink."

"We do," I admit, looking up at him. "Though I still think your winter porter needs more body."

"And I still think you're full of shit." But there's no heat behind it. Just that teasing undercurrent that somehow transitioned from genuine hostility to our weird version of foreplay.

Clover appears through the crowd, balancing Noble on her hip. The kid's gotten huge in the past few months, his chubby cheeks and grabby hands a terrifying preview of what's coming for us in a few short weeks.

"There's my favorite sister-in-law," she greets, attempting an awkward hug with Noble and my belly squished between us.

"I'm your only sister-in-law," I point out, but accept Noble's sticky hand when he reaches for me. "Unless Kasen's hiding another wife somewhere."

"God, one is more than enough," Kasen mutters, earning himself an elbow to the ribs.

"How are you feeling?" Clover asks, eyeing my belly with sympathy.

"Like I'm housing a future soccer star who's determined to break my ribs," I reply, wincing as Summit delivers a particularly enthusiastic kick. "But otherwise fantastic."

"Enjoy these last few weeks of sleep," she warns with that knowing smile all mothers seem to have. "Pretty soon you'll be lucky to get three consecutive hours."

"Don't remind me." I force a smile even as my back screams in protest. Just one more hour, then I can go home, take off this bra, and make Kasen rub my feet while I complain about everything.

Kasen doesn't miss my wince. Of course he doesn't. The man has developed some kind of freaky sixth sense about my discomfort.

"We should probably head home soon," he says, his tone leaving no room for argument.

Before, I'd have bitten his head off for that authoritative bullshit. Now, I'm embarrassingly grateful for the excuse to leave early. Even though it's our party, I don't really want to be here anymore.

"Fine," I give in. "But only because these shoes are killing me, not because you're telling me to."

His knowing smirk says he sees right through me, but he doesn't call me on it. "Of course. It's all the shoes."

We make our goodbye rounds, Kasen's hand never leaving my back as we navigate the crowd. His constant touches used to drive me crazy in the worst way. Now they're just... always there. A steady reminder that I'm not alone. That I have a partner in this mess of a life we're building.

When we finally make it to his truck, I collapse into the passenger seat with an embarrassing groan of relief.

"That bad?" he asks as he slides behind the wheel.

"Worse." I kick off my flats and rub at my swollen ankles. "I think I'm retaining more water than the Columbia River."

Without a word, he pulls my feet into his lap and starts working his thumbs into my arches. His hands should be illegal—those strong, calloused fingers finding every aching spot with devastating precision.

"You don't have to do that," I say, even as I sink deeper into the seat and let my head fall back against the window.

"I know," he replies simply.

We sit there in the parking lot, the party continuing without us, as my tattooed, beanie-wearing husband massages my sausage feet with a gentleness that still surprises me. This is the same guy who once got so mad at my keynote speech at the Northwest Craft Alliance that he "accidentally" knocked over my presentation notes right before I went on stage. The same guy who now carries pregnancy-safe snacks in his truck because I might get hungry at random times.

The universe has a weird sense of humor.

"Ready to go home?" he asks after a few minutes.

"Yeah," I say, reluctantly putting my flats back on. "Let's go home."

The drive is short, but I still manage to fall asleep. When we pull into the driveway, I blink awake to find Kasen watching me with an expression that still makes those grasshoppers jump around in my stomach.

"What?" I ask, suddenly self-conscious. "Do I have drool on my face?"

"No." He brushes a strand of pink hair back. "Just wondering how I got so lucky."

"Ugh, stop." I wrinkle my nose but can't fight the smile tugging at my lips. "You're getting sappy in your old age, James."

"And you're getting soft," he counters. "Never thought I'd see the day when Wren Callan let someone take care of her."

"I'm not soft," I protest. "I'm strategically conserving energy. Big difference."

Inside, I make a beeline for the couch, collapsing onto it with zero grace. Summit responds with a series of kicks that make my belly visibly ripple through my dress.

"Someone's active tonight," Kasen says, kneeling beside me. His face lights up when he feels the movement. "Hey, buddy. You partying in there?"

"I swear he knows your voice," I say, watching Kasen's expression soften as he talks to our son. "He always gets more active when you speak."

"Smart kid." Kasen looks so proud that it catches me off guard, and then he glances up at me with every ounce of love he feels for Summit and me unguarded right there on his face. I never knew I could feel like this before him. "Takes after his mom."

"Flattery will get you everywhere."

"I'm counting on it." His hand slides up to cup my breast, his thumb brushing over my nipple, which is approximately a thousand times more sensitive than it used to be. "These still sore?"

The seemingly innocent question sends a jolt of heat straight between my legs. "Maybe a little," I admit. "Why do you ask?"

His eyes darken. "Just making sure you're comfortable."

"I'd be more comfortable without this dress on."

"That can be arranged." He stands, offering me his hands. "Upstairs?"

"God, yes." I let him pull me to my feet. "But only if you carry me. My ankles won't survive the stairs."

Without hesitation, he scoops me up in his arms, cradling me against his chest like I weigh nothing instead of being about a thousand pounds because of his giant baby. It's a testament to how strong he is, and to how much shit's changed between us, that I'm actually letting him do this without fighting him.

In our bedroom he sets me on the edge of the bed with a gentleness that's kind of shocking coming from a guy with arms like his. It's like watching a grizzly bear handle a teacup.

"Arms up," he commands softly, and I comply, letting him pull the dress over my head. His sharp intake of breath as he takes in my lace-covered breasts sends a flash of satisfaction through me.

"When did you get this?" His fingers trace the edge of my black maternity bra, the only sexy underwear I could find that doesn't look like something my grandma would wear.

"Last week." I arch into his touch. "Thought you might appreciate something that isn't beige and ugly as hell."

"I appreciate everything you wear," he says, his voice dropping to that gravelly register that makes me shiver. "And everything you don't wear."

His hands slide around to unclasp my bra, his movements practiced now after months of undressing me. When my breasts spill free, heavier and fuller than they've ever been, he groans.

"Christ, look at you." His thumbs brush over my nipples, which have gotten darker during this pregnancy. "Fucking gorgeous."

"I'm the size of a whale," I protest, but without much conviction. It's hard to feel unattractive when Kasen looks at me like this—like I'm some kind of fertility goddess instead of an exhausted pregnant woman with a popped out belly button and cellulite on my ass.

"You're perfect," he corrects, kneeling to help me out of my underwear. "You're growing our son. Do you have any idea how fucking hot that is?"

I laugh, the sound breathy as his hands slide up my thighs.

"I might have some idea, based on how often you want to fuck me."

"Can you blame me?" His mouth trails across my collarbone, down to the swell of my breast. "My beautiful wife. Carrying my baby. Your tits getting bigger every day."

I gasp as his mouth closes around one sensitive nipple. "Kasen—"

"I know, Pink. Gentle." His tongue swirls, the pressure light. "Tell me if it's too much."

But it's not too much. It's perfect—the scrape of his scruff against my oversensitive skin, the warmth of his mouth, the way his fingers dig into my thighs. My hands tangle in his hair, pulling him closer.

When he pulls back, I whimper at the loss. "Where are you going?"

"Nowhere." He stands just long enough to strip off his own clothes, revealing the body I've come to know as well as my own. The tattoos that flow across his skin, telling stories I've learned to read in the dark with my fingertips. The muscles that flex under my hands as he moves back to the bed.

"How do you want this?" he asks, always conscious of my comfort these days. "Side? You on top?"

"Side," I decide, already turning away from him. "You behind me."

He settles against my back, one arm sliding beneath me, the other draped over my hip. His erection presses against my lower back, hot and hard. When his fingers slide between my thighs, finding me already wet for him, the growl that resonates from his chest vibrates through my entire body.

"Always so ready for me," he murmurs against my neck. "Is this what growing my baby does to you? Makes you wet all the time?"

"Don't get cocky," I manage, but my body betrays me as I push back against him. "It's just hormones."

"Bullshit." His teeth graze my earlobe. "You've wanted me since Vegas. Maybe even before."

I can't deny it, not when he's working his fingers between my legs like a pro, circling my clit in the way he's learned drives me crazy. "Maybe," I concede.

"Definitely." He shifts, aligning himself at my entrance before pushing in with agonizing slowness. "God, you feel so good around me. So wet every fucking time."

I gasp as he fills me, the angle allowing him deeper. "Kasen, please."

"Please what?" His voice is strained, fighting for control. "Tell me what you need."

"You know what I need."

"Say it." He thrusts into me, but it's too slow and not hard enough. "I want to hear you say it."

"I need you to fuck me," I breathe. "Hard."

His rhythm falters for just a moment. "You sure? The baby—"

"Is fine," I assure him, reaching back to grip his hip. "Reed said we can still have sex. I want it."

That's all the permission he needs. His next thrust is harder, deeper, his arm tightening around me as he establishes a rhythm that has me gasping his name. His free hand slides up to cup my breast, thumb and forefinger rolling the nipple just tight enough to send sparks of pleasure-pain straight to my core.

"So fucking perfect," he groans against my shoulder. "I can't wait to suck on these when your milk comes in."

I moan at his words, my body clenching around him. He knows exactly what that kind of talk does to me, how it ignites something primal and desperate in my veins.

"You like that?" His voice is rough against my ear. "Like knowing you're mine? That I put our baby in you? That I'll put another one in you as soon as this one's done?"

"Yes," I gasp as his fingers find my clit again. "Yes, fuck—Kasen—"

"That's it," he urges, his movements growing more urgent. "Come on my cock. Show me how much you love being full of me."

The orgasm hits without warning, crashing over me in waves that have me crying out his name, my body clenching around him as pleasure ripples from my core to my fingertips. He follows moments later, his groan muffled against my shoulder as he pulses inside me.

We stay connected as our breathing slows, his arm still around me, his hand on my belly where our son has gone suspiciously quiet, as if lulled to sleep by our activities.

"Think we scarred him for life?" I ask when I can finally speak again.

Kasen laughs, the sound rumbling through both of us. "Nah. He's safe in there. Besides, this is how he got here in the first place."

"Not exactly," I remind him, shifting to face him as he slips out of me. "As I recall, it involved a lot more tequila and an Elvis impersonator."

His smile is soft in the dim light. "Best mistake I ever made."

"Was it, though?" I trace the lines of a tattoo on his hand. "A mistake?"

He catches my hand, pressing a kiss to my palm. "Maybe not. Maybe it was exactly what was supposed to happen."

I settle against him, my head on his chest, my belly pressing against his side. "You think we were inevitable?"

"I think we were too stubborn to see what was right in front of us." His fingers card gently through my hair. "It just took tequila to make us pay attention."

"And a baby," I add, placing his hand on my stomach where Summit has resumed his workout.

"And a baby," Kasen agrees, his expression softening as he

feels the movement. "Hey, Summit. You wanna hear the story of how your mom and dad got together?"

"Oh god," I groan. "Are we really going to tell him that?"

"He should know," Kasen insists with a grin I feel more than see. "It's a great story."

"Fine." I roll my eyes, but can't help smiling. "But I'm telling my version."

"Which is?"

"Once upon a time," I begin theatrically, "there was a brilliant, beautiful, badass woman who made the grave error of drinking too much tequila at a craft beer convention and woke up married to her very annoying mortal enemy."

"Annoying?" Kasen's eyebrows shoot up. "I prefer 'devastatingly handsome' and 'extremely talented.'"

"Shh, I'm telling the story." I place my hand over his lips. "As I was saying, she woke up married to this man who made mid IPAs and had terrible taste in beanies."

"Mid?" He nips at my finger. "Now you're just being cruel."

"Fine, slightly above average IPAs." I concede with a laugh. "Anyway, they decided to get a divorce and pretend the whole thing never happened."

"But then," Kasen cuts in, "the beautiful, stubborn woman discovered she was pregnant."

"And the handsome but annoying man," I continue, unable to stop smiling, "turned out to be surprisingly decent about the whole thing."

"More than decent," he corrects. "Unflinchingly supportive and loving."

"Don't push it." But I'm laughing now. "And somehow, against all odds and rational thinking, they ended up falling in love."

"And living happily ever after?" Kasen suggests, his hand still moving gently over my belly.

I meet his gaze, finding nothing but sincerity in those blue eyes that once made me want to scream with frustration and now make me feel like I'm home.

"Reluctantly."

"Whatever. I think you like where this is headed," he murmurs, leaning down to press a kiss to my lips. "Especially the part where we raise our son together and you admit I was right about everything."

"In your dreams, James."

"Every night, Pink." He pulls me closer, his warmth enveloping me like a blanket. "Every damn night."

EPILOGUE
Kasen

One month later...

I CAN NOW CONFIDENTLY SAY that watching the woman you love cut open on an operating table is fucking *awful*.

"If you don't stop looking at me with that terrified face one more time, I swear to God I'll kick you out of this room and have one of the nurses FaceTime you for the birth," Wren threatens, her voice shaky but still somehow sharp as a scalpel. She's strapped down to the operating table, her pink hair tucked into a surgical cap, as the medical team preps around us like we're not even there.

I force my features into something more neutral, though my heart's thumping so hard I'm surprised she can't hear it. "Better?"

"No. Now you just look constipated."

A laugh escapes me despite everything. Leave it to Wren to crack jokes while literally being prepped for emergency surgery. It's been over thirty-six hours of labor with no progress, and now this. A C-section we never planned for. But that's been our whole story, hasn't it? Nothing working out the way we thought.

"Hey." I lean closer to her face so she's focused on me. It's only that and her arms on this side of the blue surgical barrier they've put up across her chest. "You're doing amazing."

"I haven't done anything," she says, her eyes glassy with a combination of pain meds and unshed tears. "I couldn't even get this kid out the normal way."

"You grew him," I remind her. "For nine months. That's more than enough."

She closes her eyes briefly. "What if something's wrong? What if—"

"Nothing's wrong." My voice comes out more confident than I feel. "Reed's the best. You're the strongest person I know. And our kid's stubborn as hell, just like his parents."

"Kasen," Reed calls from behind the barrier. He's suddenly acting all professional despite the fact that in the last hour, he's sent me twelve memes about dads passed out in weird places with "your future" captioned underneath. "We're about to start. Remember to stay seated and keep your focus on Wren."

"Got it." I take Wren's hand, carefully avoiding the IV line. She squeezes back so hard I feel the bones in my fingers grind together, but I don't flinch. This is the least I can do when she's lying there, about to be cut open and scared out of her mind.

"You're going to feel some pressure," Reed warns Wren. "But no pain. If you feel anything sharp, tell me right away."

Wren nods, her face pale. Then her eyes go wide. "Holy shit, he wasn't lying. That's intense."

"Good. That's normal." Reed's voice is calm and steady. "Just keep breathing. It'll be over in a minute."

I watch Wren's face, cataloging every twitch of her expression, trying to gauge her pain level. She's always been terrible at admitting when something hurts. She prides herself on being the toughest person in the room. But right now, she's pale and sweaty and she looks scared. It's killing me that I can't fix this for her.

"Talk to me," she says suddenly. "Distract me."

"About what?"

"Anything. Tell me about... tell me about the first beer you ever brewed."

I latch onto the topic and just start talking. "It was garbage. Absolute swill. I made it in my dorm room before I dropped out. Used a plastic bucket I bought at Home Depot and bread yeast because I didn't know any better."

A small smile ghosts across her lips. "You didn't."

"I did. And I made my roommates drink it. They were too nice to tell me it tasted like liquid compost."

"How did you—" She gasps, her back arching slightly against the restraints.

"Wren?"

"I'm okay." She takes a shaky breath. "Just weird pressure. Keep going."

"How did I figure it out?" I continue, rubbing my thumb across her knuckles. "My sister. Clover took one sip, spat it halfway across the room, and told me if I ever gave her anything that disgusting again, she'd tell everyone about the time I got drunk and tried to serenade my high school crush with a Backstreet Boys song."

That gets me a real laugh. "Tell me you have a video of that."

"It's out there somewhere. I was sixteen and thought 'I Want It That Way' would win her over."

"Did it work?"

"Not even a little. She recorded it on her phone and showed it to all her friends."

Wren's smile widens, but then her face changes, her eyes going wide. "What's happening? I feel... tugging?"

"Almost there," Reed calls, his voice tight.

Then a pause. The longest pause of my life.

I'm holding my breath and I think Wren is, too.

And then there's the most beautiful sound I've ever heard in my life.

A cry.

It's high-pitched, indignant, and strong.

"He's here," Reed announces. "Summit William James, born at three forty-two p.m."

The world stops. Just... stops.

Over the barrier, Reed holds up a squirming, bloody, perfect little human. My son.

"Holy shit," I breathe.

"Is he okay?" Wren demands, her voice cracking. "Why isn't he crying more?"

As if on cue, Summit lets out a wail that could wake the dead.

"Happy now?" Reed laughs, passing our son to a waiting nurse. "He's perfect. All fingers and toes accounted for."

I can't take my eyes off him as they clean him up, wrap him in a blanket, and place a tiny hat on his head. My brain can't process that this is real. That he's real.

"Kasen." Wren tugs on my hand. "Is he really okay?"

"He's beautiful," I tell her, my voice rough with an emotion I can't even name. "Perfect. Pink and pissed off and... ours."

The nurse brings him over, settling him gently on Wren's chest in the small space above the surgical barrier. She immediately brings her free hand up to touch his cheek, her fingers trembling.

"Hi," she whispers. "Hi, Summit. I'm your mom."

The way she looks at him—like he's the answer to a question she didn't know she was asking—breaks something open inside of me. I lean down, pressing my forehead to hers, my hand covering her much smaller one on our son's back.

"Thank you," I murmur against her temple.

She looks up at me, eyes shining. "For what?"

"For him. For Vegas. For everything."

"Don't make me cry while I'm being stitched back together," she warns, but a tear slips down her cheek anyway.

I laugh, pressing a kiss to her forehead, then lean down to do the same to Summit's head. He smells like nothing I've ever encountered before—new and clean and somehow right.

"Alright, Dad," a nurse says, appearing at my elbow. "We need to take him for a few minutes while we finish up with Mom. Why don't you come with us?"

The thought of leaving Wren's side makes my stomach clench. "I should stay—"

"Go," Wren urges. "Stay with him. I'm fine. Just... don't let him out of your sight."

I nod, pressing one more kiss to her lips. "I'll guard him with my life."

"I know you will." Her smile is tired but real. "That's one of many reasons why I love you."

Following the nurse feels like an out-of-body experience. Summit has been transferred to a small bassinet, and I hover as they weigh him, measure him, and wrap him in a fresh blanket. I can't stop staring at his face—the tiny nose, the bow-shaped mouth that's all Wren's, the shock of dark hair peeking out from under his hat.

"Would you like to hold him?" the nurse asks. "While we finish up with your wife?"

Wife. The word still gives me a kick every time I hear it.

"Yeah," I manage, my voice rough. "Yes."

She shows me how to support his head, how to cradle him against my chest. I've done all this with Noble, but in this moment, I forget everything I've ever learned and I'm grateful for the reminder.

And then suddenly I'm holding my son, this tiny human who didn't exist an hour ago and now is the center of my universe.

"Hi, Summit," I whisper, afraid to speak too loudly. "I'm your dad."

He blinks up at me, his eyes unfocused and dark but seeming to search my face. His hand escapes the blanket, tiny fingers flexing, and I offer him my finger. He grips it with surprising strength.

Like I'm the only thing anchoring him to this new world.

Something fractures and rebuilds inside my chest, like a dam breaking and then reforming stronger than before. I would die for this kid. Kill for him. Anything to keep him safe.

Is this how my dad felt, holding me for the first time? If so, how the hell did he ever walk away?

"Kase?" Reed's voice pulls me from my thoughts. "Wren's all stitched up. We're taking her to recovery. You and Summit can come with me to meet her there."

I follow him down the hallway, holding Summit against my body. I'm careful, but I know I won't drop him.

"This whole dad thing looks good on you," Reed says.

"You sound surprised."

He shrugs. "Not surprised. But better you than me."

Wren's already in the recovery room when we get there, looking exhausted but alert. Her face lights up when she sees us.

"There're my boys," she says, making grabby hands toward Summit. She hasn't really gotten to hold him yet.

I pass him over, then perch on the edge of the bed. She looks down at our son with a mix of wonder and fierce protectiveness that mirrors everything churning inside me.

"So," she says without looking up. "That didn't exactly follow the birth plan, huh?"

"When has anything with us gone according to plan?"

She laughs softly. "Good point." She traces a finger down Summit's cheek. "But I think we do our best work off-script anyway."

I lean down, pressing my lips to her temple. "Damn right we do."

"If one more person tries to touch him without washing their hands first, I'm going to lose my shit," I mutter, hovering near the door like some kind of deranged bouncer as our living room fills with people.

Three days after Summit's birth, and we're finally home. Wren's still moving carefully, her incision healing but painful as hell. She keeps saying she's fine, but I catch every wince when she bends or laughs. Not that it slows her down.

"You do realize no one's getting within ten feet of him with you playing guard dog," she says, settling onto the couch with Summit against her chest. "You nearly broke Kieran's wrist when he tried to adjust the blanket."

"He didn't use sanitizer," I defend, eyeing everyone like they're walking petri dishes. "That's not my fault."

Clover bounces Noble on her hip, heading our way. "Let me see my nephew," she demands, grinning. "I've been good for a whole ten minutes."

"Hands," I bark.

She rolls her eyes but uses the sanitizer I've strategically placed on every flat surface. "Happy now, psycho?"

"Getting there." I grudgingly step aside, allowing her closer to my wife and son.

"Oh my god, he's gorgeous," Clover breathes, perching beside Wren. Noble stares down at his cousin, but who knows what he's thinking. "Look, Noble. This is your baby cousin."

Noble reaches out, and I tense, ready to intercept the grabby little hand, but Clover catches it. "Gentle, remember? Like with kitties."

Wren looks up at me, clearly enjoying my discomfort. "Relax, Beanie Boy. He's fine."

"I know he's fine," I growl. "Because I'll accept nothing less."

Banks appears, pressing a beer into my hand. "Drink this. You look ready to throw someone through a window."

I take a long pull, the familiar taste of my own brew steadying me slightly. It's Timber's summer wheat—light, crisp, exactly what I needed.

"How's she really doing?" Banks asks quietly, nodding toward Wren, who's showing Summit off like he's the eighth wonder of the world.

Because he is.

"Stubborn as hell," I answer. "Won't take her pain meds because they make her drowsy and she 'doesn't want to miss anything.' Gets up with him every night despite having her stomach sliced open three days ago."

"So... like Clover after Noble was born."

"Pretty much."

Banks claps my shoulder. "Good luck, man. The first few months are brutal. It gets easier, though."

"When? Because I haven't slept more than two hours straight since he showed up."

"Somewhere around the eighteen-year mark, I hear."

I snort, taking another swig. Reed makes his way over to join our little group, eyeing Summit even though he's off the clock. It's reassuring, having him here. Besides Wren, he's the only person I'd trust with my kid.

"Has everyone washed their hands?" I call out, unable to stop myself.

The room erupts in groans.

"Yes, Dad," Navy calls back. "We've all had our flu shots and none of us has licked any door handles recently."

"Hilarious."

"Seriously, though," Reed says, crouching next to Wren to get a better look at Summit. "He's doing great. Strong vitals, good weight gain." He glances up at me with that smirk I want to punch off his face. "Almost like you didn't need to check his breathing every twenty minutes."

"I didn't—" I start to argue, then stop. Because yeah, I absolutely did that. "Whatever. Can't be too careful."

Wren catches my eye, fighting a smile. "Why don't you show Reed the nursery? Maybe get everyone out of here for a bit so this little guy can eat without an audience."

I'm at her side in two steps. "You good? Need anything?"

"Just some space."

"Come on," I tell the group, reluctant to leave but knowing Wren needs the break. "Quick tour, then we're kicking you all out."

I lead them down the hall to what used to be my office. Now it's all Summit's. The mountain mural I painted takes up one wall, with the pine tree shelves I built loaded with all the stuff people kept giving us. The crib I designed stands opposite, with the mobile of stars and mountains hanging above it.

"Dude," Banks whistles. "You built all this?"

"Most of it." I try to sound casual, but the pride comes through anyway. "I had to do something with all that nervous energy."

Navy runs her hand over the changing table, eyebrows raised. "This is some serious nesting, James. Didn't know you had it in you."

"Neither did I." It's true. Never thought I'd be the guy obsessing over crib safety ratings or non-toxic paint. Yet I did it, building the furniture myself because it needed to be perfect.

While everyone pokes around, I notice Reed and Navy

standing off by themselves, heads close together in what looks like a heated argument in whispers.

"What's with them?" I ask Banks.

He follows my gaze and smirks. "No idea, but they've been like that all week. Ever since Navy mentioned she's donating eggs for her sister's IVF treatment."

"And Reed's involved because...?"

"He's the doctor handling the procedure. They've got 'differing opinions' on the pre-donation protocol."

I raise an eyebrow. "You're using air quotes, which means there's more to the story."

"There's definitely more." Banks grins. "You should've seen them at dinner last night. It was intense."

Before I can dig deeper, Kieran calls out, "Did you seriously make a poop emergency checklist and laminate it?" he asks, holding up the color-coded card.

"Ranked by disaster level, with response protocols," I say, not giving a shit what they think. "I got tired of Wren laughing at me when I'd panic over normal baby shit. Literally. The first one is *black*, dude. It's not right."

Everyone laughs, and I use the distraction to slip out. I find Wren exactly where I left her, but now Summit's attached to her breast, working on his lunch.

"They having fun with the tour?" she asks without looking up.

"Yeah." I drop down beside her, arm going around her shoulders and my body relaxing a little. "Kieran found the laminated list."

"You're ridiculous."

"It's practical."

She leans into me, warm and soft. "How much longer until we can kick them out?"

"Another twenty minutes, tops. Then we claim exhaustion."

"It's not a lie. I'm running on fumes here."

I press my lips to her temple. "As soon as he's done, you're napping while I take him."

"Bold assumption that I can sleep on command."

"Wren. You passed out mid-sentence last night telling me about Kieran's new filing system."

"That's because his filing system is boring as hell." But she smiles, eyes already drooping. "Fine. I'll take a quick nap. Wake me if he needs anything."

"Deal."

I look down at our son, still nursing, his tiny hand pressed against Wren's breast. Something hits me square in the chest - this feeling I can't put words to. Love, fear, pride, exhaustion - all of it mixing together into something too big to contain.

I never thought I'd have this. Never thought I deserved it. But here we are, and somehow it feels right in a way nothing else ever has.

"To Summit William James," I whisper, holding up my beer bottle in the dim light of our kitchen. "The best mistake we ever made."

It's three in the morning, and we've just finished another middle-of-the-night feeding session. It's good to see some things never change.

Summit's back asleep in his bassinet beside our bed, and I've convinced Wren to join me in the kitchen for her first official post-baby beer—my special Dawn Breaker IPA, brewed specifically for our son's birth.

Wren raises her own bottle, clinking it against mine. "To our tiny terror. May he someday sleep through the night."

We both drink, and I watch her face as she tastes the beer

for the first time in months. Her eyes widen, then close in as she moans in appreciation.

I ignore the way my dick perks up at the sound.

"Holy shit, Kasen," she says when she opens them again. "This is... incredible."

Pride surges through me. She always was my worst critic. "Yeah? Not too hoppy?"

"It's perfect. Balanced, complex, with just the right finish." She takes another sip. "Best thing you've ever brewed."

Coming from her, that's high praise. Wren doesn't hand out compliments easily, especially not about beer.

"Well, I had good inspiration." I lean against the counter, watching her in the soft glow of the under-cabinet lights. Even exhausted, hair piled in a messy bun, wearing one of my old t-shirts and sleep shorts, she's the most beautiful thing I've ever seen. "You gonna pump and dump after this?"

She makes a face. "Unfortunately. Seems like such a waste of good breast milk."

"I could help with that." The words are out before I can stop them.

She nearly chokes on her beer. "Excuse me?"

Heat creeps up my neck, but I don't back down. Nah, I own that shit. "Instead of pumping and dumping. I could help you out."

Her eyes go dark, and I know she understands exactly what I'm suggesting. "Are you offering what I think you're offering, James?"

"Yeah. I am."

"You know that's not how it works, right?" She's fighting a smile, cheeks flushed. "Pumping and dumping is just to relieve pressure until the alcohol leaves my system naturally. It's not like you'd be removing the alcohol."

"Fine, ruin my fantasy with your logic." I move closer, trapping her against the counter. And yep, my dick's fully hard between us. "But you can't tell me it wouldn't be more fun than that pump."

"Not even in the top ten worst ideas you've had." Her hand lands on my chest, but she doesn't push me away. "But you'll have to wait a few more weeks. Doctor's orders."

"I can be patient." I dip my head, my lips brushing against her ear. "Doesn't mean I can't think about it, though."

She sucks in a breath, fingers curling into my shirt. "You're dangerous when you talk like that."

"Only for you, Pink." I grin against her skin. "And maybe your resolve."

She leans into me, head against my shoulder. "I've clearly lost my mind since having your kid."

We stand like that for a while, just holding each other in the quiet kitchen, drinking our beer in companionable silence.

"Did you ever think we'd end up here?" she asks eventually, her voice soft.

"Honestly? No. I spent most of the last couple of years trying to figure out how to beat you, not how to marry you and have a kid."

She chuckles. "From enemies to co-parents in under a year. We're either insane or stupid."

"Maybe both." I take another pull of my beer. "Still wouldn't change a thing."

"No?" She pulls back, eyebrow raised. "Not even when I told that bar your flagship tasted like 'someone dumped Pine-Sol in last week's malt water'?"

"Not even that." I brush my thumb across her cheek. "Nobody else would've said it to my face. You made me completely rework the recipe."

"And you made me a better person." She says it so simply, but I know what it costs her to admit it. "Less defensive. More willing to trust."

"I think that was all you, Pink. I just got lucky enough to be around when it happened."

She shakes her head. "No. It was you." Her hand comes up to cup my face. "It was always you."

I lean down to kiss her, tasting beer and something uniquely her. When we break apart, she's smiling that smile that's just for me—the one that reaches her eyes and crinkles at the corners.

"We should try to get some sleep," she says, stifling a yawn. "He'll be up again in two hours."

"Probably." I finish my beer, then take her bottle and set them both in the recycling bin. "But it's worth it."

She takes my hand, leading me back toward our bedroom. "Yeah," she says softly. "It really is."

As I follow her down the hallway, I think about how far we've come. We pause at Summit's bassinet, both of us leaning over to check on him. He's sleeping peacefully, one tiny fist pressed against his cheek, his chest rising and falling with each breath.

"He has your nose," Wren whispers.

"And your mouth." I wrap my arm around her waist, careful of her still-healing incision. "Poor kid."

"Hey, screw you." But she just shoulder checks me with a smirk.

I press a kiss to the top of her head, breathing in the scent of her shampoo. "Get some sleep. I'll take the next feeding."

"Wake me if—"

"I will." I guide her to the bed, pulling back the covers. "Now sleep, woman."

She rolls her eyes but climbs in, already half-asleep before her head hits the pillow. I stand there for a minute, watching my wife and son, this family I never knew I wanted until suddenly it was everything.

Somewhere along the way, between that first morning in

Vegas and now, something shifted. What started as a drunken mistake transformed into the most important thing in my life.

And as I slide into bed beside Wren, her body automatically curling into mine even in sleep, I realize that some mistakes aren't mistakes at all.

They're just the universe's way of giving you exactly what you need, whether you know it or not.

The End

WANT *more?*

Want to know what happened between Kasen & Wren in Vegas?

Read the FREE bonus scene here:

heatherashley.myflodesk.com/reabonus

TIMBER BREWING CO

YEAR-ROUND OFFERINGS

BACKBONE IPA | 6.8% ABV - 68 IBU
Our flagship West Coast IPA. Bold pine and citrus notes with a clean, balanced finish.

SECOND GROWTH AMBER | 5.5% ABV - 32 IBU
Malty backbone with subtle caramel notes and a touch of Northwest hops. Named for the forests that return stronger after fire.

TIMBER PILSNER | 4.9% ABV - 28 IBU
Classic German-style pilsner with a crisp, clean finish. Our tribute to traditional brewing methods.

BEANIE STOUT | 7.2% ABV - 35 IBU
Robust stout with notes of dark chocolate, espresso, and a hint of vanilla.

RESILIENCE RED ALE | 6.2% ABV - 45 IBU
Brewed first after rebuilding the brewery from ashes. Rich malt character with a hoppy finish that doesn't quit.

SEASONAL RELEASES

WINTER PORTER | 6.5% ABV - 30 IBU
Cold weather favorite with hints of coffee and vanilla.

DAWN BREAKER IPA | 6.3% ABV - 60 IBU
Special release brewed for the newest addition to the Timber family. Pine-forward with constellation-inspired hop additions and a bright, hopeful finish.

WILDFIRE HAZY IPA | 6.9% ABV - 45 IBU
Summer seasonal with tropical fruit notes and a subtle smoky finish.

MIDNIGHT OIL COFFEE PORTER | 7.0% ABV - 35 IBU
Brewed with locally roasted coffee beans.

CLOVER'S HONEY WHEAT | 5.3% ABV - 18 IBU
Spring seasonal brewed with local wildflower honey.

EXPERIMENTAL SERIES

LEGACY SERIES: WILLIAM'S RECIPE | 5.8% ABV - 40 IBU
Traditional English-style ale based on Kasen's grandfather's original recipe, found in the margins of his brewing journals.

TATTOO INK BLACK IPA | 7.5% ABV - 75 IBU
As bold and complex as the art that covers Kasen's arms. Dark as night with an unexpected hop punch.

WORKSHOP SAISON | 5.6% ABV - 25 IBU
Farmhouse ale with notes of lemon, peppercorn and oak. Created in the basement workshop between furniture-building sessions.

FAMILY TREE BARLEYWINE | 10.2% ABV - 85 IBU
Our strongest offering, aged in whiskey barrels. Complex, meant to be savored slowly and shared with those who matter most.

DIRECT-TO-BAR TRIPLE IPA | 9.7% ABV - 95 IBU
Limited release that celebrates Timber's original business model. Bold, unapologetic, and worth fighting for.

COLLABORATIONS

RELUCTANT IMPERIAL AMBER | 8.3% ABV - 45 IBU
Limited release. Rich amber with surprising depth, featuring layers of honey and toffee balanced by subtle citrus notes from rare Galaxy hops. Sweet without being cloying, bold without overwhelming. Gets better with every sip.

PORTLAND COALITION LAGER | 5.0% ABV - 22 IBU
Clean, crisp lager brewed in collaboration with our partner breweries. Standing stronger together against corporate takeovers since 2024.

Tasting flights available. Ask your server about our current small-batch experimental brews not listed here.

a letter from the author

(If you want to avoid politics, this is your warning to skip this note)

HI, friend!

After I wrote book one in this series, there were some questions from readers about whether or not this was the new direction I was going in as an author. Whether or not my dark romances were a thing of the past.

I do want to clear that up by saying that, no, the dark is definitely not going anywhere. This series is just the candy my brain needs at the moment because there is just so much chaos happening in the real world, you know?

I'm the mom of a trans teenager, and right now, things are just plain hard.

And speaking of said teen, I was talking about addictions with my him last night and how I'm pretty sure I'm addicted to reading. I can't go a day without spending at least *some* time on my Kindle, especially because I get to pretend things are great when my brain's in another world.

So I hope this book can be that for you. I hope it gives you an escape and an outlet for a little while from all the shit in the world. Life isn't easy on a good day, and right now sometimes it feels impossible.

So I say make yourself as comfy as possible, suck up as much good as you can, and take a couple of deep breaths because I think at this point we all need it.

Oh, and a quick side note: I've got a good author friend who's gone through a couple of years of fertility treatments and while she beta read this book for me, she pointed out that Dr. Walker, as an OBGYN, would not actually handle fertility stuff. That's a whole other specialty.

But for the purposes of this series, despite it being wrong in real life, he's going to handle fertility stuff. It just has to be that way, but go in to book 3 understanding that I know that's not factually correct, but I also know this is fiction and I do what I want ::said in my best Cartman voice::

Happy escape to us all and FDT,

Heather

find me

📷 @heatherashleywrites

♪ @heatherashleyauthor

f /heatherashleywrites

P /heatherwritesitall

🦋 @heatherashley.bsky.social

|O /heatherashleywrites

heatherashleywrites.com

About the Author

Heather Ashley writes dark & steamy forbidden stories with toxic, obsessive heroes. She's a PNW girl through and through and lives for foggy mornings among the evergreens.

Printed in Dunstable, United Kingdom